The
House of
Water

Fflur Dafydd is an award-winning novelist, musician and screen-writer who works in Welsh and English. She is a graduate of UEA's Creative Writing MA, a former Hay Festival International Fellow and an alumna of Iowa University's Prestigious International Writing Program. She has also been nominated for several BAFTA Cymru awards for her screenwriting work. She lives in West Wales with her husband and two daughters.

Also by Fflur Dafydd

Novels
Twenty Thousand Saints
The Library Suicides

Novella
The Replacement Centre
The White Trail

The
House of
Water

FFLUR DAFYDD

HODDER &
STOUGHTON

First published in Great Britain in 2025 by Hodder & Stoughton Limited
An Hachette UK company

The authorised representative in the EEA is Hachette Ireland, 8 Castlecourt Centre,
Dublin 15, D15 XTP3, Ireland (email: info@hbgi.ie)

1

Copyright © Fflur Dafydd 2025

A CIP catalogue record for this title is available from the British Library

Hardback ISBN 978 1 399 71112 8
Trade Paperback ISBN 978 1 399 71113 5
ebook ISBN 978 1 399 71115 9

Typeset in Sabon MT by Manipal Technologies Limited

Printed and bound in Great Britain by Clays Ltd, Elcograf S.p.A.

Hodder & Stoughton policy is to use papers that are natural, renewable
and recyclable products and made from wood grown in sustainable forests.
The logging and manufacturing processes are expected to conform to
the environmental regulations of the country of origin.

Hodder & Stoughton Limited
Carmelite House
50 Victoria Embankment
London EC4Y 0DZ

www.hodder.co.uk

In loving memory of Jennie May James
Mam-gu Dre

'A rare place, but one identifiable
with other places where on as deep a sea
men have clung to the last spars of their language
and gone down with it, unremembered and uncomplaining.'

Drowning, R.S. Thomas

PART ONE

PART ONE

1. IONA

Placing that key in the lock was the last ordinary moment of her life.

It went in smoothly enough. The grooves on the blade had always aligned with ease, knowing to do so silently, so as not to rouse her family. But this time, the door wouldn't budge. And that is when it crept up on her, that feeling of a terrible fullness inside the house. She stepped back and intuitively knew, in the way people do, that her life was about to change forever. That soon, nothing would make sense – not this door, not this house, not even her own reason for standing outside it.

Iona drew closer and peered through the living room window. On first view she could not comprehend any of it. The curtains were heavy with dampness, water gradually pulling them apart. Her mother's reading lamp floated past – upturned and no longer connected to anything – the eye of the dull, grey bulb mocking her. The floor of the living room was entirely flooded, the paraphernalia of her family life dancing about in the water. It was as if there had been a shipwreck inside her house that had thrown everything overboard – her sister's orange pet monkey, her brother's running spikes, her father's reading glasses – all casual flotsam and jetsam of a life that hadn't seen disaster coming.

Bile surged in her throat as she scrambled around the back of the house, her motor skills unsteady, not knowing which foot to put in front of the other. The weed she had smoked earlier that evening was still heavy in her veins; making her hopeful that what she was experiencing right now was a hallucination; a paranoid delusion.

All she wished for now was normality, for her parents to catch her coming home late, for them to shout at her, to scream even. For some comforting, familiar sound to block out the terrible retching and hissing of water coming from the other side of the walls. The rain continued to pelt and thrash all around her, mocking her with the way it had somehow made its way inside the house without anyone noticing.

In the end, the back door could bear it no longer. Iona heard it before she saw it, the groan and wheeze of those hinges weakening as she stumbled towards it, reaching out her arms as if she could catch some semblance of her family life in her hands. A stack of sandbags stood on the threshold; their heavy, lolling bodies conspiring against her as she tried to move past them and into the house.

The water was unforgiving. It flowed towards her, past her, knocked her sideways, clung to the hem of her jeans. She tried in vain to grab hold of any knick-knacks she could see – a spoon, her mother's scarf, a cafetière – but it was futile. She could do nothing but stand there and watch as the water that should never have been inside her house ran off into the drive, gushing down towards the town, towards the drains, working its way back to its origins. Back into the river that was bursting its banks, joining up with it, becoming one with it, trying to sneak in unnoticed just like Iona had hoped to sneak back into her own life.

Iona remained standing in a nowhere place between a flooded town and the house that had somehow flooded itself without the help of the rain, and felt she would never be dry again.

2. CAIN

'Open the shutters, I've got some deliveries for you,' Manny says on the phone. Deliveries. Plural. None of his usual pleasantries or jokes. He never usually rings me until he's right outside the morgue. I get the impression that whatever he's dealing with needs to be sorted as soon as possible.

I tell him it's a quiet night, no backlog, so he can drive straight in. I silently apologise to my current unexplained death: the post-mortem prepping will have to wait for later. Although there are many variations in death, I like to boil them down to two simple categories. Deaths that can be explained, and those that can't. The body I was prepping, that of a twenty-six-year-old male who'd fallen unconscious behind the wheel of his car and crashed into an oil tanker, was explicable enough on the face of it, but in many ways wasn't explicable at all. How could a young man like that just stop functioning, in the prime of his life?

I do a quick check on the number of vacant fridges we have – seven in total. I wonder if it's a road traffic collision – an RTC, as we say in this business – or a street brawl or something, in which case we could be looking at two or three, maybe. There's severe flooding on the south side of Pont Sulyn tonight – some say it's the worst flood this town has ever seen, with a number of flood-related fatalities pouring in; people washed off roads trying to pass a flooded culvert in their cars, knocked off their feet by the sheer power of the water, or simply dying from hypothermia and exposure as they sit in their sodden houses waiting for the water to recede. Seven fridges. It should be enough, depending on how tonight's going to go.

Of all the people you deal with in this business, funeral direc-tors are my favourites. There's a certain decorum to them, treating all corpses the same: easing bodies onto the trolley as though they could still, somehow, be made more comfortable. 'The dead don't care,' Manny always says, 'but that doesn't mean that you shouldn't.'

Manny also mentioned it's a police call, one of the ones you have no choice but to attend straightaway. I try to imagine what it feels like to be woken suddenly, a ringtone jolting you from a dream, an urgent voice telling you to come *right now*. We morgue attendants know our hours – we choose them, even – but a funeral director rarely knows anything, in reality, of what is about to unfold. They're *on call*, of course, but that, for many of the smaller, family-run businesses, means going to sleep not knowing if you'll be called into action. A kind of Russian roulette of dreams, taking your chance on a perfectly good night's sleep, acknowledging it might be cut short. Not that I've ever once heard a funeral director complain about the disruption; or tell me how tired they are like other people do. They just get on with it.

Plus, they're talkers. Funny, too. Most of them. 'Putting the fun back in funerals,' as Manny said to me once.

But tonight, even Manny can't find the words. You can see that he's trying to hold it together as he and Eddie, his dad, wheel in the bodies. One long stretch of blackness after the other, all four of them. It's unusual for them to be in attendance at a suspicious death, but Eddie tells me they're having to deal with this sort of thing more and more now, because of the lack of resources, the police being particularly stretched tonight because of the town being cut off from their main headquarters. The coroner's officer hadn't dealt with anything like this before either, but it seems like it was pretty clear to him what had happened – the absent figure in the party seemed to tell them all they needed to know.

'Killed them all didn't he, the dad, then legged it,' he says. Manny looks drained, as if he might be sick. 'No doubt he'll wash up somewhere, soon enough.'

No one tends to tell us what or how or why it happened. A body is a body. Death is death. All that's expected of us in the death trade is to know what must happen next; to know where the body goes; what, logically, can be done with it. For us, whatever happened doesn't change how we get on with the job. But as Manny's hand unwittingly comes into contact with mine, and I feel the tremor there, I see that even he, for all his professionalism, doesn't really know what to do right now. Eddie explains that all but one of the bodies are damp, that they've been lying in shallow water for hours.

Manny hands me the sheet with the names on them. One body cannot be identified and the details have been left blank. But it knocks me for six when I see who the family are: Lisa Griffri, Bri Griffri, and Urien Griffri, that final name echoing, horribly, inside me.

Three nights ago, I was with him. A memory surfaces of him turning around to look at me on that athletics track, the last of the sun's rays dancing across his face. A disarming smile. Not a face that would have seen death coming.

'Just think, the worst is over for them, son,' I hear Eddie whispering into Manny's ear, as he nods towards me, gesturing that it's OK for me to open the fridge door. But I'm not sure that Manny believes it, any more than I do.

In some ways, the worst hasn't even begun.

30 DAYS BEFORE

3. LISA

Eurov bursts into the house and tells her that the P and Q sections of his encyclopaedia have gone missing from the boot of his car.

'I mean, I've heard of minding your Ps and Qs,' he mutters to himself, 'but this is ridiculous.'

Lisa doesn't know what to believe anymore, when it comes to her husband. She doesn't seem to be able to communicate with him at all like she used to. It's like he's just acting being a husband and father. It's a consummate performance on some days; feigning interest in the kids' lives, an intense questioning bordering on interrogation, then asking what everyone wants for dinner before losing himself in elaborate preparation via YouTube tutorials – *One pot chicken rice! Creamy Beef stroganoff! Prawn curry!* On other days, it's like someone's flicked a switch, and a darkness seems to settle upon him like a shroud. It's a relief to them all, in moments like these, when he finally retreats to his study, telling them he isn't hungry, and they should have dinner without him.

He often claims the encyclopaedia is *calling*, like it's another child, and he swirls out of the room like a tornado, leaves of paper fluttering in his wake. Lisa knows he's under pressure to deliver to the publishers, but it's like he's become an encyclopaedia himself – spouting out random facts over dinner that no one really has any interest in hearing: *Did you know that some of the earliest dinosaur fossils in the world were found in Wales? Did you know that the equals sign was created by Tenby-born Robert Recorde in 1557? Do you know that Mount Everest was named after a man from Crickhowell, who never even saw it?*

'Are you sure, Eurov,' Lisa says, trying to remain calm, to say none of what she is thinking, 'that those pages were actually in the trunk? I mean, sometimes . . . sometimes you forget . . . I mean, *people* forget where they put things. You probably left it at the university. And anyway, does it really matter – surely you can just print out another copy?'

He looks at her strangely then, and she sees something dark and inexplicable in his eyes that has been festering there for weeks, ever since he began teaching his summer school at the university. A drop of tea is now running down his chin, and she surveys every inch of its journey down towards his neck, wondering why he isn't wiping it away, or why she isn't telling him it's there.

It's like that drop of tea is in on something, something too awful to mention.

'I know where I put them, OK? And now they're gone. Someone's taken them. Someone's messing with me . . . '

'Honestly, Eurov, who would do such a thing? Who would even care enough to . . . ?'

Again, that darkness glares back at her, so deep that she sometimes worries she'll fall into it herself. She tries to dampen the condescension in her voice, but what she really wants to tell him is that no one gives a shit about his encyclopaedia. For all his stress over his research output, for the high esteem he seems to hold for his fellow academics, for everything he thinks that means something, ultimately, it doesn't. He isn't saving anyone or anything by writing an encyclopaedia. It's just one more attempt to find meaning in his life.

Then again, if she were to voice these things, she knows he would strike back with the fact that she isn't making art anymore, which she doesn't need to hear right now.

'Look, Eurov, I think you need a break,' she ventures. 'I think we all do. How about we get away this weekend? Maybe just you and me . . . and . . . and . . . '

She often wonders if some quality time is all they need to get back on track. This so called 'alone time'. Then she sees the relief in his face when he realises she didn't just mean the two of them getting away. God forbid they'd actually have to be *alone* together.

' . . . and Briall!' she continues, hurling her youngest child into the scenario like a swing ball. 'Or maybe not.' She's back-pedalling now, but the truth of it is that she can't quite begin to fathom what a weekend away without any of the children would look like. More and more Lisa is grateful that they continue to provide obstacles, and she realises more and more that this relationship would not have survived without them. These new lives that she was once so ambivalent about – the lives she imagined would never come to be – have gone and filled up the gulf between her and Eurov, populating it so it cannot be recognised as a gulf at all. And although the two eldest – Iona and Urien – will be leaving for college soon, she will be forever grateful that nature tricked them by giving them a third child in lieu of the early menopause Lisa had been convinced she was having. Their delightful Briall will surely be shielding her for another few years from having to make any real decision about what she should do about the state of her marriage.

'Maybe I could ask the other two what *their* plans are,' she continues. 'If they don't mind giving up their weekend to look after her . . . And there's plenty to keep her occupied – I think there was a party invitation from Gwen on the WhatsApp. I'll text Gwen's mum, maybe she can have a sleepover . . . '

Lisa lifts her phone, and wonders at her ability to find the strength to forge on with this plan; to arrange something neither of them want to do. But soon the intent is lost as she spirals into the other myriad messages lining up there, unread, vying for her attention. *U8s Ballet Class – Registration needed. U18 Athletics Team Presentation night. Year 4 mums night out.* Her phone seems more like a ticking time bomb these days. Is it any wonder she can't create any art, with all this going on? All the forms, all the bank transfers? And Eurov gets to sit there worrying only about his encyclopaedia, carrying none of this responsibility.

'What's this about the weekend?' Their son, Urien, enters, catching the tail end of their conversation, and stopping Lisa from saying something she might regret.

'I was just wondering about you and Iona keeping an eye on Bri,' she starts, but Eurov bulldozes across her.

'I've just got too much work to think about going away, OK, Lisa?' he says, getting up to leave the room. 'It's a stressful time for me . . . The encyclopaedia is due in soon . . . '

'And they say romance is dead, eh, mum?' Urien winks at her, walking to the fridge to get some juice.

Lisa laughs. Secretly she's relived that it's all come to nothing; but she also knows she needs to try harder next time, whether she wants this or not. She has to try to save the marriage, she *has* to, because there's more to it than just marrying the wrong person. She has moved to the other side of the world for this relationship, learned another language; she has embedded herself in the land, the town, the community.

It is only the river that she would truly be happy to leave behind.

Urien squeezes her shoulder on the way out of the room, almost as if he knows what she is thinking. She seizes on the opportunity to pull him in for a hug, and he allows it for a moment, before starting to pull away. She tries to keep him there for longer, having read somewhere that it takes seven seconds for love to transfer from one person to another – a fact she is always sharing with her children, who simply roll their eyes at her.

Lisa then watches him go, marvelling at her creation, the athletic bulk of him, his tall frame, his gentle gait, his ease of being in the world.

While she admits to finding it hard to take an interest in anything these days, let alone her artwork, she has never lost interest in her children. In fact, she never surveys any of her children with anything other than complete wonder, considering her initial difficulty to conceive. That there should be so many of them, when she thought she'd have none, is continuously baffling to her. Yet it scares her a little, too, the recklessness of it, bringing all these new lives into a world that is on the verge of drowning if the news reports about Pont Sulyn's floods are to believed. She sometimes wakes in a cold sweat in the middle of the night imagining Bri, the youngest, thrashing in the pungent brown water, calling out their names as the current swallows her whole.

The easiest one to love is undoubtedly the middle child, as everyone always says it will be, her glorious seventeen-year-old Urien, named after Urien Rheged at Eurov's insistence – 'the late sixth century king of Rheged, an early British Kingdom of the Old North, when Britain,' Eurov maintains, 'had all belonged to the Welsh, or at least the early Celts who then evolved into them.'

Lisa had liked the sheer otherness of the name at the time but has grown uneasy with it over the years. It seems too heavy a name for this light-footed athlete, who never complains about picking his little sister up from ballet or gymnastics or all manner of places Lisa and Eurov no longer have any energy or desire to go themselves. Plus, there's the matter of the name being one disastrous letter swap away from *Urine*, for which he is continuously mocked at school. But Urien himself has grown into his name and Lisa still likes the graceful sound of it on her tongue – *eer-yen* – and tells herself that he will fare well in the wider world eventually with a name so unlike others.

The name of the youngest, Briall, is Welsh for Primrose. Eurov's idea, of course, but they now often just refer to her as Bri, the single syllable *Bree* seeming more in line with her uncomplicated nature, her simplicity. Plus, she has trouble enunciating the double 'll' (a 'voiceless alveolar lateral fricative, sometimes known as the "dark L",' Eurov keeps relaying to his daughter's disinterested ears) and because she is their final child, and they are simply exhausted, they would rather drop the extra syllable than try to correct the problem.

And last but not least, apple of her eye, whirlwind of her evenings, bane of her life, is eighteen-year-old Iona – *Yawn-ah* not *Aye-ona* – whose name is a derivative of Ionawr, Welsh for January. A new year, a new start. Even now, all these years later, Lisa feels guilty about how long it took her to love her firstborn in those early months, how she'd wasted the precious time by crying and raging and wanting to throw her baby out of the window. 'I don't want her,' she'd screamed over and over again at the midwives, until they put her on meds in order for the world to make sense again. Gradually, the baby's face had morphed from something monstrous into something she recognised. Something she loved. And she often wonders if this is why Iona has turned out the way she has: because somehow, deep in the spirals of her DNA, she remembers this early rejection and resents her mother; and perhaps this is why Iona has lain claim to the root of the name, unforgiving and relentless as January often is, an icy blast who seems to have detached herself from the whole family in the last few months.

And it hurts. Badly. Iona will be leaving any day now, and that will be it; the distance between them will become a solidified, geographical fact.

But the truth of the matter is that all her children, in one way or another, are slipping away now. Her shield is weakening. They no longer need her. Their friends always tell her that she and Eurov will have more time for themselves, more time together.

And that notion terrifies her. It terrifies her because, for reasons she can't quite grasp, Eurov isn't Eurov anymore, and the more time she spends in his company trying to ignore whatever darkness is creeping its way around them, the more she feels herself, too, drifting off, becoming lost in the tide of time, becoming lost even to herself, a poor imitation, like those birthday portraits she has started to paint for money in order to fund all the bank debits demanded by her various WhatsApp groups.

They are both, Lisa thinks, she and her husband, simply pretending that everything is normal. That all is well. And such a pretence will, eventually, have consequences.

ENCYCLOPAEDIA OF 'CYMRU'

THE COUNTRY ALSO KNOWN, ERRONEOUSLY, AS WALES

as experienced by Eurov Griffri

A - AWEN - (pronounced Ah-when): is a Welsh, Cornish and Breton word for inspiration via a poetic gift or a muse, specifically poetic in nature but can be applicable to other art forms. Whereas in English, one tends to think of a muse as a person, or an imaginary being that fuels ideas, making a person able to write, paint, create, the Welsh awen derives from the Indo-European root uel, meaning 'to blow'. This suggests that the awen, unlike the muse, is an unexplained force, which can fire up the neurons in one's brain as if by magic. When artists and writers become obsessive about something, having seemingly no idea why, it perpetuates the myth that ideas are mystical things. But are ideas not also born from fears, from things we think might happen to us, from things we hope will never occur? And perhaps there is a shaman-like practice in letting them go, through art?

My own particular awen has led me here, to this encyclopaedia, which will not be a conventional encyclopaedia of Wales but rather a compilation of those aspects of Wales that have been integral to my own life.

And perhaps have been responsible for shaping the terrible person that I have become.

4. IONA

Two hours ago, she was returning home. How abstract the concept seems to Iona now. *Home*. That house on the hill in Pont Sulyn, observing her lateness, like all the times before. Its white rectangular face looming over her, judging her for staying out beyond her curfew. The house that has only ever known one family, a three-storey townhouse designed especially for them, positioned well out of the reach of the river.

It was her mother who had insisted on this elevated location. As an American who can't swim, and who has never lived this close to water, she was nervous about being pulled down into the depths. She claims to be 'aquaphobic', a term none of them believe is real.

Building their house there means it stands out. They, as a family, stand out. It's had the unfortunate effect of making the Griffri family appear as if they consider themselves above the rest, as though they have taken steps to safeguard themselves, and only themselves, against an uncertain future, having built their very own ark in the guise of a town house.

Except now Iona knows it wasn't ever an ark. More like a tomb.

She recalls the way her mother always kept an anxious eye on the river levels, pacing by the large arch-style windows, a troubling, Christ-like silhouette staring down at the town below, waiting for disaster to strike. It's been getting worse recently, unpredictable flash floods creating more and more destruction and chaos. The row of riverside cottages where some of the town's elderly residents lived have long been vacated and deemed uninhabitable, their ghostly husks casting shadows across the water. The council houses behind them will no doubt be flooded tonight, as will the youth centre behind them. There are whispers of a 'decommission' (the kind which has only happened in seaside towns up until now) and plans to use the river for hydropower instead. The residents have, so far, objected to the council's proposals.

There was a time, when Iona was little, that the water was considered an asset to the town, the very thing that gave it its character – a fun thing to be kayaked upon, jumped into, fished in. That whole time seems an illusion now; a dream. The canoeing centre Iona frequented has long shut its doors, and since they built the bypass, hardly anyone travels through here anymore. Pont Sulyn is cut off from the world, left to drown.

What she saw as she ran down towards the town, away from her home, was that the water doesn't care about people. It doesn't care about homes. It goes where it wants to go, pulled by a gravitational force that has nothing to do with emotion. It's unstoppable. Water has crept uninvited into ordinary people's homes tonight, carting away entire futures; the sudden rainfall becoming a curse, heavier than even the meteorologists predicted.

As Iona waded into it, towards the rescue dinghies, vomiting her story up into the cold hands of a policewoman in a yellow raincoat, she caught sight of a shoal of sea trout – the famed *sewin* – hurtling away at speed in the dark flow under her knees, leaving a mercurial glow in their wake.

Even the fish, she thought, could not bear to hear her story.

*

The exhausted female officer who eventually put her in the car and drove her down to the station reminded her of her mother when her sister was a baby. Drowning in life, barely able to keep her head above water. Failing to comprehend what Iona's situation was. She recalls her mother at the wheel when Bri was three months old, completely dazed, going through red lights, reversing into things, half-mad with sleep deprivation. She feels guilty, remembering the many times she told her mother she shouldn't have had another baby if she couldn't handle it. 'I just need a little help, is all!' her mother said, her voice faltering. Iona knew what she was asking of her, but she was resistant to it, because, at ten years old, life was already starting to become all about her, and she didn't want to make it about someone else. Urien, her brother, the peacemaker, was trying his best to shush the screaming life force, dangling a toy elephant in front of her face. Iona still remembers the baby's large blue eyes, reflected back at her in the rear-view mirror, utterly oblivious of the chaos she had caused by just existing, a thing she was not to blame for.

Iona is left sitting in the corner of the Pont Sulyn police station waiting room, saturated, soaked through to the skin, shaking violently. People avoid her gaze as though she is just one more oddball washed in from the storm. Next to her, a girl with lank, dirty hair is cutting herself through her purple and black striped tights, the blood dripping in bold, concentric splashes across the linoleum floor. A bald man in a tattered coat keeps muttering to himself as he sways in his plastic chair, telling them the storm is the work of the saint, Saint Sulyn, the one who gave the town its name. Iona finds herself being drawn into conversation with him, desperate for any intervention that can block out the images flickering at the edge of her consciousness; a water-crinkled finger, a bloodied ribbon, an overflowing bath.

She still doesn't think any of this is real.

'It's the work of God,' the man says. 'Or the Saint, having the last laugh. Because of what they did to his church.'

'Right,' she says, almost robotically. 'Of course. The church.'

'Well now it's completely flooded,' he mutters. 'Waste of money, that climbing centre. Why do people climb, do you think? What do they think is so interesting up there that they can't find down here, eh?'

Iona looks up, as though she'll find the answer on the mottled damp patches creeping across the police station ceiling. How could it be that it was only last weekend when she took Briall to a party at the climbing centre, watched her younger sister and her friends scatter themselves across its walls like lemmings, riding around its rafters on a zip-wire, so full of life and energy? She was surprised to see that the stained-glass window was completely intact as part of the refurbishment, that the figure of St Sulyn still hung there, his red cape glinting in the sun, looking down at them in despair just as she remembered him from her Sunday school days. They'd kept the pews of the church too, which had become littered with colourful shoes, kicked off hurriedly by tiny feet.

'He drowned, didn't he,' the old man continues. 'Saint Sulyn. Baptism gone wrong – rapids were too strong. Some deranged woman pushed him in. Or knocked him unconscious. Depends which version of the story you read. But there's more to the story, isn't there? There always is.'

Saint Sulyn, Iona thinks to herself, dredging up whatever info she has on him from the quagmire that is now her mind, pushing other things down into the depths. Wasn't her father at work on that entry of the encyclopaedia only last week, didn't he ask her which version of the town's history was taught at school? The version where the baptism gone wrong was actually an act of self-sacrifice? Or the version where it was a deliberate attack on the saint by a lover who wanted to expose him for being less saintly than he claimed to be? Was her dad trying to tell her something right then, only that she missed it? She tries to recall the tone of her father's voice, but she can't, for the life of her, remember it at all right now. Every memory of him has somehow been extinguished, just like that.

'Stupid place to put a church anyway,' the man continues, 'on the banks of a river. No wonder people started moving out when the water damage started. It was a death trap anyway. Your family churchgoers, were they?'

Iona clocks that he refers to her family in the past tense, though he can't possibly know.

'Yes, yes, they . . . we . . . were,' she says, thinking of the way her mother insisted they all had to attend church until they were at least twelve, until they were old enough to decide for themselves whether they wanted God in their lives. How they all sat there dutifully next to each other, while the Saint stared down at them from his echelons. Almost a whole church row gone now, apart from her. Her mother, brother, sister, all of them. Removed, even though the pew that housed them remains, providing solace for weary mothers looking at their phones as their kids fly in the air above them.

Her father, the atheist, had sat there too, wringing his hands uncomfortably. Is her father dead too? She finds it hard to recall now whether her father was there in the house at all. She would surely remember if she'd seen him. Unless, that, is, unless . . . Something is bobbing in the fluid of her brain, threatening to come to the surface.

There was someone in her bed. Someone who wasn't her.

A young male officer, not much older than her, walks into the waiting room, head bowed wearily, and calls out her name. He's apologising for the way she's been treated, all the while trying not to look at the blood dripping out of the young girl's arm. It's been one of those nights, he says, overwhelmed as they are, understaffed. He's so sorry. She should have been taken better care of. As he's shuffling her down the corridor he's muttering that it's 'all or nothing, eh, in this town', and then seems to shudder, as if realising this is something you should never say to someone who's lost everything, lost *all*. Iona supposes they are all, every single one who exists and lives and works in this town, out of their depth now, as if this water has been poured on the town to test them, to see how shallow or how deep any of them are, to see whether they will sink or swim.

He gives her biscuits and tea and says he'll get the person in charge. He seems to notice, at last, that she's still soaking wet from the storm, and hurries out and back in again with some rough looking towels, apologising that that's the best they have. She wraps her soaking wet hair in a turban and places another one underneath her. The hot tea scalds her tongue. Unfortunate images begin to flicker again in her mind's eye, water pouring down the stairs towards her, sinking into the turquoise carpet, turning it a dark, soggy green.

'Iona Griffri?' a voice pushes away the recollection of the attic door hanging open, its exposed tongue dangling in mid-air. 'I'm Miri Pritchard,' the woman says, reaching out her hand towards her. It's cold and bony. Iona's own hand struggles to find the strength to close around it.

'I'm the family liaison officer, and I'll be looking after you from now on. A very bad thing has happened to you tonight, Iona,' Miri says. 'No one should have seen what you saw at that house this evening, let alone someone of your age. We're going to give you all the support you need to deal with this, OK? We're going to take things one step at a time. I'll be your point of contact from now on, and I'll be there with you, every step of the way, OK?'

Every step, she thinks. How many steps are there to walk away from this? It isn't until she looks down that she sees she's crumbled the biscuit to smithereens in her hand.

'There was a girl in my bed,' she says. 'A girl who wasn't me.'

5. CAIN

Urien and I used to train together, down on the athletics track, on Wednesday evenings. Travel together sometimes too, to cross-country races and athletic competitions. I don't drive, so he's given me several lifts to places over the past couple of months. I wouldn't call him a friend, but there's an ease to our being together, chatting about our PBs and our block starts, so it's a shock to realise that I'm going to be shutting him away into a morgue fridge.

I remember his mum thanking me once, for keeping him company. 'He sees you as a mentor, Cain,' she said, something I don't think I've ever been called. Though I never met his sisters, I was always vaguely aware of their presence on those long drives, the crisp wrappers and Pokémon cards stuffed down the centre console, the Patchouli perfume that lingered in the air and the mascara tubes and colouring books that splayed out of the map pocket of the car. I always got this feeling that he secretly loved being sandwiched in between them in life. I guess I was a little jealous of that, that he had so many people, when I only have my grandmother to call family.

I decide to park whatever feelings I have about it right now, as I've got a job to do. In a small place like Pont Sulyn, you can't let yourself get derailed the second you happen to recognise one of the deceased, or you'd never get anything done. Just like the funeral directors, you're expected to crack on.

The handover isn't as swift as Manny would have hoped. Although everything's complete at my end, they have to hang around for a bit longer this time. There are police officers to deal with, forms to be filled in, and they've been followed all the way here to ensure they don't suddenly abscond or interfere with the bodies in any way. One of the bodies proves more complicated than the others, because of a certain technicality that we rarely encounter – an unnamed victim, a Jane Doe. Manny is getting paler by the minute and looks as if he might pass out. He finally excuses himself to take a call, saying he needs to check in with the office – not that anyone believes that a funeral director with a staff of three has a functional office at three in the morning.

'You can't switch off the dad in you sometimes can you?' Eddie says, the second Manny's out of earshot. 'Thinking about his own girls, isn't he? They're around the same age as that little one.'

The little one. She was still clutching a pink soft toy, in the most rigid of fists, which the police officer finally removed and bagged, without betraying a shred of emotion. The disposal of that piglet, shapeless and crumpled from being loved and clung to over hundreds of nights by this little girl, was enough to make Manny retch and leave the room.

A child's death is the worst. None of us ever learn how to deal with it, not really. Even I, who should be accustomed to it, have my moments. It's the complete obliviousness of the child to the fact that something this awful could ever happen that gets me. If it's true what they say about death, which is that you have enough consciousness left after you die to *know* that you've died, then I always think of the child's disappointment that the whole world has tricked them, given them the promise of life that was all an illusion. *You've got your whole life ahead of you.* I always think that's a pretty dangerous assumption to make.

'It's odd, isn't it,' Eddie whispers, as the police manoeuvre in dark shadows around us, 'filling up that house with water. Mostly in these situations it's fire – they want to destroy everything, burn it to the ground. Water just bogs everything down. Makes everything swell.'

Then he looks at me and I see the sheer panic in his eyes, as if he shouldn't have said that. I know first-hand how heavy water can be. What it can do to a family. But this isn't about me. Plus, when

I'm at work, I rarely think of my own losses. I try to be professional about it. Tackle them all as they come in, issue the appropriate emotional response on a case-by-case basis.

After Manny and Eddie leave, and the police seem satisfied I've got the right bodies in the right order, I open the fridge again and take a good look at each one, checking if the temperature of the fridges needs adjusting. Bodies that have been in contact with water, no matter how much or how little, tend to deteriorate quicker. They're not too bad, considering. There are no obvious abrasions to the younger two, but both the mother and the other girl look as if they've been hit on the back of the head with something. Only one, the mother, has been fully submerged in water, the rest are only damp, as though they've just been doused with it. Anointed even. Maybe it was a ritual of some kind; you'd be surprised what kind of odd things people do to dead bodies. There's slight discolouration to them all, the result of the blood stopping in its tracks, no longer having a place to go. It's gravity that gives them the purplish hue, pulling the blood down, and making it accumulate. The greenness, you can tell, will eventually take hold, especially on a waterlogged body, but for now they look as if they could almost still be alive. After all, death has only come into play in the last couple of hours.

A tag needs to be placed around the wrist and ankle, with the name, the date of death, and a case number if there is to be an investigation, which there certainly will be in this kind of situation. It's the same logic as placing a tag on a baby, because they, similar to the dead, can't tell you who they are. Then, I place each body in its compartment: Briall, Urien, their mum Lisa, and then the final, nameless body.

A teenage girl, who they say they can't identify.

We've had a few John and Jane Does in here over the years of course, mainly homeless people, frozen to death outside Pont Sulyn's church, and I've learned from Manny and Eddie to treat them just as I would any other body. Just because I don't know their identity, it doesn't mean they don't have one. Underneath that skin and bone in front of me there was once a myriad of feelings and emotions and grievances and losses that made this young girl who she was. It's only her flesh that can reveal anything significant about her: a chickenpox pockmark above her left eye, and a fading scar behind the hairline, from the scalp to the ear, which indicates brain surgery of some kind. It gives us the two extremes of this nameless, history-less girl, from an ordinary childhood illness to either a devastating diagnosis of some kind or a terrible accident. Either way, it gives me something to go on, and brings me a little closer to gaining some kind of understanding of her, of why she ended up here.

There's something pure about a nameless body. Something clean. Almost something to be admired. It's life coming full circle, entering back into that initial, nameless state of oblivion, before an identity was foisted upon you without your consent, before connections and relationships wove you so tightly into the fabric of life that you couldn't untangle yourself from them. Our names, after all, mark us out, stain us; determine our place in the world. Those are the things that force us to live on; whether we want to or not. I almost envy her, this nameless girl in her chamber. Without a name, without a past. There is simply nothing we can say about her beyond the conjectures about her scars. The only fact we have is her namelessness. It gives her superiority; it gives her the power of her own existence. She, and she alone, owns her own death. They won't be writing about her in all the papers because they can't; she's made sure of that. They have nothing on her – which these days, is nothing short of a miracle.

It gives the dead girl a kind of nobility that I want her to cling to for a little while longer, so that she can be spared from entering our world as cunningly as she has slipped out of it. It's as if she's a relic, discovered centuries after her death, her past a mystery even to the shrewdest of historians. She could belong to our time, she could belong to any time at all.

She, in front of me, with her crooked half smile, her nails bitten to the quick, seems curiously free. As though in her final moment of consciousness she was glad, somehow, to return to the nothingness from which she came.

I think that, in some ways, it's what I hanker for. And one of the reasons why this place has become a kind of home. Because I've lived with death more than most.

In some ways, you could say I've made it my friend.

28 DAYS BEFORE

6. URIEN

His friends notice the girl before he does. That doesn't come as any surprise: he's long realised he doesn't really *see* girls, not in the way his friends do, anyway. It's men that he's noticing more and more now, the way the sweat pools in the back of Mr Fillmore's shirt in Maths class; the way the young new school caretaker's neck chain catches the light as he leans down to mop the corridors; the way the chef's biceps bulge as he's scooping out the mashed potato. These men, their limbs, their smells, are intoxicating to him, holding a promise of something that is just beyond reach. He loves the messiness of them, the unpredictability of their movements. He wants to be entangled in their limbs, wants to push his face into theirs and feel their skin next to his.

Girls seem plain to him, in comparison. As if there's no texture to them, like they could just float through walls, so paper thin is their existence. They all seem the same to him, with their poker straight hair sculpted into artificial ringlets, their bodies shrouded by face mists and mouth-fresheners, sanitising their way out of existence.

Not that this girl is the same as the others, though, when his attention is finally drawn to her. She hasn't even bothered to brush her hair – it's thick and unruly, cut lopsidedly, art-house movie style. She wears mainly black clothes, and a long blue coat, hands shoved firmly into the pockets as though they've been stitched into the fabric. Her head is always bowed, as though she's afraid of looking up and confronting the world. She might be older than him, a school dropout, or a uni student. She seems curiously ageless, sometimes a lost little girl, other times a threatening older woman. But she's everywhere. Everywhere he seems to be.

'I swear,' Max tells him, 'She has the horn for you.'

They start yobbishly ribbing him about his *girlfriend,* every time they see her pass by the bus stop or hover in the next aisle over to him at the corner shop. It escalates to her loitering outside school, then he starts seeing her outside pubs when he's with his mates, smoking roll ups, always on her own.

'She's wasting her time', he tells Max one morning, hoping it will finally cement to him that he isn't actually interested in girls.

'Which school do you think she goes to?' Max replies, ignoring the subtext presented to him like an opportunity. 'Never seen her in uniform.'

He's had girls follow him before, and giggle at him, and eventually talk to him, only for him to have to let them down, but there's something different about this one, it's as though she has no intention of ever talking to him. Following him around seems to be *the thing*. A ploy to unsettle him. So one day he waits until he's certain she's behind him, and then he stops in his tracks and faces her.

'What the fuck are you doing?' he turns, and says, a little too loudly in her face. 'Who even are you?'

He seems to have startled an animal in the wild, and her whole body suddenly goes rigid with shock. Her bravado deflates, as though she can no longer cope with whatever designs she had on him. Nervously, she retreats, and runs off, blue coat flapping behind her. His friends cackle behind him and continue to mock him.

'Shame – would have been an easy lay,' Max laughs, bits of sausage roll falling from his mouth. 'And no talking required.'

Their voices fade in the air. Urien isn't listening to them anymore, his blood rushing in his ears. Because there was something in the way she turned, and the way she looked so frightened of him, that seemed oddly familiar.

B – BRIDGE (in Welsh–PONT): there are sixty–seven places in Wales that include the prefix Pont, paying homage to the bridges that have been built across their rivers. But the name 'Sulyn' in Pont Sulyn not only refers to the name of the river flowing through the town, but also to the rather controversial figure of St Sulyn, a sixth century saint who baptised the town's residents in the river, and who seemed to have met his end in this way.

Ever since I was a child, I have always found myself to be suffering from a mild case of gephyrophobia: a fear of bridges. I think the main reason for this is that they symbolise a liminal space, because they are neither one thing nor another, not land and not sea, just a construct that challenges you all too often to think of the absence, the gap, the loss it is masking by just existing. There are some who cannot drive onto a bridge without thinking that it may collapse, because who is to say that such a gravity–defying concept can ever be truly safe? Can a gap ever be filled completely? Or is it still there, all around us, the potential to fall from a great height into the depths below?

And of course, when you grow up knowing that a whole place can be drowned at the drop of a hat, and that no bridge can be erected for you to cross back over into your old life, it's no wonder, in some ways, that you are not only afraid of bridges, but that you resent them, too.

7. IONA

The police station feels hazy and unreal, like a film set, as if she could just kick over one of the grey walls that surround her and find herself back in her own bed.

All would be well, and it would be her lying in her own bed, rather than a stranger.

How can it be that only hours ago she was focused on little more than her own intense pleasure as a boy she loved pummelled away inside her? She imagines Jethro, sound asleep in his attic bedroom now, having left her on the side of the road in the rain, in a dash to make sure his mother and brothers were safe from the flood. How could she have stood there, watching the rear lights of his car getting smaller and smaller in the dark, lamenting her separation from him, when such terrible things were occurring in her house?

At least she's out of the rain, she tells the family liaison officer, with a stoned smile. Miri gestures towards the cup of tea that is next to her on the table.

'Please,' she says. 'Drink. Eat a little. It might help, with the shock.'

The hot, sweet tea is an elixir. It isn't how she takes it normally but she can see why people use sugar for shock. It zings along her bloodstream, alleviates somewhat of the numbness. *Where is the way out*, she wants to ask. *How can I get back to the life I had before?*

'Are you OK, Iona? Have you . . . I have to ask . . . Have you taken anything this evening?'

She thinks of that blowback she took from Jethro just before they had sex, the blue smoke serpentining between their mouths.

'I smoked some weed, with my boyfriend,' she says. 'But I don't want to get him in trouble . . . '

'Don't worry about that for now, Iona, OK? All we need to do tonight is clarify a few things. And we need to get you set up for the night. Is there someone we can call for you?'

In truth, there is no one she can call, apart from Aunt Anna. The problematic family member her mum and dad simultaneously mollycoddle and keep at arm's length. 'Something's gone undiagnosed there,' her mother would say. 'Your family just can't accept there might be something wrong with her.' She can't have Anna here right now, misconstruing everything.

'I have an aunt,' Iona says. 'But I don't know where my phone is. Her number's on there . . . '

'Don't you worry,' Miri says. 'We'll track her down, OK?'

Miri speaks cautiously, as if measuring the potency of each word as she goes, as though each one might have the potential to shatter her. She confirms, in a low, gentle voice, that her brother, Urien, her sister, Bri, and her mother, Lisa, are dead; that they are treating these deaths as suspicious; that her father Eurov is missing and is therefore their prime suspect. The house seems to have been deliberately flooded, with sandbags placed in front of each exit point, in order to keep in as much water as possible.

Iona shakes her head: no. This cannot be happening.

'I know it's a lot to take in,' Miri continues. 'But we'll do all we can to help you.'

No. Iona shakes her head again. She will not, cannot, take it in. She is stoned and hallucinating and she just needs to break out of this room to find her way back to the beginning of the evening, before the river rose, before her house became flooded from the inside without anyone noticing.

'The officer who attended to you at the flood was very inexperienced,' Miri continues, 'and I'm sorry it took so long for someone to take you seriously. It's been quite the night for Pont Sulyn, with the flood and everything. Things were not being communicated to us as they should. The flood, just . . . well, it overwhelmed us.'

It's real, the voice inside her head tells her now. *All of it. These walls, penning you in, cannot be pushed over. You cannot leave this situation.*

'At least she listened to me,' Iona says quietly. 'And brought me here. She didn't try to put me into the dinghy with the others . . .'

'Perhaps not,' Miri continues, 'but there was a bit of a hold up in communicating to us what exactly had happened at your house. Our officers should have been up there immediately, the second they found you. I'm very sorry that they weren't.'

Miri pauses, as if bracing herself for the next question.

'Your father, Iona. Do you think your dad . . . Do you think he was still in the house, somewhere, Iona, when you . . . found them? Were there any signs that he was there, do you think?'

The attic door hangs open in her mind. The darkness both menacing and inviting. She only glanced up at it for a second. She didn't know what she was looking for, at that point. Nothing made sense. Not even what that gaping hole was. He could have been up there, she supposes. Hiding. It never occurred to her to go up there. At that point, her only thought was to get as far away from the place as possible.

'I . . . don't know,' she says. 'He might have been. But he . . . he wouldn't have done something like this. He just, wouldn't.'

'OK, OK,' Miri says, in a tone that makes it sound as if she's agreeing with her. 'OK. And then, there's the girl . . . The girl in your bed. Now that you've had a bit of time to think about, it, do you have any idea who she is? Was?'

A silence descends on the room. For the first time Iona realises that they haven't understood the situation at all. It wasn't shock that stopped her from recognising that girl in her bed. She's never seen her before.

'Her parents will need to be informed as soon as possible,' Miri continues, confusing Iona's silence for reticence. 'Most people will have been woken by the storm tonight, I don't think there are many people who won't have noticed that their daughter is missing, so it really is imperative that we are able to inform her family . . . We will need to assign someone to support that family too, you see. They will be going through . . . something similar.'

Iona wants to say it isn't similar. One death. When she's suffered three in a matter of hours. And her father a possible fourth. Death is a competition, she realises, one she never wanted to be in the running for.

'I told you, I've never seen her before,' Iona blurts out, her mind now releasing unfortunate images of those cold eyes staring up at the ceiling, covers pulled up towards her neck. 'I didn't recognise her at all . . . '

'But she was in your bed, Iona.'

'I know,' Iona answers quietly. She remembers it all too well. The moment she considered that she, too, herself, might be dead, that she was somehow outside her own body, stalking the house; a ghost. But when she pulled back the sheet and really studied her, the face wasn't hers.

'Could she have been . . . your brother's friend, girlfriend . . . ?'

'My brother's gay,' she says, firmly, her heart sinking thinking that Urien has died without having experienced his full, true self.

'Something to do with your father? Was he having an affair . . . ?'

A laugh escapes her then, the thought of her father having an affair, with a girl her age. Not impossible, she supposes, but the only affair Eurov has ever conducted has been with his research, as far as she knows.

'We found a page of something . . . ' Miri says. 'In the bedroom . . . on the bed on top of the girl's body, and another ripped up and scattered all over the floor . . . It seems either she or your father were writing something . . . by hand? It seems to be a dictionary or a . . . '

'An encyclopaedia,' Iona replies. 'Yes, he was working on an encyclopaedia of Wales.' Her father's voice comes back to her now in the abyss of her mind.

'Did you know our country has more castles per square mile than any other country in Europe?'

He'd be annoyed with her that she'd just called it an encyclopae-dia of Wales. He's been adamant from the beginning that it wasn't going to be an encyclopaedia of the colonised title of his country. 'Wales,' he so often preaches to the rest of the family over one of his elaborate garlic-and-chilli-saturated dinners, 'comes from the Anglo-Saxon word Wealhas, which means "foreigners" – Cymru comes from the earlier Brythonic Celtic word "combrogos" mean-ing "compatriot". No one wants to be considered a foreigner in their own country.'

Urien would argue with him about it. Say it was evolved from Walhaz, which described the inhabitants of the Western Roman Empire. That it was just handy for Eurov to have some beef about it to keep that chip firmly on his shoulder.

Miri smooths the page down in front of her. It's soaking wet, the words bleeding onto the page. She vaguely makes out the letter 'Q' at the top, but cannot decipher what the rest of it says. Her father's handwriting is notoriously difficult to read. 'Worse than a doctor's,' she remembers her mother saying, trying to decipher a shopping list he'd given her for one of his fanciful recipes. Underneath, Miri informs her, is a section that's been torn to shreds, possibly a P entry, that is proving equally tricky to decipher, some parts of it still missing, and the ink having spread outwards and joined up with other letters, creating its own indecipherable language.

'We will get some of our document examiners onto it, though. Do you know where the rest of it might be?' Miri says. 'The way it was positioned on the bed next to the girl suggests, I don't know, a possible . . . significance . . . '

'No,' Iona lies, feeling for the cold, second skin that is hidden under the darkness of her hoodie. How had she not seen that page on the girl's body? Or the scatterings on the floor? She should have taken them, too.

'OK, well don't worry about that for now. The most important thing is to get you set up for the night. You need rest, and food, and then we can talk further. When you feel like it. We won't rush you, Iona. This is a lot to take in.'

Iona wants to tell her that she won't be taking it in. There's no way this new situation is gaining a foothold inside her. She's outright rejecting the whole thing.

'He wouldn't do this . . . He wouldn't . . . ' she says. Her voice comes out thin as air, barely a whisper.

Miri looks at her with a mix of compassion and despair as Iona reels back in her mind to the moment before this all happened, when she was busy fumbling for Jethro's belt, easing herself down onto him, gasping as he got into her deeper, much deeper this time than before. The accompanying rhythm of the storm had seemed exhilarating, erotic even – the car being doused by the rain, the river whooshing somewhere beyond the hedge, the thrum of the wind all around them, while they were caught in a passionate storm of their own. She had always loved the sound of the rain on the glass, the skittish pulse of it. She had placed her hand against those crystal droplets and cried, when it was over, because she had loved her life, loved Jethro and loved the rain. All the while that mass of water was laughing at her, filling up her house, eradicating her future.

'Give me a moment and we'll make the necessary arrangements for you, OK?' Miri says.

'Can I see them?' she asks, looking up hopefully. 'My family.'

'Not yet,' Miri says. 'But soon, I promise.'

More than anything now, Iona regrets not staying in the house. She should have gone up into the attic. Gone looking for him. Not run away from it, leaving the sodden mess of it behind her.

'My dad,' she says, with one last breath. 'My dad, is still out there . . . is he?'

Miri turns.

'We're working on that presumption, yes.'

Iona nods. Miri leaves her in the company of another police officer while she goes to make the relevant calls to her aunt. Iona shuffles the ginger dust of the biscuit around on the table and wonders if Miri is watching her from another room somewhere. Does she know, perhaps, that she is lying about having the encyclopaedia? That the small, leather-bound book, swollen with water, that she took from the girl's rigid hand, is right here, under her jumper?

She doesn't know why she won't tell Miri that she took it. Perhaps because it is her last connection to her father, and having it there, next to her, as torn and tattered and damp as it is, the ink running across the pages and onto her skin, is a way of staying close to him.

She holds it close to her chest as if it's her brother, sister, mother. Surely this couldn't be the encyclopaedia he was working on for the university? Those illegible scrawls, sentences fragmenting in black rivulets across the page? Why would he write it by hand? Who wrote anything by hand anymore?

Perhaps her greatest fear is that underneath her jumper is a document that may well make out her father to have lost his mind. And she doesn't know if she wants them to see that.

Not yet. Not before she does.

8. CAIN

My grandmother – my *Mam-gu* – has always wanted to know the particulars. I can only guess that what happened to us both all those years ago has permanently taken the edge off death. After all, no one else's dead body could be any worse to look at than that of someone who was once a soft, newborn baby in your arms. Not that we talk about it. Not that we've ever really talked about what happened to my parents and my brother, or what a mess it has presumably made of both our lives, binding us together like this; a *Mam-gu* and her grandson, her *ŵyr*, meeting daily to devour cakes and talk rigor mortis.

It's an unspoken rule between us that I call by for breakfast after the end of my night shift – she insists it's for my benefit, so I can check she isn't dead before I go for my day sleep, whereas in reality it's more about her checking in on me and getting all the gory details. When I round the corner of Smallbrook Street I find her outside, talking to a mechanic in overalls, who hands her a full jar of raspberry jam and goes on his way.

'Who was he?' I ask.

'No idea. I couldn't open the jar so I just stood out here until someone who could passed by. Very nice man he was. Strong.'

Mam-gu is resourceful if nothing else.

'So that man, Eurov Griffri, he's on the run,' she says, after I explain the little I know of what happened to them. 'After killing the lot of them? God alive! And that boy who died, that's the one you go running with, isn't it?'

She butters her scone furiously, as though it's the last offering on earth, and then more or less pours the jam over it, a flowing red lava. There is never a tremor in that voice when we discuss death. Not a single current of emotion that could disrupt those crumbs

41

on her lips, send their debris rocketing towards me. It is always the same measured flat tone, as she munches away, considering yet another life's end.

'The police think he killed them. He'd pulled the covers over their heads,' I reply, remembering what the coroner's officer told Manny, knowing that I have to give her something; one small concession between sips.

'How very considerate of him,' she says, flatly. 'Do you want anything else? I can grill a bun if you like?'

'No thanks,' I reply, feeling the sugar spreading out through my bloodstream. 'I'll need to sleep later. Too much sugar . . . keeps me awake.'

Even before I lost my own family, I was always afraid of the worst. Preoccupied by the possibility of death from a very young age, almost as if I knew what was to come – as if I knew that I was destined to experience it first-hand, way before anyone else would.

Eventually I trained my mind to think of it as a relief. Relief that I wouldn't have to fear the worst happening anymore, because there could be nothing worse ahead of me than what was already behind me.

The worst was no longer a thing to be feared. It had already been and gone.

And I like to think that makes me an ideal person for working with the dead.

*

As I'm leaving, *Mam-gu* reads the obituary in the local paper and mentions another death: her chiropodist, Marsha. Funeral's tomorrow.

'Thirty-six she was,' she says. 'Just gone, like that, in the middle of the night. Twin boys. It's bloody awful. She was the best chiropodist in town. What am I going to do now, eh?'

Marsha was the other unexplained death I put away last week. I remember the expression etched onto her face; the split second, half-awake realisation that death was coming for her. I scoop the paper up and make a mental note of the location – Pont Sulyn's community centre. Humanist service. No flowers. My interest in funerals is a relatively new thing, but ever since I started helping Manny out as a bearer, it seems a fitting way to get some closure on the whole thing. I feel a duty, in many ways, to see those I watch over reach their end destination.

'Will you be going to the funeral?' I ask her. 'I could take you, if you wanted to.'

In many ways, it's easier if I have some sort of connection to the dead. Sometimes there's only so much bearing the weight of the dead you can do, and Manny's told me more than once to bugger off when I've offered to help out.

'You need to get a life,' he says. 'Stop collecting deaths.'

'I'll think about it,' *Mam-gu* says, wriggling her feet uncomfortably in her nylon tights as though thinking about what her feet might be missing out on from now on. 'It'll be a day out, I suppose, won't it?'

*

After I leave *Mam-gu*'s house, I take my usual daily walk through the town towards the river. There are traces of the flood's destruction everywhere, the ruins of people's lives strewn all over the waterfront, damp sofas and cushions lying in bushes, debris from people's houses having been carried along by the current – a slate here, a coving there. A garden gnome with its smile washed clean off its face. At some point, we all know the river's going to engulf the whole place – *Mam-gu*'s always reading this stuff aloud to me from the local rag, how the town's going to have to be abandoned in a decade or so, and wants to

43

know what my plans are. I turn things around and say we need to think of a plan for her first, but she says she doesn't plan on being around. That she feels both lucky and guilty that her generation can just sneak out the back door while all the chaos they caused comes for us instead. I always reply that I'm very sorry to disappoint her, but being an octogenarian does not excuse you from living on into the next decade. Whatever we do, we do it together, I say. And that she might be around for some of the shitstorm, so it's best to be prepared.

The riverfront's eerily quiet and empty, as it always is after a storm, as though everyone's sulking with the water for what it's done to the town, and can no longer see any beauty in it. It's the best time to go down there, truth be told, so I don't have to bump into anyone I know. There's a quiet path down by the far bridge – ideal for a jog – where it opens up into wilderness and it's as if you're leaving the grey Pont Sulyn behind you as you hurtle on into another universe of ochre coloured grasslands.

Though years have passed now, I can't look at the river without thinking about them. How it was the last thing my family ever knew. And yet that exact mass of water is long gone, having flowed away from that disaster almost as soon as it happened, as if it was nothing to do with it at all. It's one of the largest rivers in the country, and I know as I'm walking alongside it that I'm only seeing a fraction of it, the fraction that it allows me to see; I see nothing of its origins, of the towns it has hurtled through, the steep hills it has plundered, the counties it has divided, and all the earth and silt and rock it has shaped as it flows by. I am allowed only this moment, running alongside it with these droplets that will never be seen by me again, before they flow on their merry way towards the sea. The inevitability of it, the impossibility of ever catching up with that water, no matter how fast I run, is as soothing to me as it is infuriating to *Mam-gu*.

'Stupid river. Just doing what it wants without a thought for us poor mortals,' she says.

*

For the first five years after the accident, both of us – *Mam-gu* and I – walked together along this path in all weathers. We walked up and down and around, up the path to Pont Sulyn's church, and round again back to the town, nearly every day. *Mam-gu* said that through doing this, we were 'normalising' the route again, taking away its significance. Whenever we got to that point where it happened – no longer a point now – long fixed up and plastered over, a breakage made good again – we would stand there for one minute and think about them. Sixty seconds. *Mam-gu* timed it. No longer than that, she always insisted, or she'd be hurling herself in.

And after those sixty seconds that felt like sixty hours we'd start walking away again, which was part of our healing process, according to her. The ability to walk away from something awful. To know that we had the power to reclaim a piece of land, to make it normal, to see a river as just a river. One foot in front of the other.

We've found our own rhythms, over the years, our own different ways of commemorating things. My timeline is different to hers, of course, as I'm usually sleeping when she's at her most energetic. And I tend to jog across the path, if I can – it makes me feel freer, somehow, so that it isn't dragging me down, just co-existing quietly. And I can always run faster if it becomes too much. Walking involves too much thinking and remembering.

Now we come at separate times and at separate speeds; her, mid-morning, trudging on, me at dusk before my shift, hurtling at speed, two quietly furious journeys orbiting each other, around and around, endlessly, like a whirlpool.

C – COUPLING: in the English language a wedding and a marriage are not one and the same thing, and a necessary semantic distinction is drawn between the two. One wonders if the problem with marriage, in Welsh, is that we use the same word for marriage and wedding – *priodas. Pree-oh-dass.* To me, this suggests that the day-to-day minutiae of half-heartedly preparing a bland meal fit for a small army and washing a child's soiled knickers are somehow synonymous with a night of dancing, a three-tiered, buttercream-filled cake, and saccharine-smiling headshots. As though at any moment one will open the door of the bathroom to find the party still in full swing, a samba band playing, a miniature bride and groom in each other's arms, circling the rim of the toilet. 'Have a good wedding,' (*priodas dda!*) we say! In the same breath we are saying, 'Have a good *marriage*,' as if we are standing over your marital bed, urging that tired hand to keep roaming across the too-familiar flesh next to it, even though it would rather thumb the pages of a book.

I have often wondered whether there should be another, separate word for marriage itself, something more akin to COUPLING – cyplu – *cuh-plea* – the random pairing of two items, to stress that this is just two beings that could easily have been paired elsewhere, with different, and less disastrous, results.

Had I not been coupled with Lisa, would I have done the terrible thing that I did? Would fate have led me elsewhere, perhaps?

Should I have remained a bachelor forever, as everyone thought I would be?

To bring other people into your life is to drag them down with you. Why do such a selfish thing?

9. IONA

She wakes up in a single bed in a twin room; the room she has always slept in when staying with Aunt Anna. The room is a cocoon of rose and vanilla patterns, a colour scheme chosen by Bri, who will never sleep in the bed next to her again. And yet traces of Bri, her tastes, her wishes, her desires, remain – in the cassis-coloured cushions, in those funny little magenta lights dangling from the ceiling, in the birthday-cake-patterned wallpaper. It feels to Iona as though these things hold the possibility of conjuring her back up, as though you could touch one of them and Bri could come bursting into the room any moment, like she always did, uninvited, a tangle of limbs and hair, a side ponytail sashaying this way and that, errant, golden strands caught in the zip of her onesie. Bleary-eyed, musty-breathed Bri, who would sneak into bed with her sister in the early hours and wrap her small, warm body around Iona's.

Sometime, during the early hours of the morning, the weed has whirled its last dance in her body and the realisation that her family are gone has finally reached the edges of her consciousness. Enough for her to feel the absence now, deep inside her. Throughout the night, through fitful bursts of sobbing in her almost-sleep, she has seen them, all around her, heard their voices, felt their bodies next to her. She has even been calmed by them, telling her that it will be OK, that they are not gone if she can still see them. That they exist in these strange particles of memory, that they will always be alive to her. She imagines leaving a voice note for her brother: *You'll never guess what has happened. You've gone and died.*

By the time she wakes, she's completely numb again.

She lies on her back in Bri's bed, her fingers tracing the ridges of the textured wallpaper next to her, moving slowly from one birthday cake to the next, each one tilting symmetrically at an angle

47

along the wall, topped with bright yellow icing, a mockery of celebration.

Miri informed them that there were teams at the house now, that they would be there for several days. She imagines the bubbles rising in the wallpaper of her own home; the smiling face of her family life horribly disfigured. Ghostly white figures in protective clothing moving in and out of rooms, tagging and bagging their lives, reducing it to nothing but objects, breaking it down to the sum of its parts.

It's been a mere facade of sleep through the past few hours, her body entirely alert and restless under the thin duvet cover, her mind fragmenting and flickering like a glitching screen. Blood and water commingle in her memories, she cannot now remember which was which – was her sister bleeding in her bed, or was that her brother, his hand outstretched in hopelessness on the landing? Again, she shuts the memory down, unwilling to go any further.

She's still shivering. Although she's been given warm, dry clothes, the water seems to have pervaded every pore and crevice, sunk deep into her bones. Forged its coldness right into the heart of her, making her feel watery, insubstantial. A half person. Half alive. 'We are all two thirds water,' she remembers her father saying, 'though perhaps for a Welsh person, it's a little more than that.'

Her father knew what it was to be drowned, she thinks, because it had happened to him and Anna, a long time ago.

Perhaps she should have mentioned it to Miri.

*

The sound of padding around on the landing; soft, considered footsteps, as though Anna is trying to sneak past, unnoticed. A distant, grey light pulses from behind the pink blackout blinds. Iona scours the floor for her phone but remembers she hasn't known where it is since she got to the police station. Considering how attached she always was to it, she feels strangely unencumbered to not have it with her anymore. Her phone will be full of the life she had before. She finds herself hoping that Jethro is still asleep. And that in his dream she is still that girl he knew, untouched by tragedy, aroused and thrusting in his lap. It comforts her to think that this version of herself still exists somewhere, in particles and neurons, yet to be extinguished.

The rain, at least, has stopped.

Iona wonders if Anna has slept at all since she arrived on her doorstep last night. Her aunt, as Iona predicted, found it hard to make sense of anything she was being told by Miri. Anna kept looking across to Iona, as though it was her fault in some way that this had happened, as though these were lies that had been spun to get out of trouble. 'I don't understand, where is he, where is my brother?' she kept asking, over and over, pulling her hair into a bun before pulling it all out again, pacing erratically. After they'd gone, Anna stood there by the sink looking out at the rain pulsing at the glass, pressing the button to boil the kettle over and over, her back to Iona. The silvery steam appeared to be rising off her body, making her appear like some mythical sea creature who could evaporate at any moment.

Iona had no energy left for anything at all. She simply asked if she could go to bed.

'Stay as long as you want,' Anna had said then, turning, emotionless, the fug of boiling water still obscuring her face.

She wonders if they'll be able to talk more directly about it this morning. Whether they will be able to acknowledge the awfulness. Or whether the unhelpful denial will continue. 'Good god, Anna,' she always remembers her father saying to her on the phone. 'No. Just listen to what I'm telling you.' Endless frustrations about what Anna could, and could not process, her father having to deal with it all in the absence of a decent parent, their mother long shipped off to the care home with dementia, a disease which had begun taking hold when she was only fifty two ('trauma,' her father had said, 'meant her brain had been more susceptible to it at a younger age') which resulted in her dying long before Iona was born. But Iona always felt there was more to Anna's aloofness than a lack of mother. Numbers are one of the few things her aunt understands, rather than facts, and she manages a job from home accounting for some big company. She remembers overhearing her father talking about it to her mother – 'the company says she's the most efficient they've ever had! Her absolute blocking out of everything else, all logic and sense, actually seems useful to someone. Imagine!'

Despite Anna's shortcomings, Iona and her siblings have managed to forge a relationship of sorts with her over the years – Bri being the one she had taken to the most, without Anna making any effort to hide the favouritism. The guileless, happy-go-lucky child had come along just at the right time, when Anna was getting bored with Iona and Urien, running out of ideas of how to entertain them in their adolescence. It was a relief to them too when all her attention turned to Bri, and they no longer had to pretend to be enjoying themselves in her company. Iona feels the pang of guilt now, how she and Urien whispered about her at night and questioned Anna's oddities, the way she presented food in strange ways, cutting their sandwiches into star shapes and moulding ghoulish faces out of potatoes and peas, her fastidious manner of keeping to a precise time, so much so that if there was any chance they were going to be late, they simply wouldn't go. Anna once took them out to the beach and would be too afraid to let them out of the car, so they stared longingly at the other kids on the beach from the car window, the freedom of those faraway, careening limbs mocking them.

But Bri, somehow, had been a delight to her. Bri had been allowed to run free out of the car, onto the beach, and hurl herself into the sea faced with little objection, though she still hadn't even managed to pass her level one swim class.

'Iona?' Anna's voice sounds from beyond the wooden door. 'Can I come in? I've brought you a cup of tea.'

'Just a minute,' she says.

Iona wonders how long she has before Anna notices the manuscript in her freezer, sealed in a plastic bag and stuffed in between the tortellonis and mince. While her father hadn't been of much practical use to anyone in the town during the floods, he'd been the first to run to the aid of those residents whose documents, pictures, and books were damaged by water, and Iona knows that you have to freeze a damaged manuscript as soon as possible. Iona and Urien joked that when it came to preserving life, he wasn't interested, but if it was anything to do with preserving history, he'd be right there, helping people find suitable places to freeze their documents to avoid further damage, bringing some of them home, taking others to cafés and restaurants with industrial sized freezers, then setting up his own little book-mending counter at the Pont Sulyn community centre. If she's learned anything from her father all these years, it's that it's possible to extend the lifespan of a book, to bring it back to life, if you're careful enough.

At the other side of the door, she finds Anna staring intently back at her, mug in one hand, a pile of neatly ironed clothes in the other.

'Didn't know if you were a milk before tea or a tea before milk girl,' she says. 'I know Bri's started to take it with honey, hasn't she? In which case we'd always put the milk in after, to stop it from curdling, you know. But actually the right way to do it is milk first, because the milk heats up unevenly otherwise.'

Iona takes the mug from her. It's lukewarm, as though Anna's been holding it for a long time.

Anna places the clothes down on Bri's bed and then slumps unnaturally onto it. It creaks as she sits down, and Iona recalls Bri's lightness, how she could flounce onto beds and sofas as if she were nothing at all, no more than air. Anna's presence is heavy in comparison. The bed isn't welcoming her the way it welcomed Bri. Anna folds her hands in her lap and looks up.

'There isn't anything in the paper about it, yet,' Anna says. 'I went through them all.'

'It's too early for anything to be in there yet,' Iona replies, taking her first tentative sip of the tea. It drips down into her hollow body. She still feels woozy from the weed, and slightly hungover, though she can't remember drinking anything. When was the last time she ate? Did she even finish her dinner last night, or was she in too much of a rush to get to Jethro? Why didn't she wait at that table? See what was really going on? She can't even remember looking at either her mother or her father as she stuffed down the bare minimum of her meal so she could get out of there. Would she have seen something, if only she'd looked up?

'But if it isn't in there . . . '

'I saw it, Aunt Anna. I saw them. They're gone.'

Anna looks up hopefully.

'Even Bri?'

It comes out as a whisper. The hopefulness in it is almost too much to bear.

'Yes, even Bri. Urien. Mum. All of them. Dad, probably too. By now.'

The images have recurred in her mind for the few hours she's been resting. Eurov hanging from a tree. Washed up on the river-bank, green and bloated.

'I tried to get up there, to the house,' Anna continues. 'But I couldn't get further than Lincoln Square. They sent me back.'

Iona nods. By now all sorts of irrational thoughts are bobbing around in her head; how she wishes she'd never told anyone it had happened. How she maybe could have drained the house herself, mopped it up with towels, cleared everything up, dried everyone off. Removed that strange girl from her bed, placed her back in the rain, because she didn't belong in their house. She should have gotten into her bed instead, back where she belonged. Maybe then, she thinks, maybe then everything would have been OK. Maybe she could have stayed there with them, for as long as it took for none of it to be real.

Anna, for all she knows, is lost in similar thoughts. That maybe if she hadn't answered the door, let Iona come in, then she wouldn't have to deal with any of it. Maybe that's all there is left to do now, she thinks, to dream up ways they could never have let the terrible truth in.

'I guess you won't be starting uni today,' Anna says, flatly.

'I guess not,' Iona replies, thinking of the jam-packed car outside their house, the red pin drop on her lost phone of the lodgings in Cambridge.

'You know he didn't do this, don't you?' Iona says. 'It must have been someone else.'

Anna looks away. The question hangs there precariously in the air.

'Eurov's the sort of person who hides things,' Anna says, finally. 'From everyone. The thing is, you can't know a person like that. Not really.'

They remain sitting there in silence, facing each other, listening to the ticking of Briall's pink Trolls clock which reminds them that time ticks unbearably onwards, that there is going be a next minute, hour, and day to deal with, that they will keep moving deeper and deeper into all this. That there is no way of going back, locking themselves in, refusing to let the world prey on the detail. Their mutual trance ends, with Anna springing to her feet as though someone has slapped her, announcing that the only thing to do now is to eat, to gather strength, and to phone the police to see what they intend to do about finding Eurov. She flips up the blinds and the sunshine pours in, a gloopy syrup so at odds with last night's greyness. Anna says she will go downstairs and prepare something to eat.

Iona asks for something simple. Fresh. Nothing from the freezer, she adds, hurriedly.

Iona pulls on her aunt's oversized sweater, leggings and socks, and wanders out into the corridor. She appreciates the dryness of everything in a way she never has before, the comforting feeling of the carpet beneath her feet, the silky feel of the beige curtains, the smoothness of the lime-white walls. To be dry, secure within one's home – why had she never realised the enormity of it? How a home, a real home, was what kept the outside world out, that this is what a home was for? She wanders a few feet onwards towards the large window on top of the landing, and takes in a sight she has seen many times before from her own arched window, the aftermath of a storm down below, the flooded football fields, the skeletal tops of trees grappling with the air with their desperate, begging hands, the rescue dinghies floating past in the distance, carrying people, their possessions, the damp remainder of their lives glistening in the morning air.

And the river, beyond them all, moving relentlessly forward, as the sunlight dances across its silver back and tries to dazzle them, to disguise the shame of all it has done.

Anna's words come spurting out of the water, frothing ferociously in her memory.

You can't know a person like that.

Had she not known her own father?

24 DAYS BEFORE

10. LISA

Although she hates herself for it, she begins to spend her free mornings searching for the P and Q sections of Eurov's encyclopaedia. She has a tendency (despite all her protestations to her family that these lost things are their responsibility alone) to go into a mad frenzy of searching for any lost property so that she can be the heroine to recover the missing thing. And she usually retrieves whatever it is from the places they swear they have already ransacked, which means she can smugly raise said object above her head like a trophy shouting, 'And what, do you say, is this?'

This latest venture is no different to searching for Urien's running spikes, Iona's school tie or Bri's lost ballet shoes; she knows deep in her bones that they have to be in the house somewhere. And she trusts her husband now as little as she trusts her children; she sees him as just one more dependent, a flaky child, someone who cannot be trusted to have *looked* properly.

But deep down, she knows there's more to it than this. As she pulls out the sofa cushions and empties the drawers, she knows that spending her mornings in this way, turning the house inside out, creating a mess that she will later have to clean up, is simply easier than confronting the large, empty canvas in her art studio, which she has no idea how to fill. Isn't it so much easier to go in search of something rather than waiting for it to find you? Like this ubiquitous, inspirational *awen* that Eurov keeps harping on about, insisting that all she needs to get going again is for it to beam down on her, and fulfil the artistic promise that seems to have been draining from her for years?

Almost twenty years have passed by in a blur since her breakout exhibition, which came as a result of a period of what the doctors termed as her 'unexplained' infertility. All through those years of the frenzied (and seemingly pointless) fucking with Eurov, she remembered how her *awen* had been on fire, and she could not stop the art from pouring out of her. All her paintings reflected the arbitrariness of biology in one way or another, its visceral cruelty, animals mating and devouring each other, cubs left alone in the half-light, a woman laying eggs that cracked and fried on a hot, New York pavement. Sometimes she sat in the darkness of her studio at night and shuddered at her own brutality, her honesty, her goddamn God-given talent. Her search for explanation had become her theme; and the art critics loved it, of course. It was an antidote to the explorations of motherhood and family; this was the age where people were now open about their fertility problems, about a woman's life not taking the course it was meant to. Lisa Griffri's work was 'refreshing' they'd said, 'open'. It was speaking on behalf of a whole lost generation of women who'd actively sought motherhood but had been denied it. Her greatest disappointment had become her greatest success. And there was no bitterness in that realisation either. It galvanised her – she rejoiced when yet another opportunity came through, or another journalist from the States asked to write about her. Suddenly, her pairing with Eurov, rather than being a chemical mishap, seemed destined. Had it not been crucial for her to meet this older man whose reproductive system would not align with hers, so that she could become the famous artist she always knew she had the potential to be? 'Thank you Eurov,' she'd say, giving herself to him freely, nightly. She fell madly in love with him again, and all the unexplained things were now somehow brightly, sharply explicable. Then, of course, after months of this heightened, renewed love – after she had found peace in not being a mother – she fell pregnant. It was almost as if nature sensed that they no longer particularly wanted a child, and because they had entirely forgotten about even the abstract, distant concept of becoming parents, it had thrust a baby at them, as some kind of test. Lisa almost felt like the baby had crawled out of one of her paintings, and at the worst possible time too; due a few months before her new exhibition. Eurov came home to find her crying over a positive pregnancy test with more savagery than she had ever cried over a negative one.

The art galleries were phoning daily at that point, wanting to display her works in New York and LA, pulling her back to her home country, now that she had become big again, from the periphery – from elsewhere. But she couldn't go. It was the most difficult pregnancy ever; not a day passed without her retching or having to take to her bed. She couldn't bear telling the galleries she couldn't do it. So Eurov had to. He had to field the calls and cut off her future, while she could do nothing but vomit behind him. Offers had to be turned down. Opportunities lost. The phone stopped ringing, and in that silence she become bigger and bigger while her career shrivelled to nothing. She was sick every single day, sometimes more than three times a day, vomiting right up until the morning the baby was born. The exhibition had to be postponed. Indefinitely.

And yet, even then, even after Iona's horrendous, difficult birth, the *awen* found her again. A few months after giving birth to Iona, there was another frenzy of activity. She couldn't stop painting. Her canvasses became bigger and bolder; celebrating the topography of a woman's body. With a fine pencil she created the contour lines of stretch marks zigzagging across the stomach's mountainous terrain, before using charcoal to mark out the *linea nigra*, the bold river trickling downwards towards dark, scorched forests, the shadow of her misshapen breasts looming over them. She hoped these paintings would show how a body never truly recovered from birth, that the flesh remembered everything, and that it was, in some ways, the only true expression of who the person inside really was.

And yet, despite her efforts, despite the fact that this art was coming from deep inside herself, those paintings didn't sell. Not in the way her previous infertility paintings had. When she placed the works side by side she could see why. There was a minimalism to those earlier paintings, and imagination and conjecture – grasping desperately at all that she had missed, or believed herself to be missing. There was beauty to her incompleteness. Now that she was on the other side – having betrayed her fellow childless admirers, having betrayed, it seemed, the ghost of her dead, childless idol, Frida Kahlo – her artistic expression became somehow excessive. Disingenuous, somehow, when it had seemed so raw and truthful before. Imagination was replaced with stark realities. It was difficult to look at. Who would her buyers be, every gallery wanted to know? While rich child-free couples had time and money to spend in galleries; those likely to identify with these paintings had other preoccupations. If they related to these pictures in any way then surely they would not be at the gallery but at a soft play centre, gazing inertly into their cold cups of coffee. And even their husbands, attending the openings, did not want to be reminded of what their wives had become. They would rather have a real landscape to gaze at in the evenings, rather than being faced with a contracting womb in the guise of a mountain.

Stop this, Lisa, she tells herself now, rummaging in Eurov's filing cabinet, realising how far down the spiral of the past she has fallen. *That was then, this is now. You can still create something. Something to be proud of. You still have things to say.*

And yet she still carries on searching for Eurov's lost pages, as if there isn't a canvas in her studio waiting for her brilliance to descend upon it. Because deep down, she worries that her brilliance is gone. It's been zapped – or perhaps WhatsApped – out of her.

What she has not bargained for this morning is that her findings during her search have caused her deep concern for Eurov's state of mind. She finds printed extracts of his encyclopaedia stowed away in the strangest of places; a page slipped down behind the radiator in his study, another crumpled into a ball and stuffed into a sock, another on a shelf in the cupboard under the stairs beneath a can of car oil. And most worryingly, another lone page punctured on a coat hanger, dangling like a corpse in the darkness of their wardrobe. A quick scan of the contents reveal that neither are the aforementioned P and Q sections, and these particular extracts seemed no more than early drafts which have been scribbled all over by an editor, looking for 'deeper, more factual content,' demanding for the whole section to be rewritten.

Why on earth has he kept them lying around like this, scattering his work all over the place like confetti, showing little regard for where it ends up? If this is indicative of how he now treats his research, which was once his pride and joy, is it any wonder that two sections of the encyclopaedia have taken off, of their own accord? Perhaps this negligence is also to account for the fragmented way he deals with family life and his own marriage, only appearing in it every now and then, doing very little to maintain it? Perhaps, she thinks, if she looks hard enough, she will find her own marriage stuffed down the back of the sofa among the loose change and cookie crumbs.

But finally, in the very last place she looks – which is the front drawer of Eurov's fall front bureau desk – she finds something. Or three things, to be exact. As ever, her search has brought things to the surface that she didn't even realise were lost.

First of all, a small, leather-bound book, some kind of diary. She's vaguely aware of seeing it before, having assumed it was where Eurov kept his notes for the actual official encyclopaedia he was working on for the university. But opening it, she comes across the title *ENCYCLOPAEDIA OF 'CYMRU' (THE COUNTRY ALSO KNOWN, ERRONEOUSLY, AS WALES) as experienced by Eurov Griffri*, written in Eurov's characteristic chaotic scrawl, and as she ventures further she sees that it seems to have been written in an encyclopaedic form, starting with *A* for *Awen*. A laugh escapes her then, in realising that she has gone in search for inspiration and has found the very thing that is meant to inspire her, literally, in the pages of Eurov's book. In flicking through further, she also realises that the P and Q sections have been ripped out, and that it is this particular document – one that is almost impossible to read because of his abominable handwriting – that Eurov is stressing over, rather than his official, university-funded project that he's been working on for years and years, along with a number of other dedicated contributors and individuals across the country.

Why the hell would he care about this document, which seems to her to be nothing but a few ramblings and thoughts?

The second thing she finds seems to clarify this for her a little. Just beneath this, in the same drawer, folded into a neat square, is a printed-out email from Professor Roisin Cleary, Head of Department:

Dear Dr Griffri,
It has come to our attention that the Encyclopaedia of Wales that you are working on is no longer considered an eligible research project under the current academic guidelines. Being, as it is, an encyclopaedia of Wales rather than of Britain, it is seen as a rather provincial endeavour, and will not be considered a valid contribution to British culture. Many of our contributors have decided to work on larger, more British-focused projects, and so we are now halting the funding of the project and hope that you will present an alternative research project to the university for consideration. Failure to do so could result in compulsory redundancy, as the university will need to reduce staff by an unprecedented amount in the coming months, in a bid to create financial stability for the institution.

Lisa stares at the document in stunned silence. The encyclopaedia has been Eurov's *raison d'être* for the past seven years, if not more. The wording, she imagines, would have devastated him, the notion that his endeavour was a *provincial* one. 'We are the original Britons!' he so often hailed. 'We were here when the Romans came, before the Anglo Saxons took over!' Yet Lisa has seen how his colleagues look at him when he says this, rolling their eyes, believing him to be clinging on to some fallacy. The email confirms that there's no place for a mind like Eurov's in that department, and that he, like the original Britons, is fighting a battle that's impossible to win.

But it isn't the email in itself that worries her. It's the fact he hasn't mentioned it to her at all. The potential redundancy that could upend all their lives, especially as she herself isn't bring-ing in much income right now. The old Eurov would have sat down with her and discussed it for hours, asking her opinion on what he should be doing next, what possible other interests or obsessions could be spun into a book or a grant-worthy project. But yet again, she sees that the old Eurov is gone, and that a strange, ghostly, automaton Eurov has taken his place, one who does not mention these things to his wife, and decides, with-out consulting her, to replace a solid research project with some illegible scribbles that no one at the department is going to want to read. Even the encyclopaedia, it seems, now has a secretive double that he has also never mentioned except to bemoan the loss of its pages; a shadowy, second version of the larger thing that should be there in its place.

And as she hurls it across the room, angry with Eurov for so many things now that she cannot even pinpoint the single thing which has triggered her rage, something falls out of the document.

It's a picture, of a girl. A young, blonde girl, who looks young enough to be one of his students.

And on the back someone, in possession of a much clearer, neater handwriting has written: *I love you.*

D - DOUBLING: In Wales, all sorts of doubling occurs. The most common is the split in identity for a person raised bilingual, with two ways of seeing the world, two sets of friends with whom one converses in different ways, and a general split in frames of reference, sense of humour, and beliefs. Code-switching occurs on a daily basis, where one language catapults over the other, a phrase in one language here, a proverb in another language there, a complex dance of words and phrases which sashay across the tongue with wild abandon. Code-switchers see nothing wrong with this kind of language-pirouetting. Learners of the language are sometimes confused by it. Non-natives observing from the sidelines are utterly confused by one language's incessant need for the other, their mangled wrapping around each other.

Throughout my life, my doubling has plagued me. It has been a weapon, at times, to allow me to be someone else in another country. But it has also been a way of compartmentalising things that I would rather not think about. It has enabled me to think of the other side of myself as another person, a whole other existence, in which a bad thing occurred which I no longer wish to think about.

Doubling does not always make you bigger, it can make you smaller too. Because you must learn to halve yourself. And choose which bit you want to keep, and which bit must be thrown away.

11. IONA

Once the roads into Pont Sulyn reopen and the skies brighten, it clears a path for all sorts of unwanted guests to enter the town. Reporters and TV crews filter in. Rodents, sniffing the putrid, death-riddled air.

'Unbelievable,' Anna says, 'considering their only interest in the town before now has been the prospect of it disappearing forever.'

Iona has seen paperwork littered over Anna's coffee table, which has something to do with the potential decommission of the town. Facts and figures and graphs she cannot quite comprehend. Flood charts. Hydroelectricity proposals. From what she gathers, Anna, for all her shortcomings and what her father referred to as her 'ineptitude for life', knows more about the future of Pont Sulyn than most.

Now, the reporters seem to want the town to stay put so they can get close to the two remaining members of the Griffri clan and find out what exactly has made Eurov Griffri kill his whole family – and seemingly a stranger, too. Iona watches them creeping ever closer, a tide of eyes and bright flashes, and watches Anna boldly heading out into their midst, parting them and staring them down, giving them nothing to cling to, nothing at all. Iona has begun to admire the way her deceptively small-framed aunt carries herself, and moves through life doing things on her own terms. She sees how much of her parents' unease around her aunt was more to do with their own 'ineptitude for life', their fear of facing things.

Perhaps, she thinks, if only they had addressed whatever problems they had head-on, in the way Anna does, then none of this would have happened.

The story drips out and pools around them nevertheless, each report a slightly diluted version of the other. Anna returns from the corner shop and slams the bulk of papers down on the kitchen table. She and Iona ingest them, while the coffee and toast on the table are untouched, left to go cold. Whenever Anna is out of the room, Iona rummages again in the freezer compartment, pushing Eurov's leather-bound book further down, decorating it with a bag of frozen peas and some loose leaves of cavolo nero. What the reporters would give for it, she thinks, this insight into her father's state of mind.

She's taken it out a few times and tried to read it, but it's frozen into a solid block now, and the water damage means the words have bled into each other, blurring what was already an impossibly mystifying scrawl. It needs expert care if she's going to be able to take those pages apart without ruining them.

She needs, she thinks, her father. And all his expertise.

Miri rings just to inform them that the search for her father is ongoing. That now the storm has passed, they are able to progress much quicker.

'Where is there to hide after a storm?' Anna says. 'It either flushes you out or washes you clean away.'

The picture all the papers use is the photo taken on their family holiday last summer, which had somehow been circulated, on that very first night, without their knowledge. In it, her mother, 'local artist Lisa Griffri', is featured sitting on a wall, a sunset behind her, surrounded by her husband, son and two daughters. A perfect heart-shaped formation of heads. Lisa beams at the camera, hair pinned to the side, dressed in a flattering floral jumpsuit which billows generously around her midsection. *Father of murdered family missing*, the headline says. Iona notices how craftily the headline has been constructed, the word 'murderer' somehow floating into the reader's consciousness as they read, even though the paper cannot claim any such thing at this point.

And yet, surely, looking at the picture, you can't imagine that a man whose hand seems so limp on her mother's shoulder would be capable of even holding a paintbrush steady, let alone killing a whole family.

'He looks handsome, at least, doesn't he?' Anna says, flatly. 'I guess that's the idea, is it? They get the best picture they can of him, so it's shocking? And that's how they sell papers.'

Iona thinks of the hundreds of other photos of her father there are to choose from, where he looks shambolic and barely-put-together, squinting at the camera, tongue halfway out of his mouth, eyes fixed anywhere but straight ahead. That ridiculous departmental headshot with his blazer lapel crumpled and his tie askew, giving his best impression of an eleven-year-old boy. 'You look deranged, dad,' she remembers Urien saying when he uploaded it for him on the website.

Deranged. She looks again at her father's face, honing in on his lopsided smile, his faraway gaze. No doubt there will be people sitting down to breakfast now, poring over this picture, who will delight in saying that there are *signs*. They will be processing the horror of these three innocent children in the picture, brought into the world by a father who intends to kill them.

And what of her own pose? Does it suggest something, anything? She's looking at the camera and smiling a terse, tight-lipped smile, which she knows is how she comes out best in photographs. *Never smile with your teeth*, Jethro had said to her once, before hastily adding that it was because she looked so beautiful and mysterious with her mouth closed. Iona now feels the shame of not really being there, even though she was present. All she really thought about during that holiday was her first kiss with Jethro, which had happened in the darkroom of photography class the previous week. She, in a moment of boldness that she didn't even recognise in herself – had guided him in and had shut the door behind them, firmly.

'There's something exciting about seeing a picture develop right in front of your eyes,' she'd said, reaching for the fixer, explaining, as her eyes leaned over the lens, that the reason their art teacher believes in teaching them these old methods is so that they understand the genesis of art, the process of which eludes them when they use their phones. By that time he was standing ever so close to her, his face bathed in ultraviolet light, the potent mix wafting up towards them, the heady, dangerous scent in the air between them.

It wasn't the sort of encounter you could shake off. Ever since, the pungent aroma of the fixer and developer has always been equated with some kind of excitement for her, as though she conjured a boy into being with chemicals.

Basically, she couldn't wait for the holiday to be over so she could see him again.

Iona wishes she had smiled a real smile into the lens of that camera that evening, that she had allowed herself to *feel* the experience of the holiday as it unfolded, every precious minute of it, instead of wishing the time away. If that picture holds any artifice at all, it's the fact that she's pretending to be present, to be a part of something, when she is, in fact, in her own orbit, in her own head. Kissing Jethro over and over again in a toxic chemical cloud.

Next, she looks at the e-fit picture of the girl which, in some articles, has been situated right next to their family photo. It's the same face that Iona remembers from that night, but the girl looks alert now, and she stares back at Iona, expressionless, as Iona looks for something, anything, in that face to make sense of the whole thing. Police are appealing for anyone who recognises her to come forward, but it's been days, and no one has. Iona forces herself to look again, to look intensely, as though she can awaken some knowledge in herself that is deeply hidden. But nothing springs to mind, no familiarity, nothing. And yet this dead girl brought to life by an artist is somehow responsible – she knows it – for bringing about the end of everything.

'Iona, Iona dear, it's alright,' a voice comes from somewhere, startling her. Iona looks down to see that the e-fit picture is now

saturated with tears, as though the girl's fake outline is now showing emotion. Anna is wrapped tightly, awkwardly, around her, like
an ill-fitting jumper. 'Just let it all out. There you go. We have to find
some way of carrying on,' Anna says. 'There's no other option.'

*

That evening, there's a gentle knock at the front door. She becomes
aware of voices downstairs, the melody of the female liaison's soft,
carefully measured tone. Anna's face appears around the door, plastered in makeup. Two red lips, puffed up like miniature life jackets.
Foundation that would take a bulldozer to remove.

'That awful woman is back,' she says. 'Will you come and speak
to her?'

That awful woman. As though she is the one who made this
happen. Iona nods and says she will be down in a minute. She
remembers the way Miri looked at Anna when they first met. She
supposes Miri's seen all sorts, doing her job, but even she could
not hide her astonishment that Anna was not processing the news
fully. That while Iona stood there shivering on her carpet she talked
in a dull, unruffled tone about bedding and it being too late to eat
and whether or not Eurov would be over in the morning to pick his
daughter up.

Miri sits encased in her slightly oversized grey suit, her face pale
and beautiful, her mouth fixed in a perpetual, empathetic pout.

'How are you doing today, Iona?' Miri asks. 'Managing to get
some sleep?'

Two nights have passed in a blur. There was thrashing, sweating.
A feeling of saturation, and drowning.

'A little,' she says.

'Shock is draining, and exhausting. You'll probably feel the
physical effects of it in your body for days, weeks even. The adrenalin will be whirring around your body still. And it'll alter things,

patterns of behaviour, your memory even. So be kind to yourself, OK, take it slow.'

'I was meant to be starting uni this week,' she says, the fact hitting her like a sledgehammer. Right now she should be in Cambridge, at her university lodgings. Eurov was going to drive her there. She wonders again about her possessions in the packed car. The old Iona, locked into it. Is it still sitting there, in their drive? Why would he make her pack everything that afternoon, if he knew she wasn't going anywhere? She wonders what has happened to her lodgings at uni; the bed she would no doubt be sitting on now, missing Jethro. She and Anna agreed, last night, that she would defer her place. Anna phoned them while Iona sat there, watching her. She said her niece would not be enrolling this year because her entire family were now dead and no one knew what this meant for her.

'I know, Iona,' Miri says. 'I'm really sorry about that. Hopefully they will keep your place open for you for next year.'

Her place. The place she was meant to be slotted into, right now, in that predictable jigsaw of a young adult going to uni. Neatly positioned away from her family, staring into the face of the future. Where is her place from now on?

'I thought I'd keep you up to date with what is happening,' Miri continued, folding her hands in front of her, reaching for a leather-bound file. 'I'm afraid we're still unable to identify the girl in your house, Iona. I assumed it would become clear as time went on, but we still don't have any leads on this, so, as I'm sure you've seen, we've had to appeal for information. Are you sure you don't have any idea who she could be?'

The same question again, as if they suspect she's keeping something from them. She hasn't given her much thought, is what she tells Miri. There's no space in her brain to register the loss of a girl she doesn't know. A girl who was some sort of stand-in for her. A replica. The girl who ended up in the house of water by mistake.

The girl no one wants to claim, even in death. All she wants to know is where her father is.

'That girl must belong to someone!' comes Anna's voice from the corner of the room. 'Can't you work it out, with all your resources, and stop hassling my niece?'

'It's proven tricky,' Miri says, unperturbed by Anna's irritability. 'There have been no reports of any missing girls in the area. No concerned parents ringing the station. She had no documents on her. No phone. Nothing. Just herself. It's a . . . an unusual situation. And for obvious reasons, we cannot release a photo ID, so the e-fit will have to do.'

Iona remembers the girl's face, smattered with dried blood. Who would want to claim that?

'Why haven't you found Eurov yet?' Anna continues. 'He can't have gone far . . . '

'We still have dedicated teams out looking, Ms Griffri. Searching . . . ' She hesitates. ' . . . the surrounding areas, woodland, and the river . . . '

'The river,' Anna says, her eyes glazing over. 'Yes, that would make sense. Returning to water.'

Miri looks up, curious.

'Why do you say that, Anna?' Miri asks.

'We all return to water, don't we?' Anna says, looking away, as if it wasn't the answer she was going to give her, but it's the only answer she's prepared to give, for now.

Iona knows what her aunt means. If only Miri cared to look up, rather than being so intent on staring so directly at them, as she's probably been trained to do, she'd see the black and white framed picture of Anna and Eurov as children on Anna's wall, standing above a valley in North Wales that no longer exists.

'Did you have contact with your brother before the incident, Ms Griffri? Any contact at all?'

Anna looks guiltily over at Iona, then back again at Miri.

'He came here,' she says quietly. 'The day before it happened.'

Iona has no idea why this hasn't been mentioned before. Then again, maybe it has, who knows. The past few days have been a kaleidoscopic whirl of words and images and tears and scrolling and reading and sitting in front of twenty-four-hour news channels. Facts and figures gushing out nonsensically from the screen. 'More news as we get it,' the reporter says, in an almost sing-song voice. Iona can't tell the difference between what the presenters have told her, what Anna has hypothesised, and what she, herself, has witnessed.

'Can you tell me a bit more about his visit,' Miri asks. 'How did he seem to you?'

Anna hesitates. Iona can sense a reluctance from her aunt to share her experience of her brother with this complete stranger who has waded into their lives through this murky, horrible water. It's the same impulse, Iona supposes, that drove her to hide the encyclopaedia. But it's too late for Anna to hold back: it's already out there now, and Miri will want to scoop it up and claim it as evidence.

'He said he'd done something, something bad,' Anna continues. 'And I asked what and then he said – the same as he always did – oh Anna, I don't think you'd be able to handle it. I wish you were the sort of person who could, but you're not. And I . . . I got angry. Because he's always had this way of belittling me, even though I'm older than him, you see, and well . . . I told him to leave, and so he left.'

'I will need to take a formal statement from you about this,' Miri says, getting up. Iona can tell she's trying to remain calm but that something is bubbling up inside her, the aftershock of the tiny little bombshell Anna has just dropped on her. 'If you want to follow me into the kitchen for a second, we can do it right now. Iona, you can stay here, if it's easier for you?'

'How did he do it?' Iona asks Miri, pleadingly. Her brother's rigid hand surfaces in her memory, grasping for life on the landing.

Miri pauses, as if she's been taught to do this. Perhaps this is best practice, Iona thinks. Pause and let the bereaved know something devastating is coming for them, to give them time to get into position.

'We're still waiting on the pathologist's full report,' Miri says, quieter, this time. 'But early indications are that the cause of death for your brother and sister was asphyxiation. But we did find quite a few empty pill packets, so we think possibly that they had been sedated first, and in that case, wouldn't have been aware of what was happening.'

Asphyxiation. Sedation. The words seem to suck all the air out of the room. Anna looks at Iona and Iona back at Anna and Iona wonders if they both have the same image in their heads, that of Eurov tiptoeing towards those bedrooms with a pillow in his hand.

'Looking back now,' Miri continues, 'we cannot discount the possibility that you, too, were meant to be sedated, only that . . . well, perhaps, you didn't ingest as much as was planned. Do you remember, Iona, the way you were that night? A little out of it perhaps? Is it possible you didn't take as much as you were meant to? That it didn't work fully on you?'

She had pushed her food around her plate, she says, not particularly hungry, her stomach churning with excitement at the prospect of seeing Jethro, of being with him one last time before uni. Had her father urged her to eat more? Or had he not noticed that she'd only eaten a few morsels, only enough to make the whole evening take on a strange, unreal quality? Minutes after leaving the house she was getting high with Jethro anyway – had there been something else in her system that had attributed to her high, so much so that she didn't question where the hit was coming from?

'What about Lisa, and the girl?' Anna asks.

'No signs of asphyxiation, attempted or otherwise, but we're still waiting on confirmation of that. It seems more than likely, given the external injuries, that they had both suffered some kind of head trauma. As soon as we know for sure, you'll know, OK? We'll inform you before we release anything to the public, I can promise you that.'

'It doesn't make any sense,' Iona adds, her voice cracking now, the emotion foisting its way up her oesophagus. She tries to swallow it back down as best she can. Her father sprinkling their food with sedatives instead of herbs, then calmly smashing the skull of his wife and a girl he didn't even know. It isn't the Eurov she knows. Not at all. The Eurov she knows is the kind who can only hold a pen steady, nothing else. A man who writes an encyclopaedia out by hand, with such intensity that even those closest to him can't decipher it.

'You don't get it. He wasn't like that. He wasn't . . . violent.'

'I know it's hard to imagine your father doing this, Iona. And we'll try our best to help make sense of it all, OK? It's possible that there were things happening behind the scenes in your father's life that we don't know anything about just yet.'

Another pause, as she gears up for the big finish.

'More than likely, he wasn't thinking rationally when he did any of this.'

The sentence floats into the silence between them along with the sedatives and the asphyxiation, the new vocabulary of their reality. Echoing nonsensically in the dim light of the living room.

'Here's your phone,' Miri continues, taking a long black rectangle out of her bag and handing it to Iona. It feels odd in her hand; a stone, weighing her down. The weight of her old life. Who is there to ring, to talk to, who will understand any of this?

'We found it outside the house that night, you must have dropped it. We had our team fix it up again for you – we needed to take a look at it to see if there was anything useful on it, or if your father would try to make contact, but there's been nothing yet it seems. If he does try to get in touch with either of you, in any way, you must let me know straight away, OK? And if you can think of anything,

anything – perhaps in the house, or at the university – that could shed some light on this, then we would very much like to see it. Oh, and we'd also like you to take a look at this – an entry from his encyclopaedia which we've had restored, that was found on the girl's body.'

Miri retrieves a piece of paper from her file. It's covered in plastic, under which her father's unmistakable scrawl can be seen. The letters have run wild with water, creating an erratic pattern across the page. Miri presents them with a typed version, explaining what their forensic document examiner has been able to decode.

'From what the examiner has gathered, it looks as if it's the Q section of an encyclopaedia, and the other fragments seem to suggest a P section. Obviously this suggests to us that there's more. We really do need to locate the rest of the document.'

She looks at Iona intensely then, almost right through her, right through the wall of the living room and somehow round the corner and into the darkened compartment of the freezer, peeking under the shadowy canopy of cavolo nero where the encyclopaedia is glinting with frost. A panic surges in Iona, a feeling that she must get rid of it, somehow, get it right away from a place where they might come looking. She will not let them take anything more from her.

Anna comes to sit next to her so they can peruse the entry together. Iona eyes up the handwritten version in Miri's lap, feeling the indignation of being separated from that last real shred of her father, while Anna reads out the cold replica in front of them.

'Q,' – Anna reads – '*Q is not included in the Welsh alphabet. Neither are K, V, X and Z. It will be almost impossible for a non-Welsh speaker to fathom how people can function without these letters, any more than a Welsh speaker could cope without the digraph letter LL (known as the dark L which lives on the roof of the mouth) which is used to enunciate all manner of words and place names. But there came a day when I saw the letters that were missing from my own alphabet scattered across one name and it felt significant somehow, as though those letters were taunting me with a sense of loss. It made me shudder that two separate worlds, similar to letter patterns, can exist knowing nothing of each other.'*

There seems to be a name written down next to this, but it's been scribbled over. A frenzy of ink, a smudging so deep, it's as if Eurov was determined for it not to be understood by anyone, ever.

'We're trying to see if our experts can uncover what it says underneath, but it's proving difficult. And we're also trying to restore the P section, but it's been badly damaged and it's taking some time to piece it together. What do you think he means by . . . a sense of loss? And the name?' Miri asks.

Anna looks up.

'He had a habit of being abstract about things,' she says, but her voice isn't convincing at all. Like Iona, it's as if Anna senses how perilous and potent this document could be in the wrong hands. 'This isn't . . . really . . . a serious document, you do know that? It's not what he was working on for the university. These are just . . . musings.'

She looks up coldly at Miri. Yet her voice betrays her, ever so slightly, with its tremor. Iona feels that Anna knows, that they both know, that the more abstract Eurov was about things, the worse his state of mind.

As Miri and Anna move into another room to take the statement from Anna about her father's visit, Iona charges up her phone, and sits down to lose herself in her first moment of normality in days. It's as if she's plugged herself back into life, as she watches the messages of shock and condolence filter in on her phone. Her friends, her teachers, even her lover do not have the vocabulary for this, she thinks. They can only offer platitudes and emoticons and empty gestures, offers of help when she is beyond such a thing. She loses count of the number of girls at her school who have just sent her a crying emoji and nothing else.

As she watches Miri leave, she thinks of all the strangers now working on her case, the pathologists, the detectives, the rescue teams out looking for her father. How they will carry her momentarily, she thinks, in their minds, on their tongues, as a story to tell others as they get home, her name will be uttered as they loosen ties, undo a blouse, take off a bra, open a bottle of wine. But soon the conversation will move to something else and her story, her family's story, will be extinguished in a moment – she will be forgotten about. Radios and TVs will be switched off and she'll be gone. Erased. Except she'll still be here in this house; alone in her own story; unable to escape it like they can.

And it is this which makes her drop everything and run out of the house, to bang on Miri's window, to make her stop the car, right there, right now.

'I want to see them,' she says breathlessly. 'You promised.'

Miri looks up at her.

'Formal identification isn't necessary in a case like this Iona. The DNA will be enough . . . '

'It wasn't long enough,' Iona says. 'I didn't have time with them. That night. I left too early. I left them. I shouldn't have left them. Please.'

Miri hesitates.

'I would have to make a call to the morgue – they'd need time to prepare. And you'd have to check with your aunt too, if she'd be willing to let you go?'

Iona turns to look pleadingly at her aunt. Anna's makeup has started to crack, as if her whole face might suddenly just fall away onto the pavement in orange clumps, leaving her skeleton exposed. Her aunt shakes her head, adamantly, no. Iona knows that Anna has trouble leaving her home even in normal circumstances. The unknown is something she simply cannot deal with. The supermarket home deliveries, the cinema passes to stream new releases at home. She isn't going to be swayed. Not for this. Iona turns back to Miri.

'I'm eighteen,' Iona says firmly, turning back to Miri. 'Technically that means I don't need her permission, doesn't it?'

Miri nods solemnly and lifts her phone, gesturing for Iona to enter the car. She tells Miri she needs a few minutes to collect her things. She heads back into the house and hesitates in front of the freezer. From the kitchen window, she can see Miri pacing outside in the half light, talking quietly to someone on the phone, negotiating.

Iona opens the freezer door.

Anna remains standing on the doorstep as Iona enters the car. It's the first time they've been separated since the night of the flood, and the severing feels odd now, unnatural. As the car pulls away, Iona watches her aunt become smaller and smaller in the half light, until she's only a silhouette, a meaningless flash in the rear-view mirror.

12. CAIN

The dead are free to conduct themselves any way they want. They don't have to worry about embarrassing themselves, they can let everything go. And that's exactly what they do, sometimes many hours and days after their deaths. They secrete; they groan and expel wind. I don't mind these noises myself, though I know some of the other morgue attendants do. I see them for what they are, the echoes of an ending. There is great freedom in letting go of social norms; a body no longer having to hide its natural processes, like we have to do all our lives, hiding our discomfort, our pain, from others. Although not everyone sees it that way. *Mam-gu*'s friend Hetty was very aware of what indiscretions her body could commit after her death, and so she was meticulous about what she ate in the weeks leading up to it, fearing disgracing herself in front of the funeral director who she'd been in love with since she was a young girl. So my grandmother fed her nothing but aloe vera juice and liquid chlorophyll while she lay on her death bed, trying to make sure everything was digested, nothing left to chance. Hetty saw her death as the one chance she had to get close to him. What other opportunity would she have, she said, to have him hold her hand? To lay his head on her bosom and weep? She didn't want anything to ruin the moment, whether she was there for it or not. And maybe Manny's still right that the dead don't care, but if you want to make an impression in death – well, that's your prerogative.

Another reason I chose the night shift was so that it would keep the interactions with the living to a minimum. Hardly anyone requests a viewing in the night-time, and so apart from police visits and letting Manny and Eddie and the other funeral directors in and out, I pretty much have the place to myself. I read, I listen to the radio, and I even sometimes listen out for them, the bodies moaning in their chambers.

Just as I'm settling down to read about the use of cadavers to explore head transplants – which, some scientists say, could give us the possibility of a longer life in the future (though perhaps not for the donor) – I get a call from a Family Liaison Officer, Miri Pritchard, asking me how much time I'd need to prepare the bodies of the Griffri family for viewing.

'It's short notice, I know, Cain,' she says, pronouncing my name *Kane*, not *Kine* as it's meant to be pronounced. 'But if you could make sure they're in the best condition they can be, that would be helpful. The daughter wants to see them. She's young and it's bound to be upsetting for her. We'll try to keep it short – it's mainly a formal identification.'

I slam down the book and get to work, adrenalin surging through my veins, having no idea how much time I have before they get here. I feel I have to do this justice, for Urien. A bad viewing can change the pathway of grief from the moment it happens, so it's important to get it as right as you can at this early stage. But there's a limit to what a morgue attendant can do. The embalmers are the connoisseurs of this kind of thing – they can make a person look so good it's hard to believe they're not still alive. The best the morgue attendant can do is tidy them up. The post-mortem took place yesterday and the pathologist isn't always as precise as I'd like, so there's a bit of work to be done to hide the scars where the skin has been eviscerated and sewn back up, but it's better this way – if she'd come before the PM I'd have been forced to make her look at them through a viewing window, which is always more difficult for the bereaved, I think; to have a glass separating them from their loved ones. The whole point of a viewing, in my opinion, is to cement the fact of death, to make it appear real, and those who view from a distance still seem to walk away in a cloud of denial, as though some trick has been played upon them.

I position each head neatly on an angle, slightly raised on a block. Then I take my time to gently wash away all traces of blood on the back of the head of the mother and the older girl, and try to arrange their hair, the best I can, over their injuries. You've got to be careful with hair. While you wouldn't think it mattered all that much, a fringe back-combed here, a parting turned the wrong way there, it can change who the person was, and leave their bereft family members weeping in your arms telling you that it isn't the person they knew, not at all.

The bell rings shortly afterwards. I've done the best I can, under the circumstances, and the bodies look, if not content, then at least at peace. And I don't subscribe to this nonsense, so often perpetuated by vicars and preachers, that what lies before you is 'just a shell'. No matter how messed up those bodies are, they are so much more than just some irrelevant outer casings.

They once housed a person, a whole life. That's got to mean something.

*

Iona Griffri, Urien's only surviving sister – who I had at first presumed was the girl I'd stowed away that night – is now standing at the other side of the morgue entrance with two police officers and Miri Pritchard. I'm struck by how different to Urien his sister looks, dark hair framing her moon-pale face, arctic blue eyes staring right at me. In that moment, I'm somehow a young boy again, standing small and alone at the riverbank. I know full well that sometimes it's worse to be spared something, to be told you are *lucky*, when you consider what you have to deal with instead.

'Where are they?' she asks me in Welsh, clocking my lanyard which tells her I'm bilingual, that she's free to use either language to converse with me. It takes me a while to decide whether to continue in English. Procedurally, I'm meant to let the police lead the conversation, and use a language that everyone understands. But I see something in Iona's eyes in that instant; the desire for me to be different to the others. To somehow understand this whole thing better, our common language becoming a life raft – so I answer her quickly in my mother tongue, and lead her through a door into the viewing room.

'*Dere mewn.*' Come in.

It's a warm offering in a cold environment, and I see how much she appreciates it. I want so much to tell her that I knew her brother, but it doesn't seem it's the right time for it. Plus, the Family Liaison Officers don't approve of morgue attendants talking too much. To them we're merely functional, we should be only faintly seen, and never heard; they are the ones trained to guide the bereaved through the process.

Iona bristles at the cold as I lead her through. I've become accustomed to it, I suppose. In fact, I've acclimatised to the point that being outside the morgue feels overly warm and uncomfortable.

I lead them down the corridor towards the viewing room and open the door. We walk towards the four trays, which I've positioned neatly next to each other, and one by one, I pull back only enough of the sheet so that the head is visible. Then I look at her and tell her in our language to take her time – '*cym d'amser*' – which the police officers and Miri don't seem best pleased about.

It's her sister she heads towards first, which I'm glad about, in a way, as she's definitely the one who looks the least deceased. As if she's just asleep. An impressive performance, awaiting applause at any second. Iona's hands are trembling as she traces the outline of her sister's face, as she smoothes her hair away from her cheeks.

'Oh Bri,' she says. '*Fy nghariad i.*' My love.

We stand back as the girl rests her head on her sister's chest, and await the bestial wail or scream that sometimes comes from the bereaved as the truth hits them, deeply, viscerally. But no sound comes. She looks exhausted with grief, as if she's been wrung dry, as though she has no more emotion to give. Maybe the moment of recognition, of understanding, won't come until later. For some, I've heard *Mam-gu* say, it doesn't come at all, and they live their lives in denial that anything ever happened, that their loved one is just absent, without leave, for the remainder of their days. I wonder if that's how she thinks of her son, my father – as though he's just taken off somewhere and might come back some day to claim me. I can see the appeal of it, but it isn't for me to think that way. In fact, I've made a point of making death real for myself, so it can't trick me anymore.

She walks slowly towards her brother. Urien's mouth is contorted in this rather strange way, as if he was mid-sentence when he died. I couldn't do anything much about that, though I tried to soften the appearance of his mouth a little. As I worked on him, I couldn't help but notice all the muscles in him from the running, the way his body still contained remnants of his robustness, his fitness, even in death. I found myself wishing we'd talked more as we'd gone on our runs, that I had pushed harder to get to know him. Perhaps then I would have known what to say to him while I was preparing his body for viewing.

Again there's a quiet, still, acknowledgement in Iona's face that her brother is dead. She runs her hands across his face, kisses him gently on the top of his head, and then gestures that she wants to move on.

She recoils when I peel back the sheet to reveal her mother. It's probably because of the colour – that strange violet-green, as a result of being submerged in water. I kick myself when I spot the droplet of blood that's on her mother's shoulder, that I must have missed in the clean up.

'Are we OK to confirm that they are indeed your brother, sister and mother, Iona?' Miri asks.

'Yes. Yes they are,' Iona says, flatly. Fact.

Perhaps things would have been different had I been allowed to see my mother rather than having to live with this horrific, invented memory of the bloated purple face that *Mam-gu* says I never saw. To me, that is also definitely my mother yet *Mam-gu* says it can't be. It's an *impression* of my mother. A falsehood. Confabulation, she says. The art of inventing memories.

There's something wrong with Elaine. Whenever I think of my mother, that's the sentence that comes to mind. I can't remember who said it – whether or not it was *Mam-gu*, my dad, a stranger – maybe it was just a thing that was known about my mother. That she wasn't quite right. But I wish sometimes I could unhear it – the sentence that steals away my mother, drowning out any other happy memories with its dark, endless echo.

Miri makes notes on her iPad. The police officers nod. It's as if we're in some kind of board meeting, rather than addressing the finality of three whole lives.

Iona moves on towards the final body.

We wait for some gasp of recognition. Three days in and we are no closer to knowing who this girl is. The police probably think Iona is hiding the truth, because from what I've seen of these officers over the years, there's no one they won't suspect. The bereaved are always top of their list. Yet why wouldn't Iona tell them? And why wouldn't someone else, by now, have come forward to claim her – a beautiful, young girl in the prime of her life? But Iona's face is a pure blank page as she looks down at her. Even though she showed little emotion for the others, this is different. There is confusion. And maybe irritation, too, lurking there in the irises. This girl on the silver tray, roughly the same age as herself, who was tucked up in her bed, while she was out, means nothing to her. Nothing at all. Turning around to face me, she asks, in Welsh, 'What about you, do you know her?' That's a first for me, to be asked my opinion. I shake my head, no. *Na.*

As they leave, Iona breaks away from them and buries her small frame in my body. It isn't exactly against protocol to hug the morgue attendant; but as far as I recall, no one has ever done that. Surely I'm the last one they want to touch, the one who has spent all night manoeuvring dead people. Even *Mam-gu* makes me scrub my hands at the sink before I'm allowed to sit down, as though death is contagious. I don't know what to do with my arms, so they hover somewhere in the air, as I stand outstretched like a paper doll. I find myself worrying that my cold, surgically scrubbed arms closing in would spoil the moment; hardly the warmth she is seeking. So we stand there, Iona and I, while the police officers retreat in the corridor, and while the Family Liaison Officer waits impatiently for the moment of intimacy to be over.

And then it comes. All she was holding back before. So I close my arms around her (so that she doesn't have to think about keeping herself upright on top of everything) as it all pours out, those body-shattering sobs of realisation.

I don't know how long it goes on for. Perhaps twenty minutes or more. But we let it happen, we bear witness to it, we respect it. We give grief the time it needs.

Eventually, Iona pulls away and thanks me, again, in our language, and there it is again, something hopeful spiralling up at me from her eyes. But then she adds something, quickly, that I can't quite make sense of:

'*Cadwa fe*,' she says, in Welsh, her voice so quiet and thin it's almost inaudible. 'Keep it.' '*Rhewa fe*.' 'Freeze it.'

I have no idea what she's talking about. I assume she's no more than a jumble of incoherent thoughts and emotions; that she might not even have known who I was when she hugged me; that she possibly didn't know what she was saying, or that I misheard it. It's only later, much later, when she's gone, when the bodies have been put back in their rightful place and I'm searching for the keys of the fridge in my pocket that I realise that she deposited something in my lab coat as she wept.

A small leather-bound book, rock hard and frozen, weighing me down. And carved into the leather on the front are words I can only just make out: *Cymru: an encyclopaedia, by Eurov Griffri.*

24 DAYS BEFORE

13. URIEN

When he runs, he is free and unencumbered. Just light and particles, whizzing through the air. He thinks how amazing it is that he's been born with this ability to just run and run and run and never tire of it. Sometimes it feels as if he's cheating life, with this ability to cut through it, at speed. And while he enjoys having a structure for it, going down to the track to train with his running group at the same time every week, and will gladly compete and take all the trophies and medals that come his way, he also knows that all of it is a bonus. He would run whether there were races or not. He would run because it makes him feel powerful. And it's the only thing that can shut down the tens of thousands of thoughts that flow through his mind every day; an endless cascade of startup messages filtering down into the darkness of his soul.

Running is oblivion. Running is quietude. Running is being no one and everyone at the same time. It feels genderless and mammalian and primordial. Depending only on yourself. His friends, the rugby meat-heads and football fanatics, the so-called team players, don't really get it – they enjoy being in the throng of things, a great big bustling gang of bodies which feels way too busy to him. Cain is the only friend he has who understands the runners' psyche, and the desire to stand a lit-tle to one side, on your own, doing your thing. Easy-going, solid Cain, a few years above him in school, who sometimes catches a lift with him to athletics events. And being in Cain's company is made so much easier with the complete absence of sexual tension between them. Though he can see, objectively, that Cain is a good-looking man, he's not attracted to him in the slightest, which is helpful, as they have forged a relationship that is just about this one thing: the ability that their legs have to carry them forward. They hardly ever talk about anything else. He vaguely remembers that there's something sad in Cain's history, because he's been raised by his grandmother, and there's never any family member there to cheer him on at events, but this is the next-level kind of discussion that their friendship doesn't need to venture into. He never discusses his own family either when he's with him, it seems rude to do so, when he isn't sure of Cain's situation. It would feel like rubbing his nose in it.

But it's precisely because of this slight distance between him and Cain, and the fact that they don't discuss personal matters, that he cannot somehow explain to Cain, when they are training down at the track that evening, that the reason he isn't at his best – and keeps messing up his block starts – is because he can see that girl again, high up in the stands, watching him from a distance. He feels with certainty now that this isn't a crush, or an obsession, but something altogether more disturbing. While he knows it's probably his anxiety talking, he starts to get the awful feeling that this girl might be out to hurt him in some way. Perhaps she's one of those basket-case QAnon followers, or a religious nutjob who thinks all homosexuals deserve to be mutilated. Perhaps there's a pocket knife hidden somewhere in the dark folds of her coat, ready to stab him.

While these thoughts dissipate slightly when he's on the track, applying all the force he can to catch up with Cain as they round the bend, they return in a torrent of awfulness once he's finished the race, leaving him gasping for breath at the side of the track and fumbling erratically for his blue inhaler, which Cain has to fish out of his running jacket for him.

'Hey, hey,' Cain says, a consoling arm on his shoulder. 'You're OK. Just take a few puffs, yeah?'

Just over Cain's left shoulder he can see her now, a dark silhouette moving through the stands. Is she coming to talk to him? He inhales and feels the familiar release in his lungs. Asthma is the only thing that makes running unpredictable, he thinks. If only he didn't have it, he thinks, he'd be a record-breaker by now, running at superhuman speeds.

'I'm sorry if I was pushing the pace a little,' Cain says, looking at him apologetically. 'I wasn't trying to give you an asthma attack man, I swear.'

By the time Urien has regained his normal breathing pattern, the girl is gone. He turns and looks and there's no one in the stands, no one at all. It's getting dark now, and he wonders whether she'll be waiting for him somewhere, around some corner, waiting to do something.

'Will you walk me home? I just worry . . . my asthma might get worse . . . ' he stutters in Cain's direction.

Cain looks mildly surprised at his neediness, but almost immediately his face breaks into a genial smile.

'Of course. I start my shift in a bit and it's on my way . . . you ready now?'

'Yeah. Thanks, Cain.'

They amble quietly through the dusk-laden streets of Pont Sulyn, talking about the running competitions coming up over the next few weeks, with Urien quietly praying that each shadow and dark shape in the distance isn't hiding the form of a girl with murderous intentions. At the end of his street, Cain asks him again if he's OK, and when Urien assures him that he's fine, now, he turns and walks in the direction of the hospital.

And it isn't until Urien is right outside his house that he sees that the girl is there, waiting for him, lurking underneath the tree at the bottom of the drive.

'This town is a shithole,' she says.

He stops in his tracks when he hears her accent. She's American.

'What do you want from me?' he says, trying to hide the desperation in his voice. Nothing has ever unnerved him more than this familiar-looking girl and those dark eyes of hers.

'I want you to know that you stole my life,' she says, 'and that I'm coming to take it back.'

And with that, she's gone.

E - ENCYCLOPAEDIA: A dying artform in a world saturated with knowledge, verified and unverified. Although it seems imperative that a small country such as Wales needs an up-to-date encyclopaedia so that it can move confidently into the future knowing itself, inside and out, there are certain slippages, excesses, and nuances that the encyclopaedia cannot capture. What use is it to know of Gwen John's relationship with French sculptor Auguste Rodin, for whom she modelled, if we cannot really know the ins and outs of how it affected her to be with him? And what he gained from being with her, a woman from another culture, who blended in on the streets of Paris, harbouring her other identity like a secret inside her? What use is it to hail poet and antiquary Iolo Morganwg as a great genius and founder of Welsh traditions, without acknowledging his laudanum-impacted mind, which may have affected his ability to tell truth from fantasy?

Isn't it essential to know what people are hiding, what their weaknesses are, rather than what is readily known about them, in order to arrive at something that resembles accuracy?

Beneath the facts, there is always a different story.

14. IONA

She hunches limply in the back seat of Miri's car; the seatbelt the only thing holding her together. Her hands are shaking, and she stretches each finger out, one by one in her lap, wondering what exactly it is that creates a tremor in a person. It feels nonsensical to her now, after seeing her family laid out, that there should be currents coursing through her veins when they were so unmoving and still. The notion of moving forward, when it feels like her life is behind her, in that morgue, makes her lightheaded, as if she's sitting backwards on a train.

And yet, despite her hands' shakiness, it was somehow, impressively, those very same hands that managed to sign that statement for Miri, to confirm that her whole family were dead, and even after that, still maintained enough composure to slip that book into Cain's coat without anyone else noticing a thing. It hadn't been what she'd intended to do – she had brought it with her thinking that this might be the night she would hand it over to Miri, so they could look at it together – but once Miri had mentioned that she'd been talking to her father's colleagues at the university, that she'd obtained a search warrant for his office, it had reignited her reticence for sharing this with the police. Who did they think they were, going through her father's things? Trying to piece him together, when they knew nothing about him? And still they couldn't find him.

It's hard to fathom the impact that seeing her brother's running buddy had on her, in those very few minutes she was with him. Not that they had ever really spoken, either. She'd seen him a few times from her window, getting into the car with Urien, and remembered her brother mentioning he'd walked him home that one time after his asthma attack at the track. But she'd never really shown any interest in him, who he was, where he worked. She only remembered her mother saying Cain was a funny name for a boy, considering the murderous Biblical context, but that it also suited him, because the Welsh meaning of *cain* was beauty, and that he had one of those faces whose beauty was not immediately apparent, but that grew on you. Iona remembers him vaguely from school, a lone figure in a long black coat, who used to walk home the same route as her, always a few yards ahead, turning down Smallbrook Street while she went up Lincoln Avenue. Always alone, never with anyone, and even when he was, he somehow looked as if he wasn't part of their gang, as if he didn't like standing too close to people, like he'd catch something off them. The familiarity of his face at the morgue doors had sent her heart soaring. Finally, here was something warm and recognisable, in the midst of all these strangers in the cold. The way he had spoken to her, so calmly and gently, had soothed her; and she appreciated the way he had been with the bodies, as if he didn't mind being with them, as if he considered it an honour to be guarding them. And he'd held her. In a way no one had since this whole awful thing began. He'd held her and supported her, and in that moment, it had meant everything. It seemed he was the only one who could be trusted with any of her feelings. The only one she trusted to look after her father's encyclopaedia.

Cain presumably doesn't know any of this, of course. All he knows is that his dead friend's sister pushed some document into his hand and asked him to freeze it. They probably have procedures to follow when this sort of thing happens. That's probably him ringing Miri now, as Miri goes all quiet in the front of the car, leaning away as far as she can from Iona, in case she hears anything at the other end.

If he has contacted Miri, Miri doesn't show it. As Miri walks her to the front door of Anna's house, she delivers an envelope into her hands; full to the brim with a pile of leaflets designed to help someone 'in her situation'. When she asks Miri whether she ever remembers anyone being 'in her situation', she doesn't have an answer.

Anna is sitting on the stairs in the dark when she enters.

'How was it?' she asks. There's no feeling at all in her voice, and the dull nothingness stagnates in the silence between them. 'Did they look alright?'

'They looked dead,' she says, heading into the kitchen with her envelope, turning it upside down so that they slide out all over the kitchen table.

Anna comes to stand next to her as Iona runs her fingers through the leaflets, flicking through the odd one. These people in the photographs don't seem real. Their clothes are too tidy; their bereavement seems inauthentic, rehearsed. One of the helpline cards gives her a sly paper cut; the glossy coating of the all-too-new flyers make her nauseous. But as she is preparing to hurl them across the room, she spots a blue leaflet with gilded letters, advertising a local bereavement group. When it unfurls in her hands, there he is, dangling at the last rung of that paper ladder: Cain, Urien's running buddy, the morgue attendant, staring at her. She straightens the leaflet out. It's definitely him. Poised at an angle on a red chair, looking as if he is about to speak. Two men and a woman on either side of him, looking up at him with admiration. And he *is* real, she knows because she spoke to him, put her face in his shirt, stuffed a document into his pocket. He is not an actor. In this picture he is wearing a blue V-neck jumper and his hair, that was gelled down flatly when she met him, is ruffled and free. Although she hadn't expected to find him here, it makes sense to her that the boy from the morgue is also a bereavement counsellor. That death is his thing. That perhaps he has his own losses, that maybe it's why he does what he does.

But perhaps this is an old leaflet, as they sometimes are, and perhaps, given his profession, he was just brought in to help take a picture. There's no reason why she should find him poised in the same way, in the very same room in the Pont Sulyn community centre as advertised, just because it's on the leaflet. But there's something in her that wants to believe that this thin flimsy paper is the truth and that it will deliver what it promises.

Once Anna has settled herself in front of the TV, monochrome shadows zigzagging across her body, Iona puts on her coat and walks outside into a crisp, autumnal night. For an hour or so she ambles through the streets, familiarising herself with her home-town once again. It's a comfort to see it unchanged and solid in the shadows, the shut doors of the pharmacy, the community cen-tre, the charity shops. The steep alleyways that pour you from one street into another, the small thoroughfares that the locals burrow through like moles to get to the heart of the town quicker – it's a comfort to know it's all still there, that the town's configurations have not changed, even though her own world has been blown apart. With every turn she makes, she knows, deep down, she is searching for her father, in every shop door, under every canopy – when she sees a homeless man outside the church that vaguely resembles his build – she somehow expects to see his face there, somewhere obvious, despite the police searches. She even feels it, deep down, that he is close now, but she cannot accept the fact that this may just be because he's floating around somewhere in the dark, glittering water.

And as she walks, she imagines that girl in her house, doing the same. Just an ordinary girl, walking through town, on an autumnal night. How can someone her age be nameless, known by no one? Who was she?

The winding back streets lead her towards Jethro's house. They've had a few tense, monosyllabic phone conversations over the past few days during which she feels the frequency of his voice changing, as though he's been dialled down, put on a lower set-ting. He's just worried for her, he says, anxious about what has happened. Wants to know if she blames him for her not taking her home that night.

'Don't be stupid, Jethro, I wouldn't be here if it wasn't for you.'

And with that he goes quiet again. Murmurs, as though someone is listening.

She needs, desperately, to see him now. Jethro, her last slice of normality, will propel her back to a moment before it all happened, and it will be some kind of comfort, to be that girl again.

A light pulses at the window of Jethro's bedroom, dim and green; those LED lights taped to the coving in his bedroom that he so often sets to luminous colours when he's gaming, that makes it look like there's hazardous nuclear energy pulsating inside. Iona recalls one time when they were alone in the house, when he let her set it on softer colours, a shade of warm pink. How they had both been turned on by seeing each other in that particular light, as if they were in a dream, or back in that darkroom, and she had surprised herself by guiding his hand between her legs for the first time. How she had urged him to keep going, even when they heard the din of crockery in the nearby kitchen, his mum plopping the shopping down on the kitchen counter, his younger brothers fighting each other in the hallway.

She wonders what light setting he will chose for who she is now, and what has happened to her. Perhaps she will not be desirable to him now, marked out by the stench of death and that stinking water. Perhaps she's the kind of girl who can only get fucked in the dark.

His mother has company – she can see cars mounted messily on the pavement outside. Jethro's bedroom is on the ground floor, which makes everything easier. She taps quietly, once twice, hearing him pull off his gaming headphones. His face appears in the window frame, frowning, pushing his chestnut curls back anxiously from his forehead, shaking his head with indecision. He gestures to the left, towards the front door. A few moments later the front door soundlessly opens, and he gestures for her to follow him to his bedroom, past the closed living room door. Snatches of conversation flow out underneath the door frame. She thinks she hears her name.

Once inside, Jethro pulls her towards him.

'Jesus Iona, Jesus . . . are you . . .'

She starts peeling off his T shirt.

'What are you . . . ?'

He cannot look at her.

'Jet, I'm still me, OK?'

Pulling his face towards her, she tells him she wants to be back in the moment before all this happened; to remember how perfect it all was. She's desperate to be close to him now, like they were before the flood. Before he can say anything else, she grabs the LED remote and changes it to a deep indigo. She climbs on top of him. Reaches for his zip.

'No, no. No. Is this really what . . . Jesus Iona, my mum is just . . . What's happening with your dad, did they find him or . . . '

There is simplicity in sex, she tells him. Sex with a boy she loves. Does he flinch slightly when she says this? She isn't sure, the lighting won't catch the truth of his expression. She cannot help but remember that sex saved her, that perhaps it may save her now from whatever else is to come. She slides her hand into his boxer shorts. Jethro moans and pulls her down onto the floor. He grapples with the condom packet in his bedside drawer. With her head against the floorboards she can hear her name being uttered again and again in the living room.

'Wasn't he seeing her,' she thinks she hears someone saying. 'The daughter . . . does he know anything?'

Iona blocks it out, forgetting herself for the first time in days as she feels the initial shock of penetration, and then the let-down of her body, now pulsing with warmth, which tells her it is OK. This is OK. It gives her a strange buzz, to think nothing she does now matters, or has any consequence. Nothing to hide or be embarrassed about; she has no parents; she can do anything she likes. She can live or die, no one will care. She pulls Jethro's hand towards her and feels freer now, more than ever, to direct him, to tell him what she wants. Because she's nobody. Or perhaps just *a body*. A body that's still alive. Cut adrift from everything. Or at least she is, for that one tiny moment, as she rides the initial waves of pleasure in her new, indigo reality, before Jethro's face becomes the same colour and then it's over far too soon and she realises reality is something you cannot rise above, no matter how hard you try.

15. CAIN

Carol and I are always the first ones down at the community centre on Sunday mornings. Since we lost our funding and couldn't afford our bereavement counsellor, the only option was to run it ourselves. As we set up teas, coffees and biscuits, I notice the swell of her stomach through her dress.

'Ascites,' she says, as she catches me staring. 'They offered to drain it but, you know, I've had enough of all the prodding. Time to face the music.'

There's an exhilaration in her voice when she says this. I decide against arguing with her about it, I've done my bit over the months, sat with her in chemo, looked at the treatment options. Carol's more than ready to go, and her story's even worse than mine, if we wanted to get competitive about it. She lost her husband and only child in a plane crash seven years ago and has just been diagnosed with a very aggressive form of bowel cancer. That makes her more qualified than anyone, she says, to talk about what it is to lose people; and to then gradually lose yourself, inch by inch. But it doesn't make her the ideal leader for this group, which is what I've been trying to broach with her at the last few meetings. Call me old fashioned, but I don't think it's what people are looking for when they walk in through that door: to be told that the only hope they have is that they, too, might get to die one day. That a cancer diagnosis may well be the best news you've had all week.

'And what do you think they want to be told then Cain, hmm?' Carol asks me, overcome by a sudden wave of nausea, leaning against the rusty sink in our seriously under-funded kitchen.

'Maybe you should sit down,' I say.

'Don't tell me what to do,' she says. 'I've had a full week of that, those bloody doctors talking down to me, telling me what I should and shouldn't be doing . . . ' Her sentence falls away with the last remaining drop of colour in her cheeks. 'Don't you start, please.'

We sit there for quite a while, an hour maybe, saying very little. I rub her back, feeling her bones underneath that flimsy canopy of skin. She's so thin now, fragile as a bird. It feels that the slightest touch could snap her in half.

'When I . . . When you . . . wheel me in to the morgue,' Carol sniffs, 'you'll take care of me won't you? Make me look nice again?' Carol looks up, pleadingly. Most members of this group seem to think they'll be getting some special treatment when their time is up.

'You're not going anywhere yet,' I tell her, though I'm not sure that's true. Two years ago she looked much younger than her thirty-eight years, but now you wouldn't be surprised to find out she was double that.

'How will you feel, when you see me, Cain?' Carol looks up, tears brimming in her eyes. 'Will I have meant something to you do you think?'

Carol and I have an odd sort of relationship. It isn't romantic in the slightest, but I've spent so much time with her over the past two years that we may as well be married. She often turns up out of the blue at my flat, with some elaborate dish in her hands, insisting that I'm too thin and that I need to eat, and she often stays for hours, sharing with me almost every disturbing detail of her troubled life. I think once she knew my story, that was it, she felt we were kindred spirits who needed each other. Nothing was off limits, and I had little say in the matter.

'Anyway,' Carol says. 'Don't know what I'm crying about . . . Did you see the news . . . about Eurov Griffri . . . Bloody hell.' Carol becomes unsteady on her stool. I try to grab hold of her as she totters off and rolls onto the floor. She remains lying face down for several minutes, arms stretched outwards. I know better than to try to move her when she's like this.

'Yeah, I read about it in the paper. Awful.' I don't tell her that I know all about Eurov Griffri. That I laid out the whole family on my night shift. That I used to train with his son. That his daughter pushed a document into my hands last night and asked me to freeze it. Carol would have that info circling half of Pont Sulyn by the morning. And I was still trying to make sense of it myself: why that clump of rock-hard paper had ended up in my possession, and why I hadn't uttered a word about it to anyone, especially the police. It felt I'd committed some kind of crime just by stowing it away, folding it into darkness, just another body to be removed from sight.

The door opens and a few members of the group filter in, stepping over Carol as they go.

People start gathering chairs and putting them in a semi-circle. Carol slowly sits up. And this is when she enters, quietly, almost without anyone noticing.

Iona Griffri.

A new member for our group.

F – FLOOD: Flooding is simply an overflowing of water onto dry land. But in Wales, it just isn't as simple as that. Water is deeply personal. It's emotive. It's political. And, somehow, has been from the very beginning. It's perhaps no coincidence that Wales has an abundance of deluge myths, ranging from the drowning of the Lowland Hundred – in which a single piece of land protected from the sea by sluice gates were mistakenly left open by a drunk watchman – to the myth of Dwyfan and Dwyfach – in which the thrashings of a demonic creature known as '*yr afanc*' were purported to have drowned all the people of Britain.

I have always felt that in having so many mythological versions of drownings, that a literal drowning, such as the one that was suffered by the community of Capel Celyn (see T for Tryweryn), seemed inevitable. And that it is a particularly Welsh predicament for us not to have heeded the warnings presented to us across the centuries that this moment would arise. And because we did not listen, we were powerless to stop it. And perhaps it is only now, in the face of potentially catastrophic flooding in other parts of the UK, and the decommissioning of entire towns and ways of life, that people across the rest of the country are finally able to understand what those people experienced back then, when they were told they had no choice but to leave the community they loved, putting around eighty million cubic metres of water between them and their dead relatives.

As someone who grew up in a village that no longer exists on a map, I have felt flooded my whole life, in one way or another. As though my history was washed away. Which has also ironically led me to be just as incompetent at guarding the sluice gates of my own life.

Perhaps I am myself the archetypal drunk watchman, who should have seen disaster coming.

16. IONA

'We let the silence speak first,' the exhausted looking woman says, getting up off the floor and plonking herself into a chair. 'We sit in silence and we remember them, our dear, loved ones. We think of them without negativity, without blame, we think of them as they were. When they made us happy.'

And so this is how it begins. The silence is unlike anything else Iona's ever experienced. It is a silence filled with presences. All around her, she can see people conjuring up images of their losses. She is doing it too. As they sit in silence, they sit in presence. Presences that refuse to go away. Lisa Griffri, Urien Griffri, and Briall Griffri: she has brought them all into this room with her, and through being here she has claimed them back as her own family. Now, they are more real to her than ever before. Bri, haplessly dancing out of rooms; Urien, sprinting in great big strides around the red track; her mother, upstairs in that bright, airy loft with her brush bristling against canvas. She even thinks of him, Eurov, her father, though she doesn't know if this is against the rules or not, as he isn't technically dead, as far as she knows. She thinks of her father's gentle tread against the wooden floor of the study and thinks how much of life is defined by listening out for each other, a key in a lock, tyres in a patch of gravel, a child's laughter in a porch. The sense that someone will always return.

They have to find him, she thinks. They have to. He has to be out there somewhere.

The woman leading the group tells them about her own loss. She tells them how she had to let her husband and daughter board a flight without her because of some blunder with their holiday booking. They had only two seats left on the plane, and because they were travelling to see her husband's parents, she thought it best that they went on ahead of her – he was *their son* after all, and truth be told, she had never really liked being alone with her parents in law. She was already imagining the awkward dinner they would have and the obligatory chit-chat she would be expected to make when they got there. And after all the shouting and scream-ing she'd done at the poor girl behind the desk at the airport, her husband had persuaded her that to have dinner alone on the next plane, unburdened by small hands and repeated requests to use the toilet, would be 'no bad thing'.

But of course it was a very bad thing. A terrible thing. It meant she was airborne, eating a meal in silence, watching a film, when her husband and daughter's plane was going down – shot down by a wayward missile – although no government had ever been held accountable.

'Thanks for sharing, Carol,' Cain says, before turning to look at her. 'I notice that we have a newcomer. Perhaps she's willing to share? If that's OK?'

17. CAIN

Iona's version of events is different to what we have all read in the papers. Her brother and sister, she says, were killed way before any drop of water reached them. Urien wasn't in bed like the other two, which suggests he was involved in some altercation or other. Her mother was in the bath, and the more she thinks about it, her father was probably still in the house when she entered, hiding somewhere, processing what he'd done. Iona mentions the other girl, found in her bed, who still hasn't been identified, and says it's driving her mad, thinking about who she might be. I look around the room at the responses of those who've been recounting their own disasters, over and over, every week, and am surprised at how Iona's story has made them forget themselves, for a moment. Forced them to sit upright in those uncomfortable chairs. Behind the film of their tired eyes, they are playing out a loss heavier than their own.

Carol, of course, is crying. One of our mutually agreed rules is that we try to avoid communal hysteria. People get emotional, of course, but never to the detriment of the discussion, which, for me, is the most important thing. While we're here, it's more about dealing with those tiny little things that go around and around your head the moment someone dies, it's about trying to work out how to live rationally and normally with that pain; how to avoid getting tangled up in those invisible threads of grief inside us.

Here we have a rule that we try to respond to each other's grief in a controlled manner; that the bereaved should not have to spend time consoling others who have been affected by our stories. There's nothing worse than someone crying *for you*.

And so I ignore Carol's whimpers at my side and encourage Iona to talk more. The sound of her voice is an antidote to some of the gruff, monotone drones we get in here. It's symptomatic of her clear, lilting name: it sings.

She just doesn't understand, Iona continues, why her dad did what he did. Or even if it was him who did it. She feels that she can't even move on, or grieve, until she knows. It's not only the killings, but the strange aftermath of it, because it takes a lot of effort, she says, to fill up a house with water. To break those pipes with an axe, to smash them in the right places. To place sandbags by the doors. She can't stop thinking about it, about how, as her family lay dead, the house slowly filled up with water, as if the whole house, that way of life, needed purging, washing away. She obsesses every night, she says, over what she could have done differently, how she could have saved them, even though she knows, logically, there's nothing she could have done to change any of it.

She needs, more than anything, to find him. To get answers.

I break my own rules and wade deep into my own watery memories as she talks, thinking about the river entering the open windows of my mother's car on a hot day. *Mam-gu* said that if it wasn't for those windows, the car wouldn't have been able to sink as quickly as it did. But when you think about it, either way the water would have won. There would be nothing more tortuous than to be in a car staring out at a river through closed windows, knowing that the second you opened the window you'd sink anyway.

There's something wrong with Elaine. The sentence bobs to the surface again, like flotsam.

It's my mother I envisage most strongly in this moment, gripping the steering wheel, eyes becoming level with the water, realising what she had done. I suppose that my brother, in his car seat, just an unsuspecting little baby, would have had no idea what was going on. For all he knew this was just the next part of the adventure they'd presented to him as life. I have always hoped there would have been a moment – a realisation of sorts – as my mother's head turned to look at his little face, that this was not right, and not what she'd intended to do at all.

Iona falls silent. This is the point at which Carol is meant to thank her for sharing, and to open it up to the rest of the group. But she doesn't. Carol is shaking now. Whether it's the cancer, or whether she's just being Carol: it's difficult to tell.

'Carol . . . ' I begin, placing a hand on hers.

'Eurov,' Carol says. 'Eurov Griffri. I know him.'

Iona looks up curiously.

'You know my dad?'

Carol nods.

A few concerned looks fly my way from other members of the group.

'At the university . . . ' she continues.

'Carol,' I say. 'That's for another time.'

For Carol there is no other time. Her time is always now.

'It's important I say this, Cain. I don't have time to mess about.'

I nod and let her continue.

'I was their secretary, at the department, for a bit. Your dad, for what it's worth, he always seemed decent enough to me. A little bit lonely maybe. A bit sad. But not . . . you know . . . what they said in the papers . . . '

'Do you remember the encyclopaedia he was working on?' Iona leans in closer to Carol now.

'Yes, I do. It was meant to be their big research project wasn't it . . . and then became . . . something else. I always heard the other staff talking about it. I mean I didn't understand what they were going on about half the time, those academics, but it seemed that . . . they didn't have enough money to keep going with it . . . Is that it? And he wouldn't present them with anything else, so I gather he was a bit of a problem to them.'

'I don't really know,' Iona says, 'what he was doing with that encyclopaedia. But at the end . . . it was sort of the only thing he cared about . . . '

I'm not sure how to respond to this. I had tried, in vain, to read beyond that first page of the frozen document, but the pages were all stuck together. I spent the evening scouring the internet for salvation techniques for water damaged manuscripts, but all I gleaned is that freezing manuscripts buys you time.

'Funny little creatures, academics,' Carol continues. 'Sort of closed off in their own little world. It's why I liked working there. Because I didn't have to interact, really – as long as I could fix the photocopier for them then they wouldn't need to know much about me. They were always very grateful for my help but, you know . . . it's not as though they would really see me. But your dad . . . I mean . . . Your dad was one of the ones who did want to know, one of the nice ones. He always asked about my life. He knew . . . He knew I'd . . . lost . . . people. He'd seen the photo on my desk, noticed the necklace around my neck.'

Carol lifts a hand to her neck, where two letters on a gold chain glisten in the dim light, an L and an R for Laura and Robert.

'People who know about loss, they always ask, don't they?' Carol says, trying to control the tremor in her voice.

Collectively, we exhale. For once, this is a welcome intervention. I can sense Iona's relief that someone in this room has known her father as a real, walking, breathing entity. Carol's thoughts are a world removed from those things the newspapers have suggested, over and over again. Sociopath. Megalomaniac. Carol, now on a roll, regales a story about him dropping his research work on the floor in front of her.

We imagine a man lost in something that has overwhelmed him, as the flimsy whiteness of those loose leaves of paper cover up whatever darkness was lurking inside.

When the meeting is over, Iona helps to stack those red chairs on top of one another – 'nesting them', as we say in Welsh, *nythu*

106

– easing them gently back into their homely spaces, while I heave a sobbing Carol out into the rain and into a taxi. I tell the rest of the volunteers that I'll lock up and then it's just me and her, standing there, with nowhere to sit.

'You were friends with my brother,' she says. 'Weren't you?'

'Yeah. We used to run together.'

'And I remember you from school too.'

'Right,' I say, embarrassed now that I made so little effort to involve myself in Urien's life. In anyone's life, really.

'I was around four or five years behind you,' she continues. 'Don't worry about it, it's always the younger ones who remember the older ones, because you seemed so big to us, I guess. We were just these tiny little, insignificant things. Annoying, probably. Snotty little year sevens.'

Strands of dark hair fall across her face as she talks, coming loose from her ponytail. I remember welcoming my long fringe when it grew across my forehead. It became my armour and stopped me from having to look anyone in the eye.

'What I gave you, the other night . . . ' she starts.

'Ah yes,' I say. 'I gather that's the encyclopaedia Carol was talking about?'

'It's not the official one, not the one he was meant to working on for the university . . . It's something else . . . I don't know, it's more a diary or something . . . I found it, with the bodies, soaking wet, and . . . Miri found one of the entries and asked me about it but I didn't want her to have it, you know? But they were going to come looking for it eventually, and my aunt Anna, I didn't want her to see it either so . . . I don't know. I panicked. Did you . . . give it to them? To the police?'

'No, I didn't. I thought maybe you'd want it back.'

'There's a process,' she says. 'I couldn't do it at my aunt's house. It has to be done straight from the freezer.'

'Why don't you get the police to handle it,' I ask. 'I'm sure they'd have specialist equipment.'

'No,' she says quietly. 'No police.'

'Why not?'

'You heard what Carol said. What his colleagues said. They'll use it to make out he was . . . insane. He couldn't have done this, Cain. Not the father that I knew. And I need to find him . . . I need to speak to him, first, before they do . . . There might be something in there . . . that would suggest what he was going through, you know? Or where he might be.'

We exchange phone numbers quietly; and then she is gone. I stare at the nested chairs, still warm from our bodies, and the weight of each solitary, painful world. I switch off the light and stand in the darkness a while, listening to the room unburden itself of our particles, our skin, our words, our need for nests.

20 DAYS BEFORE

18. LISA

Because she can no longer bear to be at home in her empty house, she has started spending her morning at Bianchi's Gelateria on the riverfront, rushing there from the school run to grab a window seat, where she spends her morning sketching out rough ideas.

Ever since she found the picture of Eurov's student in his desk, she has been able to make art again. She supposes it isn't really the rational response of someone who suspects her husband of having an affair – to pour all her feelings into a sketch book rather than confront him – but she feels a strange excitement about the whole thing, as though it's broken up the ennui of their relationship somehow, and it's a feeling she desperately wants to use creatively, to propel her artwork forward to new, thrilling places. What good will come of confronting him, anyway? Being drawn into long, tortuous conversations about the whole thing? It will only place yet more demands on her time. There is every possibility he could deny it or explain it away, claiming that this student has an obsession with him, that she's misread signals, that it's just yet another predicament he's found himself in, through no fault of his own. And if the situation becomes minimised in this way, Lisa's worried that this could be perilous for her art and stop it in its tracks. And so she's decided that she's going to hoard this secret knowledge inside her, and use it to fuel the fury she needs in order to work on her next, big collection.

So many of her feelings have been dampened by all the meds she's been on recently that to be feeling *something* right now, however odd and inexplicable, is nothing short of a miracle. Seeing that picture in Eurov's bureau has given her some clarity about how she feels about her own marriage. If it's true that she has been traded in for a younger model – such a cliché! – she is surprised to find that it doesn't much affect her. In fact she feels relieved that she no longer has to use whatever little energy she has left to try to save the relationship. She can stop caring about Eurov in the way that he seems to have stopped caring about her, about his work, about his career. Perhaps her art can explore this very subject: the dissolution of a marriage, the breakdown of a family, the disassembling of a future you were certain you would have.

And somehow it feels that the water which surrounds them every day in this town of Pont Sulyn – all the talk of the floods and decommissioning – seems to be symbolic of what has also been happening to her and Eurov over the years: this slow erosion, creeping ever nearer with every small disaster, destroying everything so gradually that it's almost gone unnoticed until it's too late. And despite her hatred for water, her deep-rooted fear of it, it's where she feels she needs to be now – next to the perilous thing that could engulf her – in order to blend the destruction of the town and the destruction of her marriage together as one, huge, catastrophic, breathtaking piece of art.

She spends the first half an hour just sipping her coffee, staring out at the three-arch bridge, observing the movement and flow of the water, outlining the ripples and currents in her sketchpad. 'Paint what you are afraid of,' her old art professor had told them. How had she forgotten this over the years?

And it is at this moment, that a voice comes out of nowhere.

'Are you an artist?'

It's the girl from the picture. Lisa is dumbfounded for a second, and looks around, as though she may be imagining the girl. As though she's sketched her into being. A Pennsylvanian accent, similar to her own, bounces back at her across the table, rendering her speechless for a moment.

'Maybe, yes. Sometimes,' she replies. The girl plonks herself right down opposite her, boldly. 'And you're . . . you're . . . American.'

The girl laughs.

'How could you tell, was it the fact that I didn't wait for an invitation before sitting down?'

She smiles a broad smile at her, one with a hint of something sinister at its edges. As she sits down, she blocks the sunlight coming in through the glass-fronted face of the café and somehow absorbs it. It powers her somehow, setting her golden hair ablaze.

'I'd love to be an artist,' the girl continues.

Lisa is utterly thrown by this. What kind of game is this girl playing, coming to seek her out, the wife of her lover? Or if not her lover, then at least the object of her desire, the man she is no doubt in love with, enough to scrawl an *I love you* on the back of her photograph?

'Where are you from?' she asks, almost in spite of herself, although she knows that deep down she wants the girl to leave, because whatever beautiful space she found herself in two minutes ago, staring out at that river, it has now disappeared, ideas scattering and pixelating in the neurons of her brain. Whatever she thought she could make of this situation is drifting further and further away from her, and soon it will be gone, along with all the other ideas she has started to dream up. This girl seems to be edging towards the confrontation she never wanted to have. Forcing her to find answers to a question that she was happy to leave unanswered.

'We don't get many Americans in this town,' she says, finally, resigned to her fate of having to engage, of having to accept this situation for what it is. 'Which part of the States?'

'Scranton, Pennsylvania,' the girl says, looking right at her.

Her open-sounding 'a' spreads out; a dark cavern between them.

'Really? That's where I'm from, originally.'

111

'Well isn't that something,' the girl says. 'Two Pennsylvanians in a small town in West Wales. What are the chances of that?'

Something in the girl's eyes suggests that she knows full well what the chances are; that she has come here seeking this very chance, has secured its probability. Before Lisa can think of probing her any further, the girl turns her head slightly, to get the waiter's attention, as though she is going to order something. There is something in that gesture alone, something so self-assured and calm in the way she has just placed herself in front of her (the same way someone else did, all those years ago), that all of a sudden, Lisa sees that she is wrong in thinking that this girl is just the younger version of herself that Eurov has sought out, because that's not who she reminds her of at all.

And the realisation hits her with such force that she nearly knocks her coffee over and she has to hold onto the table to steady herself.

This girl is not Eurov's lover.

She's Eurov's daughter.

G – GELATERIA: one of the most predominant Gelaterias in Wales is the one based in the town of Pont Sulyn, run by the Bianchi family, whose ancestor, Ennio Bianchi, opened the café after having been a prisoner of war in a nearby village, returning later to marry a local girl. Their famous ice cream tastes better than any other ice cream in the world – having a secret family recipe which makes it the most popular in the whole country. My son Urien, during his short–lived stint as a waiter at the Gelateria, was sacked for giving a customer two scoops of different flavoured ice creams in the same bowl – 'that was not in keeping with Ennio's vision', the manager insisted, ignoring Urien's cries to give the customer what they want. 'Flavours should be kept separate in order to be appreciated properly.'

It is here, my love, that I first witnessed, from a distance, the union of two parts of my life that should have been keep separate. I should have intervened, yet I could not breathe when I saw you both in that window. All I could do was to consider how, if it was not for the Ennio Bianchi's darkest days on earth, something as simple as a perfect vanilla scoop, with a flavour unlike any other, wouldn't be a part of this town's history. Ennio had been brought here, to this country, against his will, and yet it had paved the way for something unique and beautiful.

Perhaps in time, my love, you can see that this is what I wanted to do for you both. And why I could not allow you to be savoured in the same life.

19. IONA

Miri places her cup of tea down on the table before she gives them the news. Anna sits on the sofa opposite them, adrift on her life raft of a sofa, another pallid stare aimed at the floral wallpaper. Iona again wonders if all Miri's actions since she got here are rehearsed, following some guidelines from the handbook of good police practice. Accept the tea first, make chit-chat with the grieving family, move them from their tense, upright positions into somewhere more comfortable, where the bad news will be more digestible. Remove boiling substance from your own hands in case you have to catch them; a hands-free, belt-and-braces approach to consolation. Secure cushioning if their legs buckle beneath them.

Then – and only then – should you let the awful words fly out of your mouth like a swarm of insects.

'Your mother had water in her lungs, which means that she drowned, probably in the bath.'

Miri pauses, waiting for them both to take it in. Iona suddenly remembers seeing the door to the bathroom ajar, the water trickling out to greet her.

'But, prior to this, we think she had sustained a head injury, which means she was unconscious when she was placed in the bath. In terms of the girl . . . she had a fracture, high up on the cervical spine, which would have been a fatal injury. The pathologist has suggested that there may have been a fall of some kind, from a considerable height. She'd also had prior brain surgery, which may have made her more vulnerable to a fatal outcome to any other injury in that area.'

Images of her father click and clack in the slideshow of her mind. Packing her possessions into his car, smiling at her. Writing down encyclopaedia entries in a frenzy. Dishing out chicken pot rice.

Standing at the edge of a large reservoir, once more a little boy. A visiting student, enticing an American woman in Pennsylvania with his Welsh foreignness. A sociopath, drowning his wife in the bath, hurling a girl away from him. How could all these selves be contained in one man, like the Matryoshka doll on Bri's bedside table?

'There's a lot to take in here, I know,' Miri continues, 'and until we get toxicology back we're not going to be entirely sure whether or not sedation took place, but it seems that we're right to think that asphyxiation would have been the cause of death of both your brother and sister.'

Eurov, her father, holding a pillow down over the sleeping faces of Urien and Bri. A cry escapes from somewhere inside her now, spiralling up from where it has so far been submerged. Anna drops her teacup on the floor and stares at the orange stain as it seeps into the shaggy cream rug, making no effort to clean it up, as she usually would. Iona keeps her eyes fixed on the stain as she cries, watching it spread outwards, becoming lost forever, perhaps, in the fabric. It will be impossible to get out, she thinks, and it will always bring back this moment.

Miri knows to give them some time before moving on to the next few details. In the last few weeks of getting to know them, being in their life, she has observed their rhythms, their moods, their tendency to feel things at different times, even to ignore their own feelings sporadically. She offers to clear up the stain herself, but Anna tells her to leave it.

'The girl,' Iona manages to blurt out through tears. 'Do you know . . . ?'

'Yes. I'm pleased to say that one recent development is that we do have further information about the girl in your house,' Miri begins. Anna looks directly at Iona. They have been wondering all morning what Miri has to tell them, ever since the early morning call, both of them imagining it would be that they have found Eurov, at the bottom of the river or hanging from a tree, hacked to pieces by vigilantes. By the time Miri was entering through the garden gate and walking up towards the house they had already accepted all three scenarios, telling themselves that 'at least it was over now'.

'A B&B owner has come forward – the girl was a guest of theirs. The place was more or less destroyed by the flood, but we've had a couple of teams down there the last few days and we managed to find some documents identifying her as Skylar Quinta Dezen. She's . . . She *was* . . . an eighteen-year-old girl from a small town in America. Scranton, Pennsylvania. We think she came over here to study with your father at his summer school. Did he ever mention her, Iona?'

'No, no, I don't think so,' she says. 'But my mother was from Scranton."

Miri looks up, curiously.

'Right. Well that's good to know, thank you . . . we're currently trying to find out a bit more about her. Apparently she's been in the UK for a few months. She does have a criminal record, which is how we were able to track her down via her DNA. The nature of the crime looks . . . a little hazy at present, but we will let you know when we have more details.'

Skylar, she thinks. Quinta. Dezen. Guttural and alien-sounding to Iona's Welsh ear. And yet this alien-sounding girl found herself in Iona's bed, the most intimate of places. Both names containing letters that don't even exist in the Welsh alphabet, K and Q. Could that have been it, in the Q entry?

And yet there came a day when I saw that strange, exiled letter in a name and it made me stop in my tracks.

'We have contacted her mother,' Miri continues. 'Who is understandably distraught, but also reluctant to give us any information regarding Skylar's father. Which leads us to assume, or to . . . wonder if perhaps . . .'

'You think this Skylar is his daughter?' Anna's voice seems to come from nowhere. She's no longer on the sofa, but pacing back and forth by the window, the intermittent light of a dark afternoon lighting up her silhouette in sporadic, golden flickers. 'You think he had some affair years ago, and that this girl came to find her father?'

'It's one possibility we are looking into, yes,' Miri says. 'We found some artworks in your mother's studio which are now drying out in a special unit at the station. But we've taken a few photographs of some of the most significant ones. Have you ever seen this painting of hers before?'

Miri hands over her iPad. Iona feels the shame bubbling up inside her as she thinks of her absolute disregard for whatever her mother was doing in her art studio, how she never even asked about the work. The painting is a pastel watercolour featuring a family dinner, the faces of the family seeming deliberately indistinct. Underneath the table, her head poking out from beneath a lace tablecloth, is a girl with sharply defined features beneath a cascade of short blonde hair, unevenly cut. A face that flashes back into Iona's mind instantly, covered in blood.

'It's her,' she says, breathlessly. 'I remember her face. That's the girl . . . Skylar.'

'It seems so, doesn't it? So if your mother knew the girl, or knew *about* her, rather, this picture could be quite significant. I'm no expert on art, but the Senior Investigating Officer thinks that your mother might have seen her as a threat to the family. And if we are going to investigate the possibility that she may have been your father's daughter, the result of some extramarital affair for example, then we need to take DNA samples from you both, if you'd be happy to provide them. We have an officer here who can do that now, if you consent. We'll be taking samples from Bri and Urien too, if that's OK with you?'

Iona nods, silently, as does Anna. Numbly, dutifully they stay still as mannequins as the police officer runs swabs around the inside of their mouths. Not that it's something either of them want to help confirm either, as it's just another gain that would convert instantly into a loss, to know that you had a half-sister or a niece only when they were beyond being either one of those things. *The girl under the table*, Iona thinks. So there was something lurking all along but she never knew it. And her mother had known about it, known that it was close by, just underneath the most commonplace of things, a dining room table. Was that the point of the painting? That something awful could be hiding in plain sight, but that you could easily disguise it with steaming platters of soft mashed potatoes and green beans?

'What about Eurov?' Anna asks. 'How come you still haven't found him?'

Anna's face is a hardened shore, betraying none of the waters at its rim. But Iona has heard her crying into her pillow recently, trying to stifle the sobs while the vibrations hurtle along the rim of the skirting board into her niece's room.

'I can assure you that this is an urgent line of enquiry, and we're doing all we can to find him. It would also be helpful if you had any idea at all, of where he could be . . . ?'

'He has to be in the river, doesn't he?' Anna says.

It's the water that Anna turns to again and again when looking for answers, convinced, she says, that filling up the house with water was only the first part of Eurov's own submerging, that he is long drowned, and never coming back. With a little coaxing, Anna has opened up a little more to Miri about their history as a family: how they had to leave the village they grew up in because the valley was flooded to provide water for a city over the border, and how they had to leave their dead father behind in his grave in a drowned cemetery.

'It never left Eurov,' Anna tells Miri now, 'that feeling that no piece of land was ever safe, that the sluice gates would open and drown us all. All this talk of the decommission of the town, it was as if it was happening again. And he probably decided . . .

119

to do it himself, before he was forced, you know? There would have been some logic to it all in his head, there must have been. But whether he's drowned or not . . . you have to bring him home . . . You just . . . have to . . . I can't lose another member of my family to water.'

Anna's voice peters away to nothing. She gets up abruptly and turns the black and white photo of their childhood home face down on the dresser.

'Well I can assure you we've had teams out here for weeks now,' Miri says. 'They're very experienced and well-trained and will be systematic in their approach to finding him . . . But I'm sure you'll appreciate that searching a river is difficult . . . Fast flowing water, tidal waters and dark pools . . . and there are further floods to come, too. But we'll keep searching, I can assure you of that.'

Though she doesn't say it, Iona senses defeat in Miri's voice, as though she knows what they have already begun to suspect, which is that if Eurov's body has been washed out to sea, he may never be recovered. That with every passing moment, that river is pulling him further and further away from them, scattering him to pieces beneath the voluminous darkness, crushing that messed-up brain on rocks, mushing a body to nothing but mud.

Fish are probably defleshing whatever is left of the truth, showing little regard for what they are ingesting.

'We'll keep searching,' Miri says, her eyes as dark and ambiguous as a riverbed.

20. CAIN

When Iona rings, I'm alone at the morgue. Her name pulses silently on the reception desk, illuminated. Those four letters conjure something up in me, a feeling I can't describe. I consider answering, but it doesn't feel quite right to allow another voice into the room right now. What most people have never understood is that my morgue life needs to be kept private and separate from all other parts of my life. To do something as commonplace as pick up a phone, to have a conversation with a living person about the life they are leading, when you are in the presence of so much death, feels a bit insulting.

The phone rings again. I consider going outside, just for a moment, to talk to her.

But I don't. The man in front of me deserves my full attention. I make a note of his name – Gerard Finley – as I haven't been to a funeral in a while, and it seems as though this man, with his cheeky, crooked half-smile, might have been a bit of a laugh.

Then I have another job to attend to – an amendment of an earlier case, that of our Jane Doe. A few hours ago, the police rang to let us know that she has been identified, that we can place a tag around her ankle and fill in the paperwork.

Skylar Quinta Dezen.

When I was fitting the tag I couldn't help but look for some sign of familiarity, to see if she resembles Iona in any way; to see if Eurov could have made a mistake in those last few minutes, thinking she was Iona. And although it's pretty difficult to compare a dead person with a live one, you can see that the hair, the mouth, the features on this girl are all completely different. Eurov must have known that she was not Iona. And if so, he must have intended to leave her behind.

121

The third time Iona rings, I am clocking off; taking off my scrubs, resigning myself to ordinariness once more. I always think of it as a renouncement, lifting the veil; discarding the part of myself that has purpose. I finally answer.

'I'm sick of the police and their fucking platitudes," she says, without even saying hello. "I need to do something Cain! Can we try and dry out the encyclopaedia? Is it still there, is it still frozen?'

I tell her that those pages have remained untouched, in a freezer compartment hardly ever used by anyone in the morgue. Every now and then I place my hand in there just to feel the sharp edges of the paper. I reassure her again that I have no intention of handing it over to the police, that I am going to help her find a way to prise those pages apart without destroying it.

'Can I come over to yours?' she asks. 'I feel like I'm going mad at Aunt Anna's. I need a change of scene.'

*

When she arrives at my flat, she has a dark hoodie pulled over her head, clutching a load of newspapers and magazines under her arm. As I let the coffee percolate, she explains how it's become a daily ritual now: to slip around Pont Sulyn like some kind of sprite, and then to buy these publications at different newsagents each time, to read lies about herself in the papers, articles that purport to be the truth about how she is meant to be feeling. She traces that outline of herself daily, moving across pages. A little stick figure; a myth.

'I take it you know,' she says, 'that the girl they found . . . she has a name.'

Skylar Quinta Dezen. We both admit to googling her. The news story about her criminality was a little muddled: she was reported to have brought a knife into school and threatened some of her teachers, and then she had seemingly just walked out of school and straight in front of a bus. She ended up receiving community service instead of a prison sentence. In all the pictures Skylar's staring back aslant at the camera in front of the court, unsure of herself, hiding behind her mother, who is named as Cassie Dezen, a lawyer who has a swirl of dark curls pinned on top of her head.

The papers are still using the e-fit, Skylar's name having been kept out of them for now. But there's still plenty of material for us to wade through: the Griffri family history having been broken down into bite-size, digestible nuggets of dates, numbers, and background information, as though they were always just fodder to fill a paper rather than people with real, full lives.

Iona wonders whether I experienced anything like this when I encountered my own loss. I look up at her then and see that she can read it all in my face; the fact that our suffering is similar, despite the different circumstances.

'You looked me up, didn't you?' I say. She nods quietly. 'Then you'll know that there's all sorts of bullshit online about the accident. Some of it true, some of it . . . I don't know.'

I was too young to read the papers then. And my family were perhaps *ordinary* – more so than hers. But I did go back, when I was older, to seek out those news stories for myself. Sat myself down in libraries and learned my way around a microfiche; made my own family's tragedy my personal research project. And what I discovered was that the local rag ran the story about my family's accident for much longer than it needed to. First of all it was covered as just as a tragic accident, a failure of construction, flimsy foundations for which the council was being held responsible, and later, at the inquest – when my mother became somehow culpable because there was *something wrong with Elaine* – the story became more of a warning to other mothers that they should not drink the night before driving, especially with their children in the car. It garnered only a microscopic mention in the broadsheets, because there were other things happening that were of greater importance: wars going on, countries being bombed ragged. My mother wasn't Eurov. She wasn't a linguist, a lecturer, or someone who'd grown up in a village that ended up being drowned. A lot of the papers seem to be making much of the fact that Eurov was one of the last children to attend the school at Capel Celyn, the village drowned in order to provide water for Liverpool.

'This paper's saying it's why he did it,' Iona says, flicking through one of the longer features, which even has a picture of the reservoir above the article, as though this hefty mass of water could explain things. 'They're trying to say he was so traumatised by it that he drowned his own family. That's why he smashed up the water pipes with an axe. Even Anna says it. It makes me so angry . . . they don't know what they're talking about. It's nonsense.'

I know more about the drowned village than most because *Mam-gu* often talks about it on our long walks around the river. It's an obsession of hers: to equate one watery tale with another; to reassure me, perhaps, that water had destroyed other worlds, other families. And that perhaps that's just what this small country was all about: submersion, drowning, being unable to keep our heads above water. 'It's just a sign of all that's wrong with us,' she would always say. 'That we let that happen. And that we have to remind ourselves all the time about it, all those slogans plastered all over Wales – *remember Tryweryn* – it's just picking at a scab, you know?'

Iona's not that interested in talking about her father's childhood now. An eighteen-year-old girl – even one as traumatised as her – is more concerned with what her boyfriend has been telling the press. From the corner of my eye I can make out that he's done an interview with one of those flimsy mags, the kind *Mam-gu* reads. Overblown stories which surely cannot be true – about children being eaten alive by dogs, or a man being married to his mother and being perfectly happy, almost boastful, about it. Abductions gone wrong or someone's eyeball being decimated by a splurge of hot liquid from a microwave meal. The kind of garish, cheap magazine

Iona should never be a part of; and yet, here she is, the focus of two pages on paper so thin her fingers leave a stain as she thumbs the pages. He's revealed to them that she had sex with him the week after her family died, that she didn't seem upset at all about the loss of her family. I don't want to read it and yet she makes me, shoving the article into my hand, asking me what I – the average reader – am thinking as I read it.

'How could he?' she looks up at me. Not knowing Jethro, I shrug. I don't know. But from the look of him, in that photo, I think he's one of the ones who always would.

'I think that maybe . . . he's simply not very clever,' I say. 'Maybe that's what you liked about him in the first place. That you wouldn't really ever need to get very deep with him about anything. Sex is so much easier with people we know we don't have a future with.'

She stares at me. I'm expecting her to flounce out, the way Carol sometimes does when I've been too frank with her. But instead she laughs. A laugh teetering on the edge of tears – as the laughter of the bereaved always is – but this one doesn't falter. It's a clean laugh which keeps going, repeating itself, without her taking her eyes off me. And I almost can't fathom the feeling it ignites in me, having made this desperately traumatised girl laugh; to have been responsible for conjuring up those light, errant, notes; to have drawn them out of their hiding place in that unhappy throat.

18 DAYS BEFORE

21. URIEN

He has decided to tell his mother about the girl. About what she said about him stealing her life. He thinks it will drive him mad, otherwise. And it'll be a chance, if nothing else, to casually mention the fact that he isn't interested in girls. Not that his mother doesn't already know this, in some shape or form – because Iona tells him it's obvious – but he wouldn't mind cementing the fact with his mother. They've never really had 'the chat', because it seems that it's just a fact to everyone that Urien is gay, and that he's going about it in his own quiet way. But he admits, deep down, to himself, that he kind of wants the big drama, wants the hugs with his mother, the assurance that of course, she loves him and accepts him, no matter what.

He's never really been worried about his parents rejecting him. They are of course liberals and, in some ways, would have almost wanted him to be anything other than a plain old boring heterosexual. But he is worried that neither he, nor his siblings, seem to be the focus of their world at the moment. There's a sort of faraway quality to them both, a feeling that they have drifted from their own centres. He sees it mostly in his father when he leans into his iPad with a confused look on his face, muttering something about resources and finances and impact statements, but he is starting to see it in his mother, too, in that frantic way she looks about the kitchen in the mornings, as though she's searching for herself somewhere in the detritus of cereal bowls and piles of clothing. He can see from their shared computer in the hallway that she's been googling the decommission proposals, and that she's preoccupied with the flooding that's been happening here in the last few months.

A cup of tea, to be delivered gently to her studio, is the way he envisages the chat will begin. His mother will turn and she'll see that something's bothering him, and she'll put down her paint-brush and say, 'Come sit, Urien. Come talk to me.'

In a way, the girl is an excuse to connect back to the mother he feels they are all losing, inch by inch, drop by drop of paint. The paint that doesn't seem to be moving in any particular direction as far as he's aware, for his mother hasn't sold a painting in years now. She says she doesn't even consider herself an artist, and certainly doesn't volunteer the information when people ask, preferring rather to say she's self-employed or 'in between projects' so that the vagueness stops the conversation in its tracks.

His mother doesn't lift her head when he walks into her studio. She's completely entranced by the painting in front of her.

'Darling, I won't stop, OK, I need to get this finished,' she says, in her perfect Welsh. He often wonders at her mother's ability to select the right grammar pattern when she speaks the language, while he and his siblings, who have grown up speaking it, play with their sentence formation like Jenga, slipping in words of English here and there in order to prop it up. It's as if his mother, a learner in later life, knows how to keep it entirely separate from her mother tongue, whereas for him – to whom it is as natural as breathing – it's the commingling of it with the other language that feels natural to him.

'I brought you a cup of tea,' he says.

'OK, darling. Well thank you, but I don't think I can stop. Unless . . . Is there a problem . . . anything you want to talk about?'

She turns her head towards him, but keeps her body facing away from him. She doesn't put her paintbrush down with a sigh, the way she used to do when he was younger and he was pestering her to assemble the marble run for him. This time, he can see that she's consumed by her art, that it doesn't pain her as much to be disturbed, because she's already decided what should take precedence.

And it's not him.

'It's just . . . ' he stops in his tracks when he sees what she's painting. It's the face of the girl. The girl who's been following him.

'Who . . . who is that?' he asks. The picture isn't yet finished but it seems she's creating some kind of structure around the girl, trapping her underneath something – a table, perhaps?

'This? This is the start of my latest collection,' she says. 'I met someone who . . . who reminded me of something . . . It's just funny isn't it, with art? It can be one little thing and then . . . it sets you on your way? Look, I really hate to ask this but if you're not doing anything tonight, would you put the dinner on . . . ? I don't know when your father will be back. Could you get Bri fed, at least?'

It seems to him that she doesn't wait for an answer to the question, and he doesn't know why, but he feels he cannot probe her any more. It's been no secret to any of them how much their mother has been struggling recently, the antidepressants she's been on, ever since her art came to a sudden halt. To see her this way, consumed by something again, even if it is by this girl who has freaked him out, he cannot bring it up, for fear it will tip the balance.

And so he leaves the room, quietly, with the question still burning inside him, haunting him, just like a girl hiding under a table, in a painting he doesn't quite understand.

H – HIRAETH – (An indescribable longing; a sweet sorrow): Perhaps the most overused concept of all in the Welsh language. It describes a sense of longing or homesickness, often for a home that is long gone or for something or somewhere that can never be reached. It has become such a platitude that one feels almost sick in mentioning it. And yet what other word succeeds in capturing a predicament that is undoubtedly at the heart of the Welsh psyche, the sense that the past is fossilised deep inside us, like those microchimeric fetal cells that remain inside a mother, even when her baby has long left the womb?

Others have described hiraeth as a long field, as though we are no more than a meadow's length from what we seek, yet are somehow prohibited from crossing. And it is often a feeling that affects me physically whenever I happen upon an actual field of any kind. The yearning for the fields of the village where I grew up, where I was free to roam, to seek adventure, to find solace. But coupled with this is the memory of the monstrous roar of those chainsaws cutting the trees down, in preparation for the flooding. Unclothing the fields of my childhood, peeling away their skin until they were utterly exposed, bare and skeletal – ready to be submerged.

If hiraeth itself is a long field, then what is the appropriate unit of loss for someone whose fields have been stripped bare and submerged under a whole reservoir of water?

I often console myself that I freed you from ever knowing the pain and complexity of hiraeth. In many ways, this was an act of kindness.

PART TWO

PART TWO

I - INSOMNIA - (in Welsh, *anhunedd*, literally translates as un-dead-ness): If we are to accept that our bodies twitch involuntarily when falling asleep - the classic hypnic jerks - because our primate ancestors used to sleep in trees, then is it not possible that for a person descended from generations of people who had to fight for survival, to be seen, to be heard, that some of them will somehow be predisposed to alertness, this constant need to not-be-dead-to-the-world? It is in all this darkness that our past and its blackness lies, our forefathers leaving before sunrise, the enemy hurtling towards us, the villages being taken and drowned, all these things and more can somehow plague the Welsh insomniac. The night is a thing to go into warily, a battle. A thing to be dreaded, while other people relish it. *Do not go gentle*, was Dylan Thomas's approach, equating the darkness with death, thus ruining the night for us forever. And yet the words of another Thomas haunt me too, that of R.S., his lesser known - or perhaps less flashy - contemporary, who once stated: *every night / is a rinsing myself of the darkness / that is in my veins.*

And though I rinse myself, nightly, somehow it sticks.

Because there is always, for me, a particular night of un-dead-ness in which the darkness rose in me like a phoenix. One night of wakefulness, which paved the way for hundreds, maybe thousands more.

The night I committed the worst crime imaginable.

16 DAYS BEFORE

22. LISA

After meeting the girl in the Gelateria, something shifts inside Lisa. She isn't sure what the feeling is, exactly, only that the veil of her depression seems to lift suddenly, and in its place comes a nervy, energetic fizzing, which makes it hard for her to concentrate on anything, and can only be calmed when she retreats to her art studio to paint. She gets to work in a frenzy each morning, painting the girl into a variety of different scenarios – clinging on to the roof rack of their car, in a potted plant in the corner of the living room, even trapped inside the cycle of their washing machine, peering out with those huge eyes that had seemed so hypnotic as they bore into her in the Gelateria.

It had been an electric shock, seeing Eurov in the girl's glances, mocking her with the ghostly presence of his DNA under someone else's skin. She had mumbled her apologies and left the Gelateria without even asking her name, throwing some money across the table towards her, asking her to settle the bill. A panic attack had ensued on the corner of Lincoln Street, and she had pleaded with a passer-by for an asthma inhaler. Everyone on the street of Pont Sulyn seemed to be looking at her as she forced her cumbersome, quivering body home, and once she got in safely through the front door she had run straight for her anti-anxiety meds, taking far more than she should, descending into a soporific heap amid a hillock of unpaired socks on the bed, completely forgetting to pick Bri up from school. She had lain there until all the light had drained from the room and until she was vaguely aware of the crockery and pots and pans banging around downstairs, indicating that life was going on around her, that everyone was home and safe, that they had somehow managed it all without her.

When Eurov crept into their bedroom later that evening and tried to rouse her, asking if she was OK, she kept her eyes tightly shut and her body utterly rigid. She could not bear to look at him; and she had no patience or strength to listen to whatever he had to say about the matter either. Whereas she had been almost indifferent to the premise of some tawdry affair with a student, this was something altogether different. A historical infidelity. A deep betrayal she could not accept or forgive; that he had fathered a child with someone around the same time she had been pregnant with Iona, if her calculations were correct.

Sleep would not come that night. While Eurov dozed next to her, she turned things over and over in her mind: who had he been close to in the years they had lived in Scranton with her mother? Perhaps it had happened just after Iona's birth, during those six months she couldn't bear him touching her, for fear of falling pregnant again. Generally she didn't let herself think back to that time because of how uneasy it made her, but she found herself remembering every little detail of it now, how she had not felt any kind of bond with the baby, and that she'd stupidly voiced this feeling, telling a midwife at the hospital that she didn't think she loved her baby at all. Her own ambition was to blame, the insensitive midwife had claimed, and that she hadn't quite accepted the situation she was in. Breastfeeding while answering emails on her phone surely showed a certain dissociation, the midwife continued, and that she hadn't even allowed herself time to be a mother. And yet even when she did give the baby her full, undivided attention, feeding for what seemed like days, the baby would only go and vomit her milk back up all over her, leaving her soaking in it, and then scream to be fed again. There were times when she wanted to throw Iona out of the window, to be rid of her, rid of the responsibility, so she could get back to being an artist in her own right.

Eurov never featured in any of her memories of this time, and perhaps she had told herself over the years that it was because it had been such an isolating experience, being the only one who could get up and feed the baby in the night (because the baby also refused the bottle, even when she had expressed milk, shaking her head fitfully, going blue in the face when they tried), and the only one on whom the baby depended on for survival. She had been forced to give everything, while Eurov stood on the sidelines, a mere spectator. But had she misunderstood why he was absent from those memories? Perhaps he had not been home as often as he should have been? He often worked late at the university, could that have been when Eurov had gone searching for someone else? Someone who wasn't a fractured mess?

It is, she realises, the reason Eurov's been so unsettled since he began teaching at the summer school, because this girl, whoever she is, has tracked him down, and is ready to confront him for being absent for all eighteen or nineteen years of her life. And the more she sees him squirming and suffering and retreating to his study each evening, the more she leaves him to it and carries on as though nothing at all has happened.

Because for once, it isn't a mess of her own making. It's his.

And this is when she starts to map out an idea of a painting called *The girl under the table*, blurring out the faces of the rest of the family, so that the girl is the only clearly defined thing, she is the very *point*, the thing that has now come to upend all their lives, and she works on the face until the resemblance to Eurov is uncanny, so that she is so much more Eurov's daughter than any of the other children combined.

And with every brush stroke, she wonders if the door will open and he will enter. That this will be the way that she'll finally be able to tell him that his secret is out, and that she knows.

But it doesn't happen. Because Eurov is still obsessed with a document that will never see the light of day, and has no brain capacity to take in anything else that might be happening around him.

And he has no idea that, deep in the heart of Lisa's art studio, the worst thing he ever did is becoming the best thing that could happen to her right now.

23. IONA

Cain invites her over to his flat to look at the encyclopaedia in the early hours of the morning, after his shift ends. He sneaks it out of the morgue in a special cool box, taking care not to let it defrost or get damaged. She sets an alarm for 5 a.m. and ambles through the desolate Pont Sulyn streets, and wonders at herself keeping these strange hours, effortlessly; she, the girl who always had to be dragged out of bed in the morning. *Grief makes time irrelevant*, or at least that's what some in the bereavement group say.

It touches her to see the amount of prep that Cain has already done before she gets there. He's bought special blotting paper to place between the pages, to soak up the water as it defrosts, and waves two pink plastic spatulas up at her as she walks in, ones he's stolen from his *Mam-gu*'s kitchen. There's something garish and comical about them, which makes her laugh in spite of the situation. Silently, they work together, brushing the frost from the pages and using the spatulas to prise one page away from another. The running ink has created a marbled effect, and some pages will not be separated, no matter how hard they try. But slowly, working together methodically, standing the book up with an electric fan to finish off the drying process and painstakingly discussing what each, scrambled letter might be until they land on the right one – slowly, but surely, her father's encyclopaedia, this strange, hand-written testament to the kind of man he really was, comes back to life.

'I've never read anything like this,' Cain says, squinting to read the first entry. '*Awen*. Ah -when. Why write it in English?' he asks her, in Welsh.

Cain has a point. Its immediacy suggests it should have been written in Welsh.

'This isn't how it started out I don't think . . . It was meant to be a proper publication, for the university,' she replies, thinking of how many times she'd heard her mother berating Eurov for getting lost in his projects. 'He had other people working on the entries for him, there was an official version that he was meant to be in charge of, but at some point he must have started compiling his own encyclopaedia. I remember he was paranoid that someone could access it. He thought someone had stolen a section of it.'

'There's no P or Q entry,' Cain says. 'I noted them all down as I went through. They're missing. They've been ripped out.'

The Ps and Qs, Iona suddenly remembers, were one of the last things he'd asked her about. 'Have you been looking at the encyclopaedia? I won't be angry. Just tell me if you have.'

Iona's ashamed now, recalling that she hadn't even looked up from her phone when he'd asked her this. She had just snapped at him to get out, kicking her bedroom door shut on the question. How many conversations with her father had actually happened through her bedroom door in the last few months? Not just with him but with all of them? Sitting with her back against that wooden barrier, scrolling on her phone, hearing their thin, pleading, voices beyond the wood.

'He thought someone had stolen those pages from his car. And they're the ones Miri found on the body and scattered all over the floor. They must be significant in some way . . . someone must have been following him . . . '

Cain reaches for a magnifying glass, holding it up above the page, head bowed in concentration.

'When you see things written down, see how easy it is for a letter to be pulled this way and that until it isn't even a letter anymore . . . You realise how precarious it all is, don't you? Language . . . meaning . . . all that,' he says, drawing in closer again to the veined pattern of the ink.

'Dad always said it was a lost art form, handwriting. That we'd lost the ability to connect with our own thoughts. That writing on a screen was just not the same – it didn't capture any kind of emotion . . . or truth . . . '

Emotional truth. Was that it? Perhaps her father was seeking something only pen and paper could give him – wanting to record thoughts which could not be tampered with. Not reconsidered or edited or deleted by a button, but which remained steadfast, in exactly the same order as they were written. She remembers now, with shame, how her father tried to encourage the three of them to write diaries, when they were younger. How he optimistically presented them with one every Christmas, how he dutifully sat at their side while they tried to get those words down on paper, no matter how commonplace or boring their days had been. Iona had found one recently, when she was packing up her room, ready for uni – a pink and silver geometric-patterned cover, with only two pages filled with her nine-year-old scrawl. *Today I had fish fingers and beans and chips. My friend Maya came round. I bounced on my trampoline.*

She'd lost interest in noting her own experiences after two days. They all had. Even Urien, who was a stickler for following instructions, had no real interest in writing anything down. And although her father had insisted it was a way of writing to yourself in the future, she saw now that it was also fallible, as the water had proved. It could be washed away, erased nonetheless. You could end up in your future with nothing from the past but an illegible smudge of ink, a pattern instead of meaning, that even a magnifying glass could not bring clarity to. As much as there was purity to it, there was naivety, too.

'I think there's a reason he wrote it in this way,' Iona says. 'The missing entries have to be significant. It wasn't just him going mad. Don't you think the ending of each one sounds a little bit odd? This confessional tone . . . as if he's murdered someone . . . '

'What could be so controversial about the Ps and Qs that you'd steal them?' Cain asks.

Iona explains that she's already seen the Q entry. That it mentions a name which was crossed out. That she thinks it was the middle name of the girl in her bed.

'OK, but what would a P stand for?' Cain muses.

Paternity, Iona thinks. It has to be.

'We can ask him when we find him,' she says, determinedly. She looks up at Cain then to see if his eyes betray any of what he's really feeling, whether he thinks she's deluding herself – that Eurov is going to be no more alive than any of the bodies that surround him every day. But he looks back at her with compassion, and trust, willing to go with whatever she believes in this moment. Or maybe he wants to believe it as badly as she does. That there might be one member of her family still out there somewhere.

Iona feels the urgency of it more than ever now. The police search has been called off, temporarily, because of the threat of another flood. And because of this hiatus in police proceedings, it feels the right time for her to do something, whatever it is in her power to do, even if it's just to mull over the blurred entries until they come sharply into focus.

'I know it would be complicated, wouldn't it, after everything that's happened, for him to be alive,' Cain says quietly, 'but maybe it would be kind of amazing too.' Iona looks up at him. She wants so much to ask him how he functions from day to day, having gone through what he did, to connect somehow to the pain she knows is stored there quietly inside him, as if it's in its own frozen chamber. But she's afraid of opening that chamber, too – afraid of knowing what it is to live with something like that for the rest of your life. Carol explained to her at the group that for the first few months she'd still be in a state of disbelief, a strange kind of limbo in which she would believe that the situation was somehow temporary. Even though she tries to resist this type of thinking, it's nevertheless there, somewhere, hovering at the edges of her consciousness, in her casual lifting of her phone to text Urien, or her sudden panic that she's lost her little sister in the crowds when she is meant to be looking after her. She simply cannot process that they will not be coming back, nor does she want to.

'And that's OK,' Carol added. 'Because for a while it will be a comfort to know that you still feel them, all around you.'

The most upsetting thing in the last two days, which has almost, ridiculously, eclipsed all of her grief, has been the loss of Jethro, who she can resurrect any time she likes, in theory. Last week she decided to go and confront him about selling his story to the papers. Not only did he try to claim that his mother made him do it for purely financial reasons, but he also told her that talking about it had been a good way of processing what had happened. She'd completely lost it with him then, screaming at him that it had happened to her and not to him, that he had nothing to process, that nothing like this probably ever would happen to him or to anyone he knew, and that dating her would probably end up being the most interesting or significant thing he had done in his life.

'You can have the fucking story,' she'd screamed. 'Because that's all you'll have left of me.'

And even as she was saying it, even as she was walking away, incandescent, feeling powerful for once for having taken control of something when so many things were out of her control, there was a part of her that wanted to run back to him, to close her body around his and continue to believe in the fantasy of a boy who had loved her and understood her. The boy for whom it had been worth spending her family's last months obsessing over, so much so that she lost sight of anything and everything she cared about.

After she takes snaps of the pages on her phone, Cain quietly packs some of the pages back in wax paper – he says he's heard that it's good to refreeze the book after the initial clean up, to avoid any further smudging. He does it with the care and attention she assumes he reserves for his bodies, all the while reassuring her that the encyclopaedia is not-yet-dead, that this mangled, stuck together, nonsensical tome can be brought back to life, eventually, if they are patient enough.

Cain offers to walk her home but she says she isn't ready to go home yet.

Truth is, she's not ready to not be with Cain.

In that nonchalant, non-committal way of his he informs her he needs to visit his *Mam-gu*. She asks if his *Mam-gu* would mind her tagging along, and he shrugs and says he isn't sure, he's never taken anyone there before.

As they approach the small green house on the corner of Small-brook Street, he tells her that it's obligatory, no matter what sustenance is offered by his *Mam-gu*, that she accepts it.

'She likes to offer something that vaguely resembles a breakfast,' he says, 'though sometimes it's cake. And I'm not always hungry, but I tend to . . . try to eat, because it's easier than refusing. If you refuse anything she wants you to eat, it's like . . . entering battle.'

'Sure,' she says. 'I could do with a coffee or a . . .'

'She doesn't believe in coffee,' he says. And in they go.

24. CAIN

I tell Iona to wait in the hallway while I explain to *Mam-gu* who she is. I head towards the marbled glass door cutting off the kitchen from the rest of the house, and the jolly cacophony of Radio Cymru trickles out toward Iona while I close the door behind me. Through the glass I can make out that she's moving closer to the hallway feature wall, staring at the pictures of me when I was younger with my mum and dad. The blonde ribbons of hair dancing across my forehead, my mother in her summer dress pressing her mouth down on my once-chubby cheek. My father trying to smile but the effort of it being too much for him, his squint against the sunlight ruining the otherwise picture-perfect moment.

'You're late,' *Mam-gu* says. 'I've cleared away the breakfast things now. But I've got cake.' 'I've got . . . company,' I say.

This notion seems to both delight and startle her, all at once.

'What? Who?' she asks, reaching out to pull the glass door open. I lay a hand gently on hers.

'It's Iona. The Griffri girl,' I say. *Mam-gu* stops in her tracks. She doesn't seem sure about it now. Perhaps she doesn't think that involving myself with yet another grieving person is the right thing to do. But then suddenly she swings the kitchen door wide open and she's smiling at Iona, inviting her to come join us for breakfast.

'Iona,' she says, in Welsh, with kindly urgency. 'What's wrong with this boy, honestly, leaving you standing out there – I haven't put the heating on yet, but it's warm in the kitchen, don't you worry. Come . . . Come have something to eat.'

Iona is guided into the small kitchen, and *Mam-gu* puts away the cake tin and starts going back to the business of making breakfast. An enormous pot of tea is plonked down on the table, wrapped in its paisley tea cosy. There is somehow an unspoken understanding between *Mam-gu* and Iona that because they have both seen awfulness, they know full well how to live alongside it. They know there is still tea to be had and breakfasts to be devoured even when you are at your worst.

And what pleases me more than anything is that Iona sits, and smiles, and the girl I have never witnessed eating a single morsel suddenly seems to find herself hungry. Ravenous even. And in silence we sit, the three of us, quietly breaking bread together.

*

By the time we get back to my flat, my eyelids are heavy. I make some coffee for us both, a strong Colombian blend that Carol bought for me for the days where the fatigue overwhelms me. It wakes me up almost immediately and has the effect of making me feel light-headed, drunk even.

And then the truth comes pouring out of me, like water.

I tell her what I remember about the day my own family died. It somehow seems easier than waiting for her to ask, and I could tell she would, eventually, simply from the intense way she was looking at those photos. They had gone to a wedding without me, I tell her. My baby brother was only a few months old, and my mother was still breastfeeding, so they took him with them and left me behind. *Mam-gu* often says how she'd pleaded with them to try to get the baby on the bottle before the wedding, but my mother would not be parted with him. The umbilical cord had not been severed – as *Mam-gu* would have it – with that baby. *Mam-gu* had felt there was something amiss when we both waved goodbye to them on the drive, but she couldn't put her finger on it. A strange look in my mother's eyes when she refused to let my dad get behind the wheel and reversed out without looking into the road properly. Nick – my dad, her

146

son – had been saying *there's something wrong with Elaine*, for months at this point, apparently.

Mam-gu however couldn't foresee that whatever it was, it would end the way it did – by wiping out entire lives. Otherwise, she would have gone running after them, and she regrets for every second of every day that she didn't. She was afraid her own anxiety about the whole thing would seem like madness, rather than a rational fear, or that she'd seem to my mother like an interfering mother-in-law. And so she dismissed those feelings and busied herself with entertaining me for the weekend.

We were eating lunch when the police came. It was one of *Mam-gu*'s specials: potatoes from a tin, some salad cream, lettuce, eggs and pickled onion. To this day I can feel the texture of that potato rolling around in my mouth when I heard *Mam-gu*'s caterwaul at the front door, a sound I have never heard her make since, but the like of which I've heard several times since from others, during viewings and formal identifications at the morgue. But she must have gathered herself together pretty quickly because within seconds she was back in the kitchen saying that we would finish our salad and then she would need to talk to me in the living room – the living room where the glass-domed, gold anniversary clock on top of the telly seemed to tick unbearably loudly. Ever since, that clock has haunted me with the way it splits a day up into tiny, perfectly uniform fragments, with those gold, spinning balls at the base of the clock turning this way and that, as though they symbolise the Russian roulette of life – every ticking second, every minute, someone – rather than someone else – gets taken away.

The way *Mam-gu* put it that day was that there had been an accident that would mean that I would now live with her, and would not see my parents or my brother again. I even remember her rationalising to me that my brother was still *new,* and so in time I probably would not miss him, and also, that because I was pretty

147

new myself, and would have many more years without them than with them, that it would be easier for me, in time. Her parting shot, from a voice trying its best not to falter, was that somehow life was strange like that but that things would begin to make sense to me pretty quickly and we would both be fine.

We'll be fine Cain, she said, unable to look at me. *Just fine*.

I pause for a moment, listening to Iona's breathing, remembering the ticking of clocks, the spinning of golden balls, and the smear of salad cream on those tinned potatoes. Having been at the bereavement group for years, I've heard all manner of ways that the news of death has been delivered, but never have I heard anyone trying to rationalise it in the way *Mam-gu* did that day, measuring time out like ingredients, rationalising that a year of love here, a year of dependency there, would not mean much in the large scheme of things. To this day it is the *large scheme* we both cling to – the triumph of our long lives together, me and her, the fact we made it through. Perhaps she's right to see things in this way, because what is the alternative? To spend a life wallowing about what we've lost instead of what we have gained?

In any case, she was perfectly right in saying that being with her would be the only life I really remembered. But not so for others who remembered me, and knew my story. I was somehow indelibly marked out by everyone I came into contact with, as the boy the bad thing happened to. Until that, too, began to fade. Other kids had stuff happen to them. Mothers died of cancer; fathers died in accidents. A brother or sister drowned on a camping holiday or killed themselves in their bedrooms. Soon enough, it seemed that some awful shit was happening everywhere, and I wasn't special anymore. Iona, passing me in the school corridor as an oblivious year seven wouldn't have known anything about it, and there is comfort in that; that the further away you travel from your loss, the more it becomes your decision whether you want to share it or not. It's not like it's written all over you; it fades, like a henna tattoo.

We sit in silence awhile, as Iona quietly sips her coffee next to me. She asks me if I think this is what she'll be like, ten years from now, sitting there, just reeling it all off so casually like it happened to someone else. It hadn't occurred to me that this is what it sounds like to her, but I tell her that my story probably has this quality because *Mam-gu* has kept me guarded from the reality of it for so long.

'So was she suicidal, then, your mother? Did she . . . do it on purpose?' she asks. No one's ever asked me this before, even though it's the thing I wonder about, more than anything else. I guess the bereaved can ask each other these kinds of questions, without fearing overstepping. There are no rules; nothing's off limits.

I know there are versions I would like to believe about what happened, I say. That my mother simply lost concentration for a split second. And yet, it's my father I can't account for in this picture, sitting sullenly at her side, having again let her drive despite knowing *there's something wrong with Elaine.*

A narrative verdict, that's how they categorised it in the end. I hate the term now just as much as I did when I first heard it. The way it makes the whole thing sound like some stupid story. The details of which can be changed at any time. A way of not attributing the cause to an individual, but rather convincing yourself that some other factors around that person had to be the cause. My mother's drinking the night before, they said, could be a factor, although she was not over the legal limit. Her condition was not classified as depression by the doctors – it was more a kind of *peri-natal* anxiety, common in mothers of small babies. The baby could have been vomiting, my mother could have been worried that he was choking. My father could have been arguing with her about it, perhaps telling her it was all fine, to let him be. A splay of arms, a wrangling of wrists. A moment of tension that proved life-altering and death-inducing. It could be all those things and none. And yet deep in *Mam-gu*'s eyes, I have always felt like the rest of the story lies just beyond that thin, glistening film. A nar rative that only she can provide. Which would explain things once and for all.

'But you've never asked her?' Iona says, incredulous. 'All these years?'

I think of all those times I tried. Knowing somehow, that I was pushing beyond a boundary she'd so carefully placed around herself like police tape. Apart from that one time in the hallway, *Mam-gu* had never cried about it, and I suppose I feared I would push through the tape to the tears, and I didn't want to hear her crying again. I need her to remain what she had been my whole life – a calm, dry shore, that was never bogged down by grief.

'What does it change, knowing more?' I say, which is what I've rationalised to myself all these years. That understanding more of that manoeuvre over the bridge won't change the outcome. And so we've always left the truth buried somewhere underneath that heavy sentence: *there's something wrong with Elaine.* Elaine, my beautiful mother, who that day let her anxiety get the better of her. 'It isn't worth upsetting someone over something that just can't be changed.'

'There aren't many people like you, you know Cain,' Iona says, looking earnestly at me. I can't tell if she means it as a compliment or not.

I offer to walk her home, and we amble through the streets of Pont Sulyn, arms dangling limply at our sides, like we don't quite know what to do with them. It reminds me of that night I walked Urien home, how I listened to his erratic breathing gradually become steady in the night air. I tell Iona how he seemed nervous that night about something, something I couldn't quite grasp.

When we get back to Anna's house, the police are outside. Miri, the detective I met at the morgue, is leaning against her car, looking anxiously at her watch. She looks up at Iona, then at me, faintly recognising me but perhaps not being able to place me. That's the case with most people in this town, I'm a silhouette to them, a ghostly reminder of something they'd rather not think about.

'What is it?' Iona asks. 'Is Anna . . . Is Anna . . . OK . . . ?'

'Anna's fine,' Miri says. 'It's just . . . the DNA samples have come back . . . and . . . Can we go inside, and discuss it . . . and maybe your friend could . . . '

She gestures towards me as though I'm something to be brushed off, sent away.

'You can say anything you like in front of Cain,' she says. 'And you tell me now, whatever it is . . . you need to tell me . . . '

Miri hesitates, looking at me again, as things perhaps click into place. *The morgue attendant.*

'It's been confirmed. Skylar Dezen was your father's biological daughter,' she says.

J: The Welsh alphabet – *Yr Wyddor Gymraeg* – does not include J. And yet unlike some of the other excluded letters, it has crowbarred its way into Welsh vocabulary over time – perhaps not surprisingly so, considering its shape. And yet the letter J also physically resembles a rather cartoonish outline of those aristocrats who carried it into Wales from England, with their top hats and straight backs, their outsplayed feet bringing the Joneses and the Johns and the Jenkinses to town, trampling all over the system of patronymic surnames upon which Wales historically relied, where every person was marked out as the son or daughter of the father.

Under such a system, my children's rightful names should be:

Iona Eurov. Urien Eurov. Briall Eurov. Similar to the Icelandic surnames which indicate the father (or mother) of the child and not the historic family lineage.

These days even those who do use the patronymics say they tend to cause chaos in airports, despite being perfectly legal. 'Are these really your children?' the immigration officers will ask a family whose names are all different to their mother and father. Perhaps they will even detain them. It seems absurd to elevate a problem of lettering to the status of a crime, does it not?

And so J, like so many other errant letters, slides into our vocabulary, and we forget that it wasn't ever meant to be there. Because as a people who have been oppressed for centuries, why should we not take extra letters, and have more than anyone else? Have we not suffered centuries of having less?

But the real reason for not using the patronymics in naming my own children was that I felt I could not burden my children with my name. Because one day they would know the kind of man I was, and they would carry that name forever, like an albatross.

14 DAYS BEFORE

25. LISA

Eurov has burst unannounced into her studio and is now staring aghast at her painting of the girl under the table. He's so still he could be a statue himself, a piece of art carved by her own hands. The fug of acrylic paint still hangs in the air, the finishing touches not yet dry.

'What the hell . . . is this, Lisa,' he asks. It comes out like a statement, rather than a question, his voice small, like a child's.

Lisa feels like laughing, but she swallows the laugh back down.

'It's good, isn't it?' she says, circling the canvas. The face of the girl under the table she has painted with precision, sketching out the delicate features, making them even more beautiful and haunting. Sitting back to look at it afterwards she felt satisfied for the first time in years, becoming excited about working up a whole new collection. It would secure her re-entry into the art world, she thought, a late flowering of the potential that had always been there.

'So when did you have time to have an affair? Eh? Was it when Iona was little? Who was she? Someone at the department at Scranton? Oh don't tell me it was the secretary, that old cliché, please . . . '

'I saw you . . . at the Gelateria . . . I was following her, to see where she'd go . . . God, I wish I could have stopped her from speaking to you,' he says, his voice dull and flat. 'But she's . . . she's dangerous Lisa . . . You need to stay away from her.'

He has this odd, faraway look in his eyes. Her husband is a relic, she thinks, crumbled to nothing with age. The looks he could depend upon, well into his forties, have now fallen away, and he's a husk of a man, with nothing left inside. No energy to even stand up to his stowaway daughter.

'To be honest, I'm sort of glad she came into our lives,' she says. 'I mean, look at what she's given me. She's given me something to paint about, Eurov! And let's face it . . . our marriage is dead, anyway, isn't it . . . '

'Lisa, please don't say that, I love you . . . Our love . . . means more than anything to me.'

The sentiment catches her off guard. She hadn't expected him to say it. She's been utterly convinced for months that her marriage is over. That it has happened quietly, without fuss, somewhere in those bouts of swapping children in and out of cars between sports events and conferences, in the monosyllabic exchanges about school pickups and grocery lists, in those nights of reading and painting in separate rooms. Just gone and died, just like that, like a cat does; taking itself off to do it quietly, sneaking off when no one is looking, without even looking back over its shoulder. This declaration of love from Eurov, so earnest, has rather interfered with the narrative going on in her own head, and she doesn't know how to feel about it. In fact, she tries to unhear it, to erase it from her consciousness.

'You . . . betrayed me . . . Eurov,' she says, trying to cling desperately to the facts now, keeping all emotion at bay. She cannot access those feelings she once had for him; even though they must be there somewhere, deep down. 'And what's worse . . . you let that girl, whoever she is . . . wait all that time to find you. Perhaps, had I known . . . she could have been accepted, as part of our family. She's a sister to our kids, Eurov . . . she's their blood . . . '

Eurov is shaking his head vehemently now, like a dog being chastised.

'Look . . . I didn't think . . . I didn't know she existed,' he says, finally. 'You have to believe me . . . '

Lisa doesn't know what to believe at this point in time. She feels as though she's somehow floating through life now, that she skims on top of it rather than engaging with it, and that she cannot allow Eurov to pull her back down to reality, when floating away from it has enabled her to truly lose herself in her art.

'Who was she?' Lisa asks. 'Her mother?'

Eurov is crying now. His shoulders are heaving with the weight of it all.

'Cassie, she's called Cassie,' he splutters. 'But it doesn't matter who Cassie is, all that matters is . . . '

'Just get out please Eurov,' she says.

'Lisa, please . . . '

'Out, now!'

Out of her comes a grief-stricken bellow, almost choking her with its ferocity. She has not expected it from herself any more than Eurov has.

'I'm worried about you, Lisa . . . I think you need to see a doctor . . . Are you taking your pills, because . . . '

And with that she slams the door in his face and walks back towards the painting in the far end of the studio.

It is, without a doubt, she thinks, the best thing she's ever painted.

The best thing, at the worst of times.

Thank you, Cassie, she whispers to herself, as an errant dollop of red paint splashes onto the wooden floor.

26. IONA

When Miri informs her that Skylar is her father's daughter, there is a sense of relief. A sense of having something to cling onto, that can help her navigate this new reality of hers. A half-sister she never knew about. But then, just as swiftly, after this feeling of connection, comes the severing she had never expected.

There is something else, Miri forewarns her, urging her now to leave Cain outside so they can head into the house for some privacy. This can only mean that something worse, much worse, is coming. Cain promises he'll wait for her, and their bodies meet in an almost-hug that ends up being an awkward squeezing of each other's shoulders.

She hurls her body into Anna's living room sofa. She knows how this goes, now.

'Just say it,' she tells Miri. 'You've found him, haven't you? He's dead, isn't he?'

Miri's eyes widen, caught off guard, for once. What could be worse, Iona thinks, than that?

'There's no easy way to say this Iona . . . ' Miri says, looking right at her now. 'But Skylar is also . . . your mother's biological daughter,' she adds. 'She's theirs, and you . . . I'm very sorry to have to tell you this Iona, but the DNA test shows that you're not related to them at all . . . '

The sofa seems to fall through the floor, plunging Iona into darkness, hurling her, it seems, into the sewers of Pont Sulyn, where all the dirty stinking water washes over her.

'No,' she says, trying to scramble out of the darkness that's descended on her. 'No . . . That's . . . impossible.'

Miri tells her that she's sorry, but that the DNA is conclusive, and that there is no genetic connection between herself or Urien or Bri. That whoever she is, she isn't a Griffri.

Iona's mind cannot help but wander back to the night of the flood, seeing those images differently now, as if they have suddenly been unscrambled along with sections of the encyclopaedia. Her mother – not-mother – in the bath. Her brother – not-brother – on the landing. Her sister – not-sister – with the covers pulled over her head, the pink teddy dangling limply from her tiny fist.

Nothing at all to do with her, this woman seems to be telling her.

She asks Miri one last time if there could be some mistake. Miri assures her that the tests are 99.9 per cent accurate and that their processes are meticulous. It's science. Not conjecture. There is no way that she would be presenting these facts to her if she wasn't sure herself, if she hadn't done her due diligence, and checked that they were the most accurate representation of truth they could be.

'But it doesn't *feel* true,' Iona says quietly. No tears come, this time, even though she knows they are there, somewhere, sloshing around in those sewers.

'But what . . . How . . . ? How can she not be theirs?' Anna hollers. 'It doesn't make sense . . . '

'We will be investigating this thoroughly, we can assure you of that,' Miri continues. 'We have the records of the hospital in Scranton where you and Skylar were born, and one of our officers will be travelling out there to conduct interviews, look through birth records, and hopefully get to the bottom of this.'

Iona cannot bear it any longer – just being in this room with Miri and her aunt – not-aunt – with rigid facts and results that seem to have no bearing on how she is feeling, or any understanding of what this news takes from her, is suffocating. She needs to get away from them, to be outside, and it isn't until she has run out of that stifling living room and out into the front lawn that she remembers that Cain is still there. And she needs him now, more than ever, as she takes off her shoes and socks and stands in Anna's front garden, feeling a deep visceral need to ground herself, to connect with the earth, the only thing she knows for certain belongs to her and she to it. The lawn she has swung her sister around on and where she once raced slugs with her brother during a slow-moving summer. *This earth has seen and felt us*, she thinks, *it has witnessed us as a family. As siblings.*

Cain does not try to calm her or rationalise or explain any of it away. He simply absorbs the news and listens to her as she tells him that she no longer knows what she is; only what she is not. That she doesn't know how to redefine herself against this negation, this not-being-related – not-being-daughter, not-being-sister. It feels as though Miri was telling her she should separate herself from those bodies still laid out at the morgue. But the fact that her blood is not their blood does little to curtail the grief; in fact, it twists and turns with a renewed agony in her unrelated body. The implication that she doesn't need to mourn them; that she has no claim to them, makes her angrier than she was before. She has lost, she thinks, more than everything in being told she's lost nothing at all.

'It's why he looked at me the way he did, Cain!' she cries. 'He knew all along I wasn't his . . . He must have done! We have to find him. We have to!'

Cain promises her that they will. Not that they will try. But that they will.

And looking into his kind eyes, for the first time ever, she believes it may be possible, and that not all is lost, even if she's now lost to herself.

K – Kin: a group of persons of common ancestry: clan. And yet in Wales it feels as though kin has a slightly looser definition, because to be Welsh is to seek out other Welsh people constantly, which means that even people who are not related to you can be your kin. There is a tribal element to it. We are a *llwyth* (tribe) as much as we are blood relatives. Our language and shared history are thicker than blood. Kin, in Welsh, has many translations, the most common of which is *perthynas*, which also doubles up as the word for 'relationship'.

And so if kin is simply relationship, can it not be forged with anyone?

Over the years I have tried to reframe my crime as an experiment of sorts. To prove that anyone can be brought up bilingual, no matter where they were born, or who their parents were, or what they might be predisposed to.

It has helped me to think of my crime less as depriving someone of something, as gifting someone with something.

And I hope, my love, in time, you will forgive me for keeping an open mind about my own kin, and for causing this loss as a result.

You are of course, my kin, my firstborn. But Iona is too. I made her so.

12 DAYS BEFORE

27. LISA

She and Eurov do not speak for two whole days. They somehow manage to weave a facade of normality around the tension, so much so that the children do not notice. If anything, it's impossible to hear the heavy, burdensome silence between them because it is simply drowned out by the din of cereal bowls crashing into the sink, the repeated requests for lifts and permission slips, and the opening and shutting of doors as the family leave and return, return and leave again.

Mealtimes have become increasingly frenetic affairs, which means that their physical distance is also easier to hide from the children; often broken down into several sittings to accommodate their children's schedules. Bri often claims to be starving by 5 p.m. and so is allowed to eat in front of the TV, Iona spends all her free time with Jethro or packing for uni upstairs, and Urien is always late coming home from the track, at which point Lisa needs to cook yet another – preferably nutritious – meal for muscle-recovery, being thankful for the distraction it provides her. By the time Urien has finished eating, Eurov is safely stowed away in his study, shutting his door on them all for the rest of the heavy day.

They have gotten away with it, she thinks. None of the children have yet sensed the complete mess they're in.

Or perhaps Bri does. Despite not being able to concentrate on much of anything when it comes to sitting down with her homework, she has a sort of sixth sense when it comes to honing in on people's emotions.

'What's going on between you and dad?' she asks one morning, on their walk to school.

'Nothing!' She feigns a sing-song voice, far too high pitched. 'Why would you ask that *cariad*?'

'Because . . . Because you look at him oddly, Mum,' she says.

A look, she thinks. So it isn't the silence that's the giveaway, it's the look she gives him. It must be written there on her face in a way that only archaeologists of emotion, like Bri, can unearth.

Your father had a child with another woman while I had post-natal depression, is what she wants to blurt out, a sentence that scrolls constantly across the message board of her mind in bright, neon graphics.

He betrayed me in the worst way. And he won't even tell me how it happened.

But then, things take a turn. The worst possible turn there is to take.

When she returns from the school run one morning, she is horrified to see the girl there on the doorstep. Eurov's daughter, staring boldly back at her, a wild thing, unwilling to be tamed. She remembers Eurov's warning that this girl is dangerous, and wonders if this is it, if this is the moment she will be stabbed on her own doorstep and her children will be left motherless.

'You knew who I was, didn't you, that day at the Gelateria?' the girl says. 'It's why you left the way you did.'

Lisa is dumbfounded. Again, it's the accent that throws her, more than anything. It's like looking at and hearing her younger self, like being spun back in time to being that girl in Scranton who did not know anything about Wales, or the Welsh language or drowned villages, who had not yet met Eurov Griffri, who had not yet been sent on a track that had led her here, to this town, to such devastation.

'I guess I . . . worked it out eventually, yes,' Lisa says.

'Well don't you think we need to talk about it?' she says. 'Talk things through?'

Lisa has no idea what to say now. To allow the girl to actually enter her home, to cross that boundary, feels perilous. It feels like there would be no coming back from that.

'I think we should wait until Eurov gets back, don't you?' she says, trying hurriedly to find the right key in her chunky sprawl of silver so that she can get inside and leave whatever this is outside. Her hands somehow do not recognise the key anymore; they all seem the same to her. *Which is the key back to the life I had before?* she thinks, as she loses her grip and drops the whole lot on the pavement.

'Lisa, please,' the girl says. 'Please, let us talk about this . . . I need to know how it happened. Look, I've had just as much of a shock as you . . . We need to work through it together . . . don't you think? It was him, wasn't it? Who did it? Not you? He stole me, didn't he?'

Lisa is staring at the girl now, looking intensely at her features. It is like seeing herself in a dream, and again that strange feeling ignites in her, like maybe none of this is real, like her life hasn't been real from the beginning somehow. Like maybe this girl is just her, at an earlier time in her life.

'I need . . . I need my meds,' she tries to say, but it comes out in an incoherent mumble. She cannot remember now whether she has been taking them or not, or what Dr Gloria said would happen if she stopped. Perhaps this girl is a symptom, a hallucination? Perhaps all she needs is a pill to make her go away, just like all she needed were meds to make Iona look like a baby she recognised.

The girl heads towards her, picks up her keys, and hands them to her. Lisa finally knows which key is which, and the moment it clicks into place in the lock, it's as though the ground beneath her tilts sideways, and Lisa realises she's read this whole thing wrong. That Eurov has deceived her in more ways than one.

'You know you're my mother,' the girl says. 'Don't you?'

Lisa experiences the sensation of being up to her neck in water. It's as if the whole of the Atlantic Ocean merges with the brown bulge of Pont Sulyn's river, and intermingled with it is the water that broke from her eighteen years ago, through which she sees a baby's face, a face she only saw for a few, devastating moments before a wave carried it away and another baby came to take its place.

A changeling.

'Yes. Yes I think I do . . .,' she tries to reply, but no sound comes out because the water is gushing into her mouth and flowing down into her lungs, pulling her down, down, down, and drowning her.

28. IONA

A 'mix up', the police said was still the most probable cause, as if those two small words explained everything away.

But there are other things that can be explained away. Or at least on the face of it they can. Now that their house has been drained, a damp, horrible picture emerges of what happened on the night of the flood.

A timeline is established, delivered by Miri in characteristically digestible chunks, only as much as she thinks they can handle. Toxicology results have revealed that both Bri and Urien were sedated by benzodiazepines, administered more than likely by being crushed into their food. Bri was the first to go, then Urien, then Skylar, then her mother. Iona whispers their names to herself at night, trying to imagine the whole thing playing out. Knowing that Bri was knocked out, adrift on dreams; that she wasn't conscious of any of the awful things going on around her, feels a relief.

Miri asks her again whether she remembers who prepared the food that evening. Iona has tried, several times, to re-enter that particular memory, but it's as if her brain hasn't recorded it. Her mother and father are stick figures in a dream, dark shadows moving around the kitchen island, hands obscured, passing things to each other, the extractor fan of the oven whirring in the background. Had they done it together? Sprinkled those sedatives over their food, spread an invisible dust around the rim of their water glasses? Had it been done right in front of them? Perhaps her parents had concocted this plan together, to remove themselves neatly from life, a whole family unit packed away. No descendants, ending the family line cleanly, without fuss.

But the girl. The girl had turned up. Had she been expected? Or had her presence changed the course of the evening? There is also something about Urien that still bothers her.

'He was on the landing, wasn't he, Urien,' she says. 'I remember now. I tried so long not to remember . . . seeing him lying there, but he was . . . '

'I'm afraid that your brother might have been conscious for long enough to sense that something wasn't right,' Miri says. 'But the drugs would have wiped him out pretty quickly, so it's unlikely he would have realised the full extent of what was going on.'

A sob escapes Iona then, somewhere from the depths of a hidden vault where she keeps all her feelings about Urien and Bri – her not-brother and not-sister, who she still loves deeply – under lock and key. Her Urien. Lying in the crook of her arm watching telly. How she would start humming a tune and Urien would tell her that it was the exact tune in his head at that moment, as if a strange musical telepathy existed between them, that the melodies and rhythms of their brains were indelibly linked.

'And the water,' she asks. 'The water, was . . . later? Or during? Or . . . ?'

'We think the house was flooded afterwards. We see it sometimes in cases like this . . . The perpetrator sets fire to the house . . . But it seems your father wanted to do things differently . . . Perhaps, as your Aunt said, to symbolise something.'

Iona nods, and looks out across the river, towards the bridge. She thinks of Cain's parents going over the edge, of those houses being swept away, of how they are saying now that the whole town, someday, will be underwater.

Maybe her father thought the whole thing was inevitable.

Miri then shows her hospital records from eighteen years ago, in which her name is registered as Skylar Quinta Dezen, not Iona Eira Griffri. She is shown another photograph of the woman she recognises from the online articles. Cassie. Whose DNA matches her own. All teeth and hair, oozing confidence, staring down the barrel of a lens like she's going to war. As unlike Lisa as it's possible to be.

'This woman is your biological mother,' Miri says. 'From what Cassie Dezen has told us, they'd only just found out about the whole thing recently, following an accident that Skylar had. She needed a blood transfusion from her mother and their blood types revealed that they weren't related at all. Since then her daughter – or whom she believed to be her daughter – had become fixated with tracking down her real family. She was in a real rush to reach out, her mum said. Whereas Cassie wanted to wait to do things properly, through the authorities.'

'So she knew about me . . . this Cassie,' Iona says. The name shimmers on her tongue. Cassie. So this is what her mother is called.

'Only for a few months. It was traumatic for her, too, you understand, to try to get her head around it all. She only met your father briefly, in a hospital corridor, and she thinks that he deliberately switched the babies.'

'But why?' Anna hollers from the corner of the room. 'Why would he do that?'

'We're not sure,' Miri says. 'We're still looking into it.'

Iona tries to imagine her inept, fumbling father carrying out this devastating act. There is part of her that is almost impressed by this consummate act of criminality perpetrated by someone who, in the last few years, has become an almost insignificant player in their family lives, orbiting around them at random; a person who could not steal a cat, yet alone a whole human life. But along with the rage and injustice of it all also comes compassion, thinking about how much she's been cared for. How much she's been loved. By Eurov. By Lisa. By her brother and sister. She, a stranger in their home. This doubling of who she should have been. Two languages, rather than one. She wonders what kind of dynamic their home would have had with Skylar living in it. A totally different one, perhaps. Enough for them to stop at two. For Bri never to have existed.

'You still don't know where he is either, do you?' Anna hollers. 'And you don't know why he did this, did any of it. You just keep coming here to tell us how much you don't know, expecting us to be OK with that.'

'Anna,' Iona says, clamping down on the nonsense in a way her father would. 'Please.'

'Cassie had a lot going on, she's had a tough few months of dealing with Skylar's erratic behaviour. And then Skylar just left one day, when she was meant to be attending a therapy session, and her mother had no idea she was even in Wales. And from what we've deduced, your father – Eurov – would have known who she was . . . Some of your father's colleagues had noticed odd behaviour during the teaching of the summer school. We think possibly that Skylar turning up, being confronted with the truth that his daughter was not his, in the midst of a particularly stressful time at work, facing redundancy . . . It might have been the perfect storm, you know?'

The perfect storm. Like the one that started everything, the one that worked its way into her house without anyone noticing. Iona feels she is closer to understanding the way Eurov looked at her now, that mixture of astonishment and love. What had it been like, to see her every day, and know she was not his child? To sit at the table and know for certain you had taken something that belonged to someone else? Not just a possession but a whole life? And that the child had gone hurtling on into that life with energy and enthusiasm, happy to accept any reality presented to her?

'And Cassie . . .' Iona begins. It is the question she has been holding back, afraid of the answer.

'Cassie is looking into flights as we speak,' Miri says. 'She wants to meet you.'

29. CAIN

Now that the coroner is satisfied, the bodies can be buried. Iona tells me it almost hadn't occurred to her that the morgue was a temporary measure, and that decisions will now have to be made about whether her family (not family) are buried together, and whether or not she is entitled to make any decisions at all. But because her American grandparents have both passed away, and her mother had no siblings, it is left to her and Anna to sort it out.

I tell her I'm happy to help, so I call Manny and ask him to come over. Manny's good with people. The common preconception about funeral directors is that they deal with the dead; but what they really deal with, and do so expertly, is the living. With life. Life in its trembling awfulness; but life all the same, felt keenly, horribly by those left living it. His father Eddie was the funeral director who buried my parents and, being the same age as me, Manny was brought along to keep me company while *Mam-gu* and Eddie discussed the particulars. I remember meeting him for the very first time when he was thrust into a living room by his father. No introductions. Just the arrival of a boy on a carpet, smiling shyly at me. I remember thinking that if I ignored him for long enough – sitting huddled at the far end of the living room, clutching my brother's toy train – I could make him disappear. But he was like one of those energy-saving bulbs, gaining power and momentum with every passing second, endearing himself to me, suggesting we put the train track together until I found myself building it with him, just to have something to do. Track upon track, sentence upon sentence, we found a way of communicating. And then we watched together as the tiny train moved around and around on the carpet, orbiting what was left of my old life, and Manny looked at me and said there would always be a way of fixing things, of moving forward, no matter what.

Iona makes it clear that the meeting cannot take place in Anna's house – because now Iona knows she isn't related to her, she says that arranging a funeral in her house would give Anna the upper hand. I know, from talking to Manny, that this is how some families feel when they are arranging funerals; like they are entering a battleground. Nothing brings out the insecurities of the living like arrangements for the dead, so Manny says.

And so Manny, who is used to navigating fractious families – tells me he will call by early, before they get here. He says it will be easier if he's already there, already part of the furniture, having already been casually hanging out there for half an hour or more drinking coffee with me, because a funeral director turning up at your door – there's still something very terrifying about that. This way, Manny's just there, just a friend. Iona will be just happening upon him in my living room, and she won't forever connect him with a dreaded knock.

The only thing Manny miscalculates is the effect his presence has on me. I hadn't anticipated it either, really, having greeted him at those shutters almost weekly. But when he walks in, dressed in his characteristic black suit, it is as though he shrinks right in front of me and he's once again that boy on the carpet who came to replace the life I once had.

Manny knows to ask Anna if she found us OK and proceeds to ask Iona if she'd like to take her coat off, before offering cups of tea as though it were his place rather than mine. A man who knows how to take his time – to get everyone seated and comfortable. Even *Mam-gu* remembers this about Manny and his dad: the fact that they make you feel as if they have all the time in the world. And the fact is, they haven't, because he's already told me that he's got several funerals on the go this week; but none of this comes across in this meeting. The frenzy of death arrangements that must be going on behind those lids, weighing on his mind, is completely hidden. Manny makes Iona and Anna feel as though he pauses to reflect on what has happened to them as much as they do. He doesn't offer platitudes. He does not say that he knows how difficult this must be for them.

What everyone has to acknowledge – and there is no getting around it – is the scale of this funeral. Three coffins. A coffin each for Lisa, Urien and Bri. Three coffins is going to mean a lot of bearers. Does Iona have any idea about bearers, he asks, although it seems pretty obvious to everyone that Iona doesn't, and so I pipe up at this point, confirming I'll make myself available. Anna mentions cousins up north; she is sure she can ask them to help out. Manny says that if they give him the contact details he'll speak to them; no one else needs to lift a finger. It is what he is for; to take away the burden of the asking, the negotiating, the arranging. Because he knows that death throws people into a muddle, and they should be allowed to be in that muddle for as long as they want.

They discuss ideas for music; Anna sits there sullenly and says, 'What music is there, for such an awful thing?' Iona mentions something by Mozart that her father liked but then her face pales when she wonders if it's right for her father's tastes to be considered, under the circumstances.

'Bri liked musicals,' she says, quietly. 'Didn't she?'

Manny tells them not to worry, that he can have a think about it, come up with some options and they can choose later. Manny's a musician himself, plays every Saturday night down the Stag and Pheasant with a cover band. I see people looking at him sometimes like they can't quite equate the guy on stage playing guitar with the guy that's so calmly been managing all the deaths in this place. But it's his outlet. He's an ordinary guy like the rest of us, and to see him on his day off you wouldn't even think he was a funeral director – sitting under the eaves in the centre of town in his lumberjack shirt, eating a pasty, a little girl walking around in circles around his long gangly legs.

'He should sell the business to one of the bigger companies and be done with the stress of the dead,' *Mam-gu* always says. 'Can't be good for you, can it, spending all your time with people who are upset?'

Mam-gu adores Manny. It's why she seems to want another life for him. But I know full well that if Manny ever did decide to sell and bugger off to the Maldives or somewhere, she'd be the first one pointing the finger. The fact is, she loves Manny because he would never do that. Manny is Manny because he *doesn't* look like a man sitting on a lucrative business prospect for some soul-less big company. He looks like a man who wants to do the right thing, although it's shit and difficult. Manny once told me that if he sold the company tomorrow to one of those companies, they'd keep his family's name, and bring in a whole load of new staff from elsewhere, under the pretence of being a local business. So Manny remains Manny so that he can be the kind of person who assures people they can have the funeral they want, in the language they want, with the customs and practices and traditions he under-stands, having grown up here.

It's an odd sort of thing: sticking to your principles for an event that people aren't even around for.

I wonder if he ever thinks these things to himself, as he sits under that plastic canopy eating his pasty, while his daughter cartwheels around him. Probably not. Because doing the right thing is just second nature to him, and I wouldn't imagine he gives it much thought at all.

It's crazy to think that for these kind of people, people like *Mam-gu*, to get the funeral they want – a funeral that's true to who they really *were* – is dependent on people like Manny being like Manny and not just taking that cash and running away to a far-flung island to sip a cocktail and fill his boots with the all-inclusive buffet.

One day, I worry the world might run out of Mannys, a man so rooted in place and principle that to take him out of it would change the whole world order somehow. Because maybe lovely Manny and his easy way, his easy smile, and his preference for a pasty over a goldmine is all we've got to stop us from disappearing behind the curtain and sinking down into oblivion forever, to the tune of a hymn in another language that means nothing to our dead ears, nothing at all.

PART THREE

L – LOVE: love is never straightforward in Wales, bound up as it is with all sorts of other things – duty, obligation, legacy, principle. The niggling realisation that whom one chooses to share one's life with could actually have a cultural impact on the future of your country.

When I moved to the States all those years ago, it broke my mother's heart, because not only was her husband now dead and buried and suspended under hundreds of feet of water, but now her only son was on the other side of a vaster body of water, potentially never to return.

I would have loved to have been able to stay in the US, to embrace the All-American Life, and hide those problematic parts of myself from Lisa. But once she knew about them, about the drowned world which I had come from, she made the ultimate sacrifice and said that she would move to Wales, with me. That she would learn my language. Learn all about my history. That she would come and gaze with me across the Tryweryn reservoir and would make sure our children knew that a whole way of life lay beneath.

And so, considering such generosity, how could I have let her leave that hospital without a baby? Without the future we had planned in her arms?

8 DAYS BEFORE

30. LISA

A large proportion of her antidepressants have gone missing. They are no longer in the drawer under her bed, the boxes empty, haunting her with their cardboard skeletons. Her search for them is not methodical, as it would be for the other lost items in the house, she just spins wildly about the room, moving from one corner to the next, running her hands fleetingly across shelves and surfaces, and turning to implausible hiding places – the laundry basket, which she empties all over the floor, her husband's trouser press, which she more or less dismantles, and finally her jewellery box, whose necklaces and bracelets seem to glint menacingly at her, making her dump them all into a black bin liner, to take to a charity shop later.

Eurov has hidden the pills from her, she thinks. He is trying to drive her mad.

She must find some way of getting them back from him, but now he seems to be guarding his study with his life, working and sleeping there throughout the night, and rarely leaving it during the day. She often finds herself pottering around on the landing at three in the morning, seeing the dim light filtering out from beneath the door, damning him for still being awake. Eurov tells the rest of the family that the deadline for the encyclopaedia is looming, but Lisa's not sure they believe him.

'Have you actually seen him doing any proper work?' Urien asked her one evening, leaning against the door frame of her studio. 'I think . . . he's writing it out by hand. By hand?'

Lisa tells Urien that whatever he's seen Eurov doing is surely just his usual note taking, after which Urien looks at her intensely and asks her if everything's OK with her. Like, really OK?

'Of course it is honey,' she reassures him, reverting to Welsh as she reels him in for a hug. '*Paid â phoeni amdana i.*' Don't worry about me.

But she can see that Urien is worried about her, deeply, in a way Briall, for all the twitching of her emotional antennae, can only grasp at. Somehow this middle child of hers has been put on earth in order to see through her, to see things as they are, while Iona, wrapped up in her teenage romance with Jethro, hasn't noticed a thing.

But how on earth can she tell Urien what she is really feeling? That she's become unmoored from life, like a free-floating balloon, drifting higher and higher up into the air, looking down on everything and everyone from a distance. The fewer pills she takes, the more this feeling increases; and the lighter she becomes, the less any of it seems important. Or real.

She has been questioning whether Skylar, in fact, actually exists at all. And yet then she remembers the familiarity and ease she'd felt in being with her at the kitchen table. The flashes of resemblance as Skylar turned her head this way and that, her face hosting the very same brown beauty spot above her lip, the one you had to look carefully for, not big enough to announce itself as such. The one that Lisa's covered up for most of her life with concealer.

'But how?' Lisa had wept at the kitchen table that day. 'How could you be mine? And who is Iona?'

The girl said she did not know how it could have happened, but perhaps the hospital had made a mistake. Either that, or Cassie or Eurov would have done it deliberately.

It was too much to process. She had asked the girl to leave, with the promise that they would speak again soon, once they had cleared all this up. As though a misplaced childhood of eighteen years could be sorted, just like that.

It was only when she was gone, and her meds were nowhere to be seen, that Lisa started to wonder whether she had conjured the girl up from thin air. That she may well be an apparition that had emerged from the fissures of her broken brain.

She can't be real, she whispered to herself. *She can't be.*

Because if she was, then that would mean Iona, the daughter she had loved for eighteen years, the one she was so reluctant to let go of, was nothing but a fiction.

31. IONA

At the funeral, Iona has no idea who half of the guests are. Their faces make no sense to her, and she cannot seem to look anyone in the eye. She focuses rather on things like the diamanté pattern on a dress, the brown stain on the underside of a stiff collar, the rise and fall of a brooch catching the light in frightening, glittering dashes. She is used to walking into a room with her parents – with Eurov and Lisa – standing behind them while they talk; folding into them, along with her brother and sister. Her mother always knew what to say to people. Even if she secretly hated them. She knew which questions to ask each person; when to keep it light, or when to delve right into the deep stuff. She said it was something to do with being an American, that there were simply so many people to talk to, with such varying opinions on everything, it kept you on your toes; you had to know how to adjust. Her dad mused that in Wales there was only ever one approach and one question – 'Where are you from?' – which inevitably then led to the scramble to find a friend in common or some shared appreciation of a familiar place. Her mother would say: 'Nonsense. You don't have to find something in common. And anyway, everyone is connected by something Eurov, it doesn't have to be about land, about a place.' Her dad would say: 'That's the big country talking.'

The minister talks in terms of Iona having lost a *mother, brother, sister*. News has not broken yet of her un-belonging, which helps her to feel a little more in control of the situation. Miri continually talks about 'keeping a lid on things', as if Iona were a tiny person inside one of her mother's (not-mother's) Tupperware boxes. She thinks of the fact that she wouldn't mind stowing herself away like that for a while, for there has been so little silence since everything happened, and she has been expected to talk more than she ever has in her life. And this is what she relishes about the funeral service (the little she remembers of it) – that it's a perfect hour of her own, understood, silence. Sitting there in the front pews with Anna, clutching her aunt's (not-aunt's) hand, while all the other people are asked to talk and pontificate and try to find the right words, when everyone knows there are none, for a situation like this. She is not even expected to sing along with the congregation.

She is excused from everything.

Her friends, those she used to call her friends, are huddled together with their mothers on the chapel balcony, all cascading hair and lip gloss and awkwardness, and when they approach her later and try to offer some words of condolence, they seem to be physically clumsy, like newborn foals. She thinks of how easy it was for them to disappear from her life; for the words of their WhatsApps and Snapchats to get fewer and fewer, until they were reduced to a flurry of emojis. Even though she's known these girls since primary, some of them since nursery, now they are simply this: a mass of strangers thronging around her outside the chapel, trying to reclaim her because her situation makes her more interesting, more of an asset to their group, than ever. Jethro and his mum are there, in the far distance. His mother probably made him come, she thinks, and he doesn't approach her or speak to her at all.

They should never have been her people in the first place, she thinks. She should never have even known this place existed. It wouldn't even have featured on her map of the world.

When she heads outside, she relishes the freedom of the crisp autumn air. A welcome few days of dryness in their wet town. That's when she sees Cain standing there, under a birch tree. It's the fact of him not wanting to be noticed that draws her attention. It's such a relief to see him again. This boy she's known for a few short weeks seems like the only family she has right now, because he's part of the tribe of the dead and the mourning, the only place she knows for certain that she belongs.

'*Ti'n iawn?*' he asks. You OK?

That's all she needs right now, for someone to ask the simplest of questions, in her mother (not-mother) tongue. She nods.

Cain doesn't know what to do now – she can see he isn't sure whether to hug her or not. He admits to being out of sorts because nothing is asked of him – the funeral directors are taking care of everything. Finally, she takes one of his fidgety hands in hers, and it takes him a while for him to register what she's doing, to see that she isn't clinging to him because she thinks she might fall or buckle or need pulling up or down like all those other times he's helped her. She's putting her hand in his because she wants to. And finally, he seems to understand, and smile at her. And loops his morgue-cold fingers back around hers.

32. CAIN

Carol is hunched outside the flat. Drunk. Or weak from chemo. I can't tell.

'Are you sleeping with the Griffri girl?' she says, swaying as she reaches out for me. I haul her off the doorstep and get her inside quick, before the neighbours see.

'Come on Carol,' I say. 'Stop talking nonsense now, yeah? Let's get you inside.'

Of course, she was at the funeral. I remember now; she knew Eurov. But more to the point, she knew I'd be there. She must have seen me with Iona. My palm is still warm from her touch.

She starts rummaging around in the cupboards for something to drink. I'm not a great drinker; she knows this. She has always berated me for it: *if you don't do it for yourself, do it for me, Cain.* She wanted me to lose myself with her, to sway and slip and slide along life like she did. *Why are you always so upright, so sober!* she'd shout. I used to buy her those little cans of G&T and stack them up in the cupboard. I thought of them as artillery, like Carol and I were indulging in some sort of warfare during those angry, shouty, drinking sessions. Now, as she plods through the flat, opens the cupboards and leaves them flapping open like someone's ransacked the place, she berates me for the fact that all the alcohol has gone. Then comes the real reason for her visit.

'You're taking advantage of a grieving girl,' she said. 'It's not appropriate. It's one of the rules of the group, isn't it? No relationships for the first year.'

'That's AA, Carol,' I tell her. 'We don't have rules like that.'

'You know she's in no fit state to be in a relationship!'

'I'm not in a relationship with her Carol,' I say, which is the truth. Iona and I have something deeper than that. An indelible binding,

187

stuck steadfastly to each other with the glue of our collective sadness. A bond almost impossible to understand from the outside, like the words of that mangled encyclopaedia.

And I can't muster the strength to explain it to Carol right now – that nothing at all has happened between us yet, nothing but the promise of something in the way we clung so desperately to each other at that funeral. And I don't like the insinuation that Iona is a poor bereaved girl to be taken advantage of. Carol doesn't know about the many nights we've spent sitting here side by side watching TV, our legs maintaining the necessary, painful distance. How we've stood together by the kitchen island in complete, comfortable silence watching the town come to life below us. The way we text each other back and forth incessantly about those encyclopaedic entries, every time we think we've decoded a letter or a word. How our losses, and even our lives, now seem like a joint effort. Carol, who claims to either love or hate a person, who always goes off first impressions, won't understand that one doesn't simply arrive here, feeling this way. Relationships have to be given space to grow. Impressions change.

'Well that's it, you know. I'm fucked,' Carol says, a sentence to reel me back in when she senses me not giving a toss about what she thinks about me and Iona.

'What do you mean?' I say, although I know what it means.

'They say I've got five weeks. It seems like a weird number doesn't it? I mean, who gives you an odd number for the rest of your life?'

There's much of Carol that has been lost already, so many bits of her that went and died when she lost her husband and daughter, there isn't much left of her to take. I tell her this; although it's a bit of a gamble and it possibly isn't what she wants to hear. But she laughs. She laughs, and with it comes a spark of life; the little of what is left in the tank.

'Fucking hell Cain. I've been waiting so long for someone to say that, you know. That it's OK to be, well, OK about it.'

She curls into my shoulder, suddenly soft and vulnerable, and I put my arm around her. I tell her that we all have our own unique relationship with death, which sounds like therapy group jargon, but I mean it. Despite everything it's taken from me, or how it's shaped my world, I'm not like Carol, and I've never wanted to head willingly into it.

What a pair we make – me, post-funeral, still in my black jacket, with a dying woman in my arms, thinking about the fact that every day we don't die is some kind of triumph.

All I have ever wanted – surely all anyone wants – is to get to the end of their lives without dying first.

And as far as I see it, Carol's made it to the finish line she always wanted. She's earned it.

M – MERCH – (mer as in merry, ch as in Bach): Another word in Welsh that has to encompass two meanings is *merch* – synonymous for both *girl* and *daughter*. This however is not the case for the male species, who have their own separate words for son (*mab*) and boy (*bachgen*) dividing them into two distinct identities.

Over the years, I persuaded myself that, on some level, this ambiguity concerning whether the newborn in front of me was, in fact, my daughter, or whether she was just a girl, plucked at random from another life, had somehow directed me to take action in the darkest of moments, in order to make sure that this anonymous girl indeed became someone's daughter, in a way she was never intended to be. For while there are some merched (plural for merch: girls) who are meticulously planned, yearned-for, long-awaited, there are also those others that spark to life against all odds, even when the women who carry them have done everything in their power to stop it from happening – which is also a right every merch should be afforded.

In many ways, what I did in the hospital that night was a response to the sadness and panic I saw in one merch's eyes, that she could never be a real mother to her child, and the horror and agonising grief I felt in knowing my own merch had slipped away.

It was driven by a desire to make all those feelings go away, and to unify the endless echoing of that word – merch – down that sterile corridor – to make it mean something again.

To set a woman free, who had never wanted to be a mother.

To bring a warm, living baby back into my beloved's arms, not a dead one.

To unite both a girl and daughter and think of them simply as symbolising one entity, one huddled inside the other, an embodiment of the word merch itself.

6 DAYS BEFORE

33. LISA

More and more now, she dreams of water. The irrationality of it, the voluminosity of it, the way it doesn't care if stupid, fallible humans, who cannot swim, are in its way. There is talk of another, far more serious flood coming their way in six days.

Part of her hopes the storm will come and sweep the girl away, leaving the rest of them on dry land. But another part of her knows she shouldn't be thinking these things, because this girl is her daughter, and Iona is not.

She stops painting and defaults back to the time-wasting endeavour of scrolling on social media, becoming obsessed with the ocean-driven melting of floating ice-shelves in the Amundsen Sea. The algorithms deduce that someone of her disposition will also likely be interested in age-defying wrinkle cream, spine-aligning pillows for sleeping, and raised toilet seats for those with bad knees. The age-defying products and the almost certain death by water seem at cross purposes, but still she clicks on the adverts and buys the product, because she knows she's still vain enough to want nice skin when she goes under.

Leaflets are shoved through their letterbox announcing further meetings about council plans for decommissioning the town. It feels that everything around her will soon be washed away.

She finds herself obsessing over tsunamis, even though she knows it's unlikely to happen in Wales. ('One did!' Eurov once told her. 'In the seventeenth century! There's a flood plaque at Goldcliff Parish Church in Newport! Thousands of people got caught up in it – they weren't sure if it was a tsunami or just inadequate flood defences!' She remembered how she'd hated hearing that, knowing that it would prey on her mind for days, weeks, months afterwards, when she was feeling fragile, the thought that something could sweep them all away one day. That nowhere, not even a small Welsh town, would be safe.)

Next she googles the Thailand tsunami, watching home videos of people in their hotel rooms, up to their necks in water, filming themselves grabbing onto light fittings and perched on coving, only their terrified eyes visible above the rising water level. She remembers how she and Eurov had spent that gloomy Boxing Day in Scranton, watching the news reports filter in on her mother's blaring kitchen TV as they worked up the sugar pie between them. Eurov was particularly disturbed by it, because of his own history with water and drownings, and spent most of the holiday explaining to his mother-in-law how they'd drowned the village he grew up in, while behind him on the screen images flickered of the debris of entire villages hurtling past in the rush of water.

'But surely it's not the same, Eurov,' her mother had said, in that lazy drawl of hers. 'You were warned, you got moved, you got out. Not like these poor souls. This is a *natural* disaster.'

As ever, Eurov could see that this conversation with her mother was a non-starter and returned to marking his papers. Lisa spent most of the Christmas season thinking about the enormity of that wave. At what point did that tiny swell become something dangerous, at what point did the distant and far away become close enough to engulf everything? She often thought of those people on the shore, sunbathing, relaxing, watching the wave gather height and strength. At what point did they realise that it would be the last wave they would ever see?

'Mum! Mum, hello!' Urien calls to her now, waving his hand in front of her face, noticing she's in one of her morning trances, 'You remember I've got training down at the track tonight? Can you come pick me up at 4.30?'

Sometimes Lisa finds it hard to understand how these two worlds can co-exist, the awfulness that goes on in her head, those raging storms, natural disasters and catastrophic events, while a teenage boy is just stuffing a pair of running spikes into his bag as though the world isn't going to end anytime soon, never questioning whether he will make it to four-thirty that day. It's love; that impossible, deep, terrifying love for her children that lifts her out of it, every time, and brings her back to life.

Of course life continues. Of course it's a given, she thinks. Of course it is all going to be OK.

They will find a way of slotting Skylar into their lives. It will somehow all be sorted. Iona will understand. She will continue to love them.

But then just as suddenly, she thinks – what if it's not that easy?

34. IONA

They are finally permitted to re-enter the house of water.

A whiff of wet plaster and paint, mixed with something else too, rises up into Iona's nostrils as she and Anna cross the threshold, remnants of the aromas of their family life over eighteen years, their perfumes and scents, their particles of skin and hair; it's all there, submerged, yet faintly present, in the air.

Miri says she'll stay outside and give them a moment.

Anna has brought her a box to fill up with keepsakes. One by one, objects and artefacts of a life start to get assembled, a pink headband which belonged to Bri, an erase board on the fridge that is filled with their weekly meal plan, Urien's headphones, her mother's brushes, Eurov's old typewriter, high up on a shelf in his study. As Iona watches the box fill she cannot believe how small and pathetic their family life looks, reduced to trinkets and paraphernalia, but at the same time she sees that their family life can never be conjured up with things. It is memory and laughter and remembered conversations, which will live inside her forever, that make up this family. Not this.

Anna takes down the framed picture of the aerial view of their farmhouse in Capel Celyn. Last night, Anna told Iona that these last few weeks have brought her a kind of peace about what happened to her village back then. It's reignited an appropriate amount of fury to fight to make sure that these precious resources do not get taken over. If they are to forge ahead with the decommission, the drowning of Pont Sulyn has to mean that they, as a people, become more powerful. Not weakened by it. Not traumatised by it. But heading on into the future with determination to keep hold of what is theirs; their water, the most powerful thing in the world, the commodity that everyone will soon want in this soon-to-be-parched, yet drowning world. She remembers Eurov telling her that one of the reasons the river kept overflowing was because it wanted to go back to its natural course, the one it had before the Romans came and built the roads and the bridge; it comforts her to think that what is happening here is a return to nature; that the river has a memory, spilling back into his origins, making its point that humans were never meant to decide its direction.

Iona gathers up some things from Urien and Bri's room, trying not to loiter in either one for longer than necessary. On the floor of Urien's bedroom is his crumpled up running parachute, the one he strapped to himself to improve his performance. It feels light and crisp in her hands, so at odds with the heaviness she feels when she thinks of him. Maybe she should start running, she thinks, take the baton from him. It makes her smile, the thought of how he would laugh at even the notion of his unfit, uncoordinated sister taking up any sport at all.

Bri's bedroom is immaculate, still, the only bedroom in the house that her mother habitually tidied and organised. She peels off the rainbow and heart stickers from the light switch, and finds an old Peppa Pig T-shirt with her own name stitched onto it, a childhood item of hers which Bri loved to wear as though it were a fan item, as though Iona were her idol.

Perhaps she *had* been, she thinks sadly, without knowing it. Perhaps the more unreachable she became, in those months wrapped up in her relationship with Jethro, the more they tried to get her attention.

Eurov's study is the last room she enters. Where his project, the encyclopaedia, started. A simple task, she thinks, to give this country the facts it needed to know about itself in order to move forward into the future. And now the entry of her own life is erased, left blank, free to construct as she wants. To take as much or as little from this country's history as she needs.

She takes nothing of Eurov's. She isn't sure she wants to, not until they've found him.

She opens the skylight, letting the dampness out and the crisp, new autumn air in. And that's when she sees Cain, just waiting there for her on the other side of the street. His eyes glowing, and urgent, as he waves her down, wanting to show her something.

35. CAIN

An American woman visits the morgue with Miri, wanting to see the girl she thought was her daughter. I wonder if the impact of seeing her will be different now, knowing that she isn't hers, but there's a ferocity to her response which betrays the polished exterior of her perfectly painted-on face. Her pinned-back, black hair suddenly becomes loose, its ink spreading across her shoulders, and as her guttural sobs echo around the room, her makeup leaves orange stains on the white sheet. It is a full body reaction; the raw, unashamed truth of grief.

'If only she'd known,' she says, through her sobs, 'how much I really loved her.'

Miri thanks me for my time and I watch them retreat down the corridor, Miri's hand sliding across the woman's shoulder; a feather boa of consolation. What I wanted to tell her, but couldn't, was how much she reminded me of Iona, in the way she spoke, the way her eyes seemed to look not at you but deep into you somehow. Curious to think that there are some things we carry genetically, from those who give birth to us, no matter how, or by whom, we are raised. That there is some invisible force pulling the strings of our actions, our quirks, our mannerisms.

I get a call from Nerys, a nurse on the palliative care unit, to come up to see Carol. She says it won't be long now, and it would be nice for her to have someone with her. While I'm not entirely sure if it's what Carol wants, when I found out that she hadn't had any visitors since being admitted, it feels the right thing to do.

When I get there Nerys is inserting the syringe driver. Carol now seems a miniature version of the woman I first met, a tiny doll, a random arrangement of limbs in the white bed, her face hollowed out so that I can see almost the shape of her skull, her mouth open-ing and closing, a fish strenuously taking in the final lungfuls of air.

'There, there, lovely,' Nerys says quietly. 'Cain's here.'

It's not clear whether this registers at all. And so for a while I just sit, and wait, and observe the rhythms of her breath. The haunting death rattle of each laborious one. And yet although so much of it is unpleasant, this end-of-life stage, there's also a sort of beauty in bearing witness to it. A great honour. And a departure for me, too. End of life isn't really what we process in the morgue, it's the beginning of a different journey.

And for a few brief, wondrous moments, she wakes up and sees me sitting there, a smile flitting across her face. Her hand begins to move as if of its own accord, drifting across the vacuum between us. I vow to myself to never forget the feel of it – as weak as it is, it still has warmth, and gratitude, an appreciation for being here, no matter how painful it has all been. There is also relief in it. Relief that finally, she's here now, all signed up for the end destination, all strapped in and ready to go; and even if it's just random old me at her side watching the departure, at least she has someone who understands how much she wants this, and who isn't making her fight.

'They were never gone,' she suddenly whispers. 'I saw them every day, you know. The past is just there, always isn't it. It never goes. They were just hiding in plain sight . . . '

Suddenly her hand goes limp in mine. And with her very final intake of breath, I reach over and place the picture of her little girl and her husband on her chest, and whisper to her that everything's going to be OK.

The porters bring the trolley and we gently ease her onto it, her body still pulsing, particles of her skin escaping into the air around us. I then accompany her on her final journey through the secret thoroughfare between the hospital and the morgue. I take my time. 'There's no rush, my love,' I tell her. When we arrive at the morgue, when I transfer her from the trolley onto the tray, it isn't like all the others, somehow. And I dare say there's grief surging inside me somewhere, a feeling that's been dormant for years. It makes my hands unsteady as I open and close the fridge, and I lose my bearings for a second, needing to sit down with my head in my hands until the feeling passes.

'You see Cain,' I can imagine her saying, 'you *do* have feelings.'

Damn her. I close the drawer and take a few moments to gather myself and think about her last words. The notion of hiding in plain sight makes me think of Eurov. The police saying they'd looked everywhere, yet something niggles at the back of my mind that he wouldn't have left Iona to fend for herself in this situation.

*

When I get home I head straight for the kitchen. I took the encyclopaedia out of the freezer again a few days ago, and with every thawing comes another surprise, another phrase or word that reveals itself to me. This time I study the B section, specifically. It's been bothering me for a few days, because it seems thicker than the others, and when I inspect the bottom of the page it seems that there's another page underneath the entry, folded underneath, stuck fast to the first. Prising it apart with a spatula doesn't work, so I boil the kettle, holding it above the steam, sliding my fingers under the paper to try and find a gap.

The more I delve into Eurov's encyclopaedia the more convinced I become that the man he was is all in those pages, that it's the only way we're ever going to find him, by decoding every single entry one by one, until we've reassembled him, somehow. Because unlike my own parents, he's left something behind, and when you do leave something behind, death doesn't have to be the end.

It can be the beginning of something. B for beginning, I think, as I finally prise that last piece of paper from its hiding place, and spread it out carefully in front of me.

The addendum to the entry, as far as I can tell, reads:

Pont-Sulyn's bridge is also the most impressive of its kind in Wales. It has three arches made with reinforced concrete, each span consists of an arch barrel, with columns supporting a beam and a slab deck. It is travelled across day after day by hundreds of residents, taking them in and out of the town, with the majority of them being unaware of the secret vault inside, which only the select few know about.

Hiding in plain sight, I think. Unknowingly Carol's last gift to me.

N – NOSTALGIA: A particularly complex emotion for a Welsh individual. There is a tendency in Wales to hanker after a long-gone past, to remember past glories; being unable to shake the feeling that, once, the Welsh were a powerful nation, before that power was taken away from them. But there is also a sense in which Nostalgia itself, coming as it does from the Greek *nostos* (homecoming) and *algos* (pain) could indicate some psychological instability. In fact, it was once categorised as a mental health disorder, linked to individuals who had problems connecting with others, and who tended to have fractured, unstable relationships; people who lived in the past.

There is a sense that I have lived with nostalgia more than most, having grown up in a place that was later flooded. But it has come to my attention that not everyone is as affected by these things. For, when another village in Wales, another N – Nant y Moch – (literally 'the pigs' stream') – was flooded to make way for a hydro-electric scheme, there wasn't much fuss about it at all. In fact, the archive footage seems to show that some of the residents were quite jolly at the prospect of being moved out of the valley in which they had lived all their lives. Why let the nostos and the algos get in the way of an exciting new future?

And yet for me, the algos has always been something that festers within me, the pain I cannot shake off, the one I must endure. And the nostos is an incessant reminder of the homecoming to Wales that was far too complicated to be enjoyed, all because of a wrong turn in a hospital corridor.

2 DAYS BEFORE

36. LISA

Finally, Eurov sits her down and tells her about that night at the hospital. It takes her by surprise, this need of his to explain everything away, when he has been so elusive about it all from the start.

'Why have you not asked?' he cries at her. 'Any normal person would want to know!'

Normal person. She laughs at this. What can he claim to know about normality?

He shakes his head, avoids her gaze, and begins.

*

Many years ago, Eurov tells her, he took a life. Lifted it, unsuspecting, out of a plastic crib, and ran away with it down a corridor.

While Lisa was in theatre after the birth, with surgeons trying to stop her haemorrhaging, he had been left alone with the baby, wheeling her all around the hospital in Scranton in an attempt to get her to stop screaming. He remembered looking down at her in complete wonderment, at those strikingly large eyes taking in everything around her, while the sound she made seemed to be taunting him, telling him she was opposed to him, opposed to the life she had suddenly been given. And then, just like that, the crying stopped. He could never remember if it had been a sudden realisation that she'd stopped breathing or if it had crept up on him gradually, but it seemed that time both slowed down and sped up at the same time and seemed to contain every minute moment in his life that had led to this.

A few minutes before, he had been drawn into conversation with another new mother, Cassie, who he could still hear weeping in the corridor behind him. A young woman who had not known she was pregnant, and to whom giving birth had been a terrible, painful, traumatic shock. And the baby in front of him, the one he'd so proudly introduced to her minutes before as their very much longed-for firstborn, was now unmistakably dead. Had it been his fault? Had he perhaps pushed the crib too quickly, or rocked it in a way he wasn't meant to? Reaching a trembling hand down towards her, he came into contact with the agonising, cold truth: that his firstborn was gone, and that he had failed at being a father within the first hour.

It was Cassie's wails behind him, those wracking sobs, that had seemed to signal what should happen next. Cassie's insistence that she had never wanted that baby, that she would not know what to do with it, came clanging into his head. She would never love it, she had said. *It*, rather than her. And there in front of him was the baby he and Lisa had so desperately wanted to love which they would now have to spend the rest of their lives loving in the most unimaginably painful of ways.

How on earth he had managed to walk so calmly back towards Cassie, to suggest to her that she head to the restroom and freshen up, while he looked after the two cribs, was beyond him now. Cassie's baby had been wrist-banded, but his had not, such had been the frenzy and panic of delivery, and it had been this oversight, more than anything, that would later make the whole thing possible. As much as he would forget so many of the little details of this awful night, there was one thing he would never forget in his life, and that was the feeling in his arms when he had lifted a leaden, dead baby up into his arms and placed it back down in a crib next to a living baby. And how the other baby screamed with the sheer horror of it, knowing, somehow, exactly what he was doing. And how he rocked and rocked and rocked that baby in his arms until

Cassie returned, assuming that at any moment, she would recognise her baby's cry and take her baby from him. But instead she had looked at him with dull eyes, thanked him for minding the crib, and wheeled the still, quiet baby away from him.

He stood there and watched her pushing his own dead future away from him while her own future lay there screaming in his arms. And that was that. Cassie turned a corner and disappeared from his life. Cassie's full name he would remember forever, as though it had been tattooed on his heart. Baby of Cassie Evelyn Dezen. The womb he had betrayed; the set of genes he had so mercilessly taken away in a bundle; the wristband he'd cut away with his key and slipped into the darkness of his pocket. A murderer bagging a memento.

He rushed back to the ward with the screaming baby that was not his. Not Iona. At that point, it still wasn't too late to turn back. What he had done was terrible, yes, but it could have been rationalised as shock or trauma or some kind of cerebral incident, he was sure of it. He had not slept for days at this point – due to Lisa's long labour and then the sudden rush of blood and complications – and everything around him had taken on a kind of a distorted, illusory quality. As he cantered on back to the ward, he suddenly felt with certainty that Lisa would be dead. That it would be his punishment for what he had done, subtracting one life for another.

'But I didn't die, did I Eurov?' Lisa now says in a dull, quiet voice, that she does not even recognise as her own. 'I came around, and I looked at that baby and said – she isn't mine. Do you know how much I tortured herself over voicing that doubt, for years?'

Lisa now recalls every lurid detail of those hours – how Eurov pointed out that they had not yet given the baby a wristband, and they duly apologised, as if commending him for noticing. The midwives continued to reassure her, to tell her all was well and that this was her baby, and he joined in with their chorus of confirmation.

It's normal to feel like this! Things will get better! Things will start to make sense soon!

It is this, more than anything, she tells him, that riles her: that he allowed her to feel mad. That she was the one in the wrong.

'And you're doing it again, by taking my meds from me,' she says. 'Aren't you?'

Eurov seems stunned, but does not refute this, either.

All light has drained from the room. Lisa is dimly aware of the amber warning on the radio turning to red, but Eurov reassures her, in a thin, whispery voice, that he'll get the sandbags from the garage. Place them outside the doors, just in case. But they'll be fine. Their part of Pont Sulyn is always fine.

But nothing is fine, she tells him. Nothing will ever be fine again.

She leaves the room and he does not go after her.

37. IONA

As she and Cain peruse the new section together Iona finds it hard to believe the police have not gone looking for Eurov inside the bridge. It is, now she thinks of it, the most obvious of places. The way he kept going on about bridges, and crossings, when they were in the car. *The liminal space.* Both terrifying and liberating. Like you could die crossing it, but that weirdly you were nowhere, and nothing mattered.

Because who is to say that such a gravity-defying concept can ever be truly safe? she reads. *And can a gap ever be filled completely? Or is it still there, all around us, the potential to fall from a great height into the depths below?*

In any case, this is their best bet now. The police resources have run thin, almost to nothing. The divers have long moved on to other tragedies, other rivers. There's simply no more money to look for Eurov, to have those boats out on the water day and night looking for a murderer when there are good, honest people to be evacuated from their own lives. Plus, there is another storm, another battering, coming soon, they say. *Storm Lisa*, it's called, the irony of which is not lost on Iona.

Iona remembers Eurov taking them inside the bridge once, when they were younger. Beaming with pride that he was letting them in on a little-known secret of the town, as he placed the yellow hard hats on their heads. Bri had skipped around happily in the grey shadows as Eurov had given them yet another history lesson about the bridge's various reconstructions over the years, and Urien had rolled his eyes at her in the darkness. Iona had paid as much attention to it as she had her mum's exhibition, because your parents' obsessions were something to be endured at this stage in life, not to be taken seriously. Once again, she finds herself wishing she had really seen her parents for who they were, but just as suddenly she remember they are not her parents. That the girl inside the bridge that day was just a stranger, trailing a random man and his two kids in her yellow hard hat, which could never protect her from the destruction that was to come.

Cain sits down on her pink bedspread and tells her earnestly what he thinks has been happening, running his hand down the side of his face, as he always does when he's trying hard to focus on something. Iona finds herself tracing the movement of his hand, being envious of the way the hand attached to him is allowed to roam over such lovely terrain.

'The police have been scouring the river, the fields, right? They've been looking for a drowned man, or a man hanging from trees. They have not been looking for a man who wanted to stay alive, who was maybe biding his time. Wouldn't it be the perfect place,' he asks her, 'the perfect place to disappear for a while? I mean, I doubt many people even know about it. I only know because . . . because of course, when it was repaired, after my mum and dad . . . I remember my grandmother saying something about the structure being damaged. That the construction workers worked on it from the inside – that there was another way in, from the river. Some kids got washed downstream once, and everyone thought they were dead, but they found an opening from beneath it. It's only when the water levels are really high that it carries you close enough to climb in. And that night, the water would have been high enough, wouldn't it?'

As much as she wants to listen to him, she's distracted now by his earnestness, thinking of all this water that's between them, thicker than blood. And how the bridge that could be housing her father is the same one that threw Cain's own family into the abyss.

'I think we should go down there,' he says. 'Tonight.'

'Tonight. Sure,' she says, 'why not?' Her tonights stretch end-lessly in front of her, meaningless and without purpose. She checks an app on her phone that says the next storm is over twelve hours away, so they have time.

Iona asks Cain what he thinks the other version of herself would be doing now, the one who had woken up, slightly woozy and hungover that morning, and climbed into her father's car and headed to Cambridge. Would she be out now, perhaps, with her uni friends, enjoying herself?

'I don't think it helps to think of the other versions,' Cain says quietly. 'Because, well, we are where we are. And we are who we are, because of it.'

'And what's that, group jargon?' she laughs. 'Carol would love that.'

He goes quiet, all of a sudden.

'Carol . . . Carol died,' he says.

'Oh Cain, I'm sorry, I didn't know.'

'It's OK,' he tells her. 'I was with her. It was peaceful. And it was what she wanted, you know?'

Another one gone who knew her father. Another fragment of her father's story chipped away. And she tries her best not to be jealous of the emotion she can see glistening in Cain's eyes when he talks about Carol; but this is the way she is about him now. Even a dead woman has more of a claim on him than she has. Her eyes trail the perfect slope of his spine as he leans down to put the encyclopaedia back in a protective plastic envelope, the way the few wisps of dark hair curl at the nape of his neck, holding the promise of a fuller mane. Nothing, still, has happened between them since they held hands at the funeral. Never before has she felt so close to someone, so sure about them, yet paralysed with fear about moving things forward. Something deters her, every time, from kissing him. Somehow she imagines that he would find her frivolous if she did so, especially now, when there are so many more important things to be done.

They move silently downstairs and Iona crosses the hallway to close the living room door. Anna is asleep, her hair bathed in the blue light of the TV, spilling like lava over the side of her designer sofa. They take what they can from the kitchen, stuff Anna won't miss: unopened Christmas edition biscuits in the back of the cupboard, some slices of bread, a hunk of cheese. Some water. Just in case he is there and needs sustenance, which Iona is starting to think might be some pure fantasy on Cain's behalf, something to distract her, to stop her from falling into a pit of despair. And yet he's trying. He cares. She again thinks back to that boy, Jethro, writhing on top of her a month or so ago – how he wouldn't be doing any of these things for her now.

In fact, she never thought a boy would do the things for her that Cain has done. Waiting patiently outside Anna's house for her at the same time every week in order to take her to the bereavement group, knowing she has no desire to go, because he knows it will ultimately make her feel better.

Guiding her forward because he knows, more than most, that you can't look back.

38. CAIN

We head down towards the river, working our way through the back streets of Pont Sulyn until we reach the river. I don't think I've ever walked this route in the dark before, certainly not with anyone by my side. Yet now, it feels stranger to be without Iona than it is to be with her. I think of all those funerals Manny asked me to help with, all those lives and deaths I just dipped in and out of, making it almost a rule that I would slip quietly away – a peculiarity only to be discussed briefly between family members – *Who was that young man at the funeral? That sixth bearer?* Iona's actually the first person I've met through my work who has become part of my life. And I'm not entirely comfortable with the space she now occupies in my brain, although *Mam-gu* insists it's good to care about *something*. A person, a thing, even a hand-written encyclopaedia.

I find Eurov's preoccupation with Wales bizarre, especially as I've never felt particularly indebted to Wales for anything, or even considered this patch of land as anything other than happenstance. But perhaps Eurov has a point, perhaps there are emotional repercussions of belonging to an overlooked, underestimated country, even if we don't think about it all that much. Who am I, if not the languages I speak, the patch of land I've occupied for twenty-two years? Pont Sulyn must have moulded me somehow, like a river rock carried downstream, without me knowing. He's got me thinking that when a Welsh person dies, especially a Welsh-speaker, there are things they are taking with them to their graves that could disappear forever, a way of speaking that will never be heard again. I think of *Mam-gu* berating the woman next door she calls a *menyw ddihareb*, a proverbial woman, or how, when she had the flu she kept saying her legs were weak, *fel brwyn*, like rushes, like those that congregate around the riverbed. It makes you think about what exactly you are pushing away into those fridges at the morgue. It's not just people, or bodies for that matter – collectively, they represent a way of life. A way of being. Something you can never get back.

As we're hurrying along towards the bridge, Iona and I chat about the fact we've been living in this same town for all of Iona's eighteen years and it's taken something this big to bring us together. I haven't yet told her about Cassie's visit to the morgue and it sets me on edge, keeping it from her. But it doesn't seem helpful either to share it with her right now. How can that be right, that I have met Iona's mother before she has?

So I don't say anything. Tonight is about Eurov. Not Cassie.

We stand now at the foot of Pont Sulyn's bridge, looking up at its three huge arches curving above our heads. And it seems stupid, all of a sudden, that I should have suggested this, because of the ramblings of a confused man on a piece of paper. I'm afraid of disappointing her, of making things worse.

'Cain, you could never disappoint me,' she says, looking up at me. 'You've been there through this whole thing. I may have lost everything, but you're the one thing . . . I've found.'

She gives me a look, and stands almost unbearably close to me. It seems she wants me to do something, but I'm not really sure what. We just stare at each other awhile, until it becomes a bit awkward. Eventually I turn away from her and head down the stone steps to the foot of the bridge towards a large wooden door, which is fitted with a padlock. I've run past it countless times, but never once have I seen it open. I take out a pry bar from my bag and manoeuvre it into the gap between the door and the wall, and bear down on it, as much as I can. I press and press but the door itself doesn't budge. It stands against us, warning us not to go further, not to enter. I turn back to Iona, wondering if it's best we leave it alone. Or for another time. But Iona is kicking at the door now, whacking a hammer against it until some of the wooden slats start to weaken and come away. I kneel and join in with her until eventually, enough of the slats have been removed to leave a gap. One we can both squeeze through.

To be inside a bridge is disorientating. The tremors of cars above your head, as you walk into a cavernous space, make it feel like the world is upside down. The arches of the bridge, from inside, resemble the structure of a church, and as we walk around each arch it feels like the medieval origins of the town were somehow always here, lurking. Bats dart in the air above us like dark angels as the water gushes on noisily below. We walk deeper into the structure, holding on to each other, for fear the other might disappear. And just as we venture around the third arch, slumped on the floor is a body.

The body of Eurov Griffri.

And above him, in carvings and markings on the wall, are the etchings of Iona Griffri's life story.

O – OBSOLESCENCE: why do some words survive and others die a death? Over the centuries some Welsh words have simply fallen out of use, or they have been forced out, being replaced by English-isms. Obsolescence is not something that happens overnight. It is a slow process, where a word here, a phrase there, is kept so exclusively on the lips of a certain generation that, when they die, the word dies with them. It has always frightened me, as a logophile, that such obsolescence can happen, which is why I insist on a substantial collection of dictionaries so I can hold all these words close and dear to my heart.

Consider the poetry of a language that refers to a tomato as an *afal cariad* - a love apple - or a railway as a *ffordd haearn* - an iron road - or a tortoise as a *llyffant cragennog* - a shelly toad! All these terms have now somehow slipped through the cracks of time and become lost to the ether. These days a tomato is simply a tomato, and that which distinguished it from its English counterpart has long been forgotten.

Still clinging on to common usage is the term *tafodiaith*, for 'vernacular', *the language of the tongue*. But a vernacular needs a live tongue, not a dead one, in order to survive. It needs passing on, from mother to son, from father to daughter. It needs a dedicated speaker in order to make sure that the loose change of language does not slip down the back of the sofa, never to be retrieved.

To what extent can it be said that I was successful, in keeping obsolescence at bay? I failed you by passing none of these things on to you, but in other ways I succeeded in bringing them to the consciousness of another, who may have spent their whole life not knowing our language existed.

Yet perhaps my own obsolescence is the price I will pay, ultimately, for all this.

1 DAY BEFORE THE FLOOD

39. LISA

Everyone around her seems to be talking strangely. They seem to drift towards her as if they are underwater, and she will catch only a fraction of what they've said, with the rest of their sentences trailing behind them as soundless bubbles. She actually checks to see whether they have left damp prints on the carpet. When the children give her odd looks when she fails to answer, to engage, she tells them her ears are playing up. '*Diplacusis echoica,*' she says: she's hearing her own voice repeated back to her, making every conversation difficult to follow.

Her explanation is almost the exact opposite of what she is actually experiencing: her words do not come back to her, they disappear meaninglessly the second they are uttered, sinking from view, and she watches them go without feeling any attachment to them whatsoever. They bob around like fish in a tank.

The world is dissolving, ever so slowly, all around her, because Iona is not hers, and never has been. Her daughter is the stranger who appeared on her driveway two days ago. She remembers how Eurov had stood back when he'd delivered the news as though he'd expected her to rage and cry and throw things at him. The fact that she did nothing seemed to scare him even more.

And yet there is a little voice inside her head, tinny and automated, that tells her that she needs someone to haul her back in from wherever it is she's drifting off to. Sometimes, she allows that voice to be heard, and picks up the phone to dial the number of their GP, Dr Gloria. Dr Gloria with her lovely face and calm, cold hands, who will surely be able to tell her if what she thinks is happening is really happening. And she finds herself on the doctor's line, with seven patients in front of her, listening to the fuzzy saxophone muzak and wondering what ailments or woes those seven people in front of her have, and suddenly they are right in front of her, dancing to the music with their bleeding, ulcerous mouths, and their paunches of ascites and bulging tumours, calling out for someone to help them. And she looks at herself in the mirror and sees how rosy-cheeked and healthy she looks, how idiotic it is to think that she's ill, so that by the time the 'Hello, surgery!' comes, perhaps sixteen minutes later, it all seems ludicrous, and she puts the phone down.

Last night she attended the open meeting at Pont Sulyn's hall to discuss the plans for the decommission of the town. It seems it's not a matter of if, but when. Angry villagers shouting at councillors, some having to be removed forcibly. People arguing that by decommissioning the town they are decommissioning history. She was the eye of the impending storm, sitting there, taking it all in. And in the back of the hall, there she was, Skylar, looking accusingly at her, making her question how on earth she had found herself in this place, with these people, how she could show no objection to her world being swept away.

'We're done for,' a drunk, swaying man in a tattered coat kept muttering, 'whether we move out of here or not. You can only run from a wave for so long.'

Lisa no longer feels safe in Pont Sulyn. She has started to suspect that the councillors know more than they are letting on, and that disaster is imminent, not a year or two away as they claim. What if her family isn't safe on that hill, after all? What if that river will someday thunder through their bifold doors, showering them with glass and water and the debris of the rest of the town? What Lisa fears most of all is that feeling of separation that will come when the water knocks her off her feet in the kitchen, sweeping her away so that she won't be able to hold on to any of them, any single one of them. It horrifies her most of all to think of Bri, her baby, being swept away like a piece of driftwood, while she looks on, unable to do anything to stop it.

And what will she do, if that flood water comes for them all, and it is Skylar and Iona standing in front of her? Will she grab hold of the daughter she has loved and fought with for the past eighteen years, or will she disregard her love for her now, and grab hold of the other?

And as she ponders these things, deep into the night, listening to the first, seemingly innocent drops of rain tapping against the window, that's when she sees Eurov, outside, clutching sandbags in his arms, his eyes hollow and empty, a husk of a man, on the precipice of disaster.

And she knows, somehow, with certainty, that something terrible is about to happen.

40. IONA

'Dad!' The name has an unreal sound to it when she calls it out, its single syllable booming in the cavernous space around her. The effect of uttering it after such a long time takes her off guard and makes her legs buckle, so that Cain has to grab hold of her to stop her from falling to the ground. Two dark eyes glimmer at her in the far distance, a wild animal taking her in, yet seemingly not knowing what to do about her presence at all. He remains perfectly still, perhaps hoping that he can retreat into the darkness and remain hidden there forever. It is the first time she considers that she may have been wrong about everything; that the man she is stupid enough to still consider her father, even though she knows he is not, could also be capable of all the other awful things they say he has done.

But then again, what else to call him? There is no other narrative but the one she's been given all her life. Iona, daughter of Eurov Griffri. No matter what happens from here on, that cannot be undone. Her life is such a specifically chosen one, this town of Pont Sulyn with all its myths and history, the two languages that have existed together with ease, all her life, on her tongue: those things won't disappear no matter how many other truths expose themselves to her. If he's a murderer, then he remains the man who raised her, the only father she knows. And she becomes the daughter who never really knew him.

A flutter in the shoulder blades. He's trying, but failing, to sit up.

'Can you hear me, Eurov?' Cain asks, as he moves towards him. 'Are you hurt? Can I help you up?' The unfamiliar voice seems to startle him. Enough for him to look up with confusion, having no idea who this stranger in front of him is. *This part of my life*, she wants to tell him, *this part I have chosen for myself. Yet I would not even have him in my life if it weren't for you.*

Eurov nods silently. His face is smattered with blood, soil and debris. All around him lie the detritus of the few provisions that have kept him alive; Iona recognises the cream and blue wrappers of those high-protein bars he used to keep in his raincoat for Urien, a red slice of one of Bri's dried fruit rolls lying there like a cut off tongue, the case of his reading glasses a mini trough from which it seems he's been drinking the dirty river water, Cain pulls out a blanket and puts it over Eurov's shoulder. A small gesture of kindness, towards a man who may have done such awful things, makes Iona ache for him; this boy who has lost so much yet carries it all so lightly.

'That better?' Cain asks, before reaching into the bag for provisions. He pours out the hot, sweet tea into the small silver cup and hands it to Eurov. Eurov looks at it as if he's never seen a cup before. Cain lifts it to his mouth and encourages him to take a few small sips.

'Oh Iona I'm so sorry for taking you,' Eurov croaks. 'I should never have taken you . . . you know I took you, don't you? That you weren't mine?'

Iona is stunned to find him acknowledging this so readily at last after eighteen years of secrecy. She still cannot fathom how Eurov could have carried this knowledge with him for her entire life. She's thought so much about it in the last couple of weeks – whether or not there were any real signs that he did not love her – but it has been the opposite. If anything, he's loved her too much. Always the first at the Christmas concert, in the front row, beaming, clapping loudly; the first to help with her homework when she was little; sucking poison out of her hand when she was bitten by a fish on holiday. Urien, rolling his eyes, referring to Iona as 'the golden child'.

'I was trying to make sense of it,' he says, gesturing up at the wall in front of them. Iona shines her torch on the drawings he has scratched onto the stone wall with rock and soil, and what looks

222

like his own blood, and sees one that features the stick figures of a family of six, perhaps the family he had convinced himself they could all be.

'The thing is, the town will drown, won't it? But the bridge, maybe the bridge remains. Our story, could remain,' he says, his voice now petering away to a whisper, as if he has expended the last shred of energy he has.

And suddenly he slumps.

'Eurov,' Cain says, gently. 'Eurov, we need to get you out of here now, before another storm comes. And we need to ring Miri,' Cain says, lifting his phone.

'Not yet,' Iona says, reaching out for his hand. 'Please Cain, not yet?'

'If we don't, we'll be assisting an offender. There could be serious consequences for you . . . I mean it's up to you . . . but . . . we need to do the right thing, don't you think?'

Iona needs time to slow down now. Yes, she remembers Miri warning them on that very first night that any contact with her father needed to be communicated to them immediately. She had looked at Anna sternly as she said this, still convinced, in those days, that her aunt knew more than she was letting on.

Offender. It's almost not until Cain utters the word that she can face up to the fact that her father (not-father) is indeed such a thing, and that they still don't know the extent of his crimes.

'But what is the right thing?' she asks Cain. None of this has been right, from the moment it happened. She only knows that she needs to be with her father – not-father – for a few more hours before she has to give him away, like he gave Skylar away, all those years ago.

41. CAIN

I called Manny and said we needed help with something. He pulls up outside the old snooker hall at the corner of Bradford Street, a few yards from the bridge.

'Jesus Cain, why so cloak and dagger?' he says as he gets out of the car. 'Don't tell me you've started murdering people to give business a boost.'

Then he spots Eurov, crouched on the pavement behind me.

'No. No way,' Manny says. 'I can't have him in my car. He killed those kids.'

Iona looks up at Manny, imploring him to do this one last favour for her. It's uncanny how similar she and Eurov look, both with the dark hair and the penetrating eyes, considering they are not related. I guess we create fictions for ourselves when we want something badly. All this time, Eurov has seen in Iona the capacity to really be his daughter.

Manny takes another look at Eurov's shrivelled frame and somehow sees that he isn't the person in all the papers. That perhaps he, too, is grieving, and should be allowed the solace of the black car. I guess Manny's seen it all in that rear-view mirror. Heard all the murmurings of grief in the back seat. Absorbed the uncomfortable silence of shock and disbelief as it spreads all around him. Manny, I'm sure, could compile his own encyclopaedia of all the ordinary but incredible lives of Pont Sulyn that slip away unnoticed.

He's always insisted that you learn more about someone at their funeral than you do through their whole lives.

We get Eurov into the car, where he falls asleep on Iona's shoulder.

'I've got you, I've got you,' she murmurs to him, in Welsh. 'I won't let anything bad happen to you.'

225

Considering what he's done – and that this isn't even her father – there is still a curious intimacy between them. Then again, who am I to judge? If my own mother rose out of that river right now, her hair matted with fronds, who's to say I wouldn't immediately rush towards her, and forgive her for the destruction she caused?

We wind our way through Pont Sulyn's streets. Past the climbing centre that was once a church, past the bingo hall that now sells mobile phones, past the community centre where I was with the group earlier this evening. All these places now shrouded in darkness, with no indication of the rhythm and chaos that's been inside them. I tell Manny to turn down side streets to avoid the town centre, just in case we run into any police and they wonder what a funeral car is doing out this time of night.

Through our tinted windows the town is spectral and unreal. The sad and solitary drunkards ambling home, attached only by the invisible thread of their aloneness. It strikes me that I hardly ever see Pont Sulyn at night, because I'm at the morgue. Even at this hour there's so much life in this small town: the line of taxi drivers hunched as if in prayer by the wheel, waiting to deliver customers safely home; the newsagent getting his morning's papers in order; a dedicated baker getting in early to fire up the ovens.

And yet all this, my grandmother says, will soon be gone, if the evacuation plans go ahead. All these streets, all these connections – the tapestry of a town, a community, dating all the way back to the fifteenth century – all this will be picked apart, bulldozed to the ground. Perhaps this is why Eurov felt the need to document it all. Because you can't just give someone the cold facts of a place and expect them to understand it. Statistics, measurements, numbers: they don't give you any of the real truth of a place. What it feels to belong here, how it would feel to have to leave, against your will, when the place is so tightly bound to who you are. How those streets will always be knotted up with your intestines so you don't know where you end and Pont Sulyn begins.

Eurov's breathing is laboured and heavy. Each and every one of us feel as if we are breathing with him, for him. Manny says that maybe we should take Eurov to the hospital first.

'No,' Iona insists, 'please. Just ten minutes. We'll ring an ambulance from the house. And Miri. But he needs to see Anna first.'

Manny indicates to turn down into Anna's estate. Every single light in Anna's house is on. I catch sight of her figure at the landing window before she disappears, and reappears suddenly on the drive in front of us. Iona gently grabs Eurov by the shoulders, telling him what's going to happen as though she's the parent and he the child: 'We are going to go in and you are going to tell us what happened, OK? And you don't get to die on me. Not now.'

I stand above the car door with Anna, watching Eurov gather strength, as though the touch of her hands on his body are endowing him with some new energy. I think of *Mam-gu*, then – of her determination to live, despite all that pain, because she had me to live for. I guess our lives are always lived because of others, continuously pulling us forward, giving us purpose.

If you know that someone in this world needs you, sometimes it's enough to keep death at bay.

R – REVENANT: a revenant is a person who returns, after a long absence; sometimes to haunt the living. Stories of revenants are present in some of the earliest Welsh writings – such as those found in the work of twelfth-century courtier Walter Map (probably a Welshman, though not entirely confirmed as so), who recorded an array of various stories of the dead rising back up to terrorise their communities.

For eighteen years of your life, I believe you had died. And I would have believed it for the rest of my life had you not turned up as a name on an enrolment form, a few months ago.

Skylar Quinta Dezen. When I saw that name, my heart plummeted into my feet and the ground beneath me disappeared. I had never forgotten that name on the wristband. It had been imprinted on my heart, because that is the person I had allowed you to die as. I had chosen to let Iona Griffri live and I had let you go.

By the time I spotted your name on the enrolment form, I could do nothing to stop it. My very own revenant was hurtling towards me through the sky, and my day of reckoning would finally come.

I had become my own myth.

42. IONA

With Cain and Manny's help they manage to get him upstairs, and into the bathroom. She tells them both they can leave, imagining they will want to absolve themselves, but they offer to wash him, to save her and Anna the indignity of it.

'We wash all sorts,' Manny jokes, trying to lighten the mood. 'Don't we Cain? A live person is a bit of a novelty.'

Iona stands back and watches Manny bagging Eurov's clothes, advising them not to touch them in case the police will want to analyse them. Again, it forces Iona to acknowledge that Eurov is a wanted man, a fugitive, and that they don't have all the time in the world to squeeze the last remaining drops of truth out of him. It must happen now. They are all already in danger of being arrested, just by allowing him space and time.

Anna wraps Eurov up in one of her fluffy robes and brings him to sit at the kitchen table. Iona stands at the window watching the silhouette of Cain's head moving away in the long black car.

And behind her, as though he can only begin when she is no longer looking at him, Eurov finally relays to them what happened on the night of the flood.

'I'm so sorry I didn't see it,' he says. 'I didn't see what was happening right in front of me. I should have seen it. But I was too bound up in myself. In what I'd done.'

Iona hears the clatter of china, followed by Anna's hurried steps across the kitchen floor. Eurov's hands – those capable of stealing a baby; of filling up a whole house with water – can no longer even hold a tea cup.

'Skylar sought us out . . . Enrolled on my summer school . . . She toyed with me for a while . . . sent me letters and pictures of herself, telling me she loved me, and when I didn't respond . . .

she told your mother everything,' Eurov continues. 'It was a relief in some ways, that your mother knew. But the way she reacted, it wasn't . . . like . . . anger or . . . sadness or . . . It was like nothing. Like she wasn't taking it in properly. What it meant.'

He spotted Skylar outside their house, he said, on the night of the flood. Perhaps she'd been watching the house for a few days. He'd first noticed her through the kitchen window, just before they sat down to dinner, dripping wet in the rain, standing completely still, as if she was in some kind of trance. And rather than address it, or go out and talk to her, he'd simply pulled the blinds down, hoping that it would signal to her that, whatever her intentions were, she was not welcome here. Not tonight. Not on Iona's last night home with them all. And then he'd sat there, his whole body numb with fear, trying to force that food down his throat, trying to feign one last happy meal with his family, looking with confusion at the calm, composed way Lisa now conducted herself as she dished out the food, carefully doling out these perfect, uniform portions on each plate. And he could not remember how they had all gotten through that meal, but somehow they had, and when they had all scattered and he'd been left alone, that's when he'd gone out to fetch the sandbags. A perfectly rational thing to be doing, he told himself, with a storm coming. But he knew that those sandbags were for keeping Skylar out, and not the storm. Before he could pile them up against the front door, however, he heard a knock at the window and opened that blind to find that she was not on the other side of the street anymore – she was right there, on the other side of the glass.

Skylar could not, *would* not be kept from entering their lives anymore.

And because Iona had already run off with Jethro, he'd opened the door and invited her in. Once she was inside – though he couldn't quite explain it – it felt like they had both relaxed around each other; she no longer seemed threatening or aggrieved to him, but amiable and grateful, as though she'd been reassured by the very fact of being welcomed by her own father into his house, as though this was what she'd been waiting for her entire life, to gain access to the life she'd missed out on. There was a childlike curiosity to her as she had run her hands across Urien's trophies, Bri's dance certificates, Iona's framed poems; tracing the photographs of the family at various gatherings with her fingers, stopping to gaze at the aerial view of his parents' farm before the flooding.

'It was as if she was imagining herself in those pictures, wondering what could have been,' Eurov said. 'And because she was no longer outside our lives, but right there, right in it, I felt maybe it was possible for us to make room for her. I know it sounds stupid, but I hoped everyone might understand why I did it; that maybe everyone, in time, would have been able to forgive me.'

'So it was her you were afraid of, all those weeks?' Iona says. 'The one you thought was following you . . . stealing your work?'

'It was one of the first things I asked her – whether it was her who'd taken those pages. She wanted to unsettle me, she said, wanted me to feel what it was like to lose something important. She kept those entries because they were proof, I guess, of sorts. The Q entry she was fascinated with because it showed how different our language was to hers . . . '

'And the P?' Iona asks, though she surely knows what it stands for, before he even answers her.

'That entry is . . . well, I guess, a kind of confession, I suppose. You know my handwriting, it's illegible at the best of times, and I was upset, you know, crying as I wrote it . . . But somehow, she could read it, as though . . . I don't know . . . as if it was genetic somehow . . . She could decode me when no one else could . . . and for her, it was the confirmation she needed that I was her father. Because, to tell you the truth . . . the whole book . . . I was always writing it for her. So that she would be able to make sense of how

I'd become the kind of man who could have done . . . something like that.'

For a moment Iona imagines them together, at that table, discussing the encyclopaedia. Skylar, so unlike any of the three of them; interested enough to hoard those pages as if they were her own personal treasures. Eurov was a novelty to her, the way his mind worked, the way he thought about identities and borders and loss, the way he could only express himself through writing. Just a girl and her father, heads bowed in closeness, mutually engaged in each other's ideas. A girl who could somehow make sense of the looping, angry, sloping letters she and Cain had struggled with.

'But then, something changed, and she got angry, really angry,' Eurov continues. 'She said that she was fed up of being an only child and wanted to connect with her brother and sister and that you all needed to know who she was. And she wasn't going to let me do it in my own time, she wanted it done right there and then. And I was sort of exhilarated by the idea of it, the idea that this thing that had been inside me for so long would finally be let out . . . But it was too much. I knew it was too much, so I tried to get her to leave, and she started shouting at me, threatening to go upstairs to talk to Lisa . . . And I knew that even though Lisa knew by now, what had happened . . . she wouldn't cope with Skylar approaching Urien and Briall . . . She wasn't ready for it.'

And that's when it came, he said, the first trickle of water.

'I couldn't understand it. I thought maybe it was the rain, you know, because that night the rain was the worst it's ever been here, but then . . . It was coming from inside, and not outside . . . and Skylar came to stand next to me and we both looked up at it, and . . . I think that's when I knew. Oh god, Iona . . . I knew something was wrong.'

Eurov asked Skylar to wait downstairs. For once, she listened to him. He found Lisa at the top of the stairs kneeling over Urien, a strange look in her eyes, the bath water sloshing out into the corridor from the nearby bathroom, soaking into the carpet, pooling around them both. Lisa looked up at him and her eyes had a wild, faraway look about them; almost as if she could not understand anything he was saying to her as he pushed past her and tried to rouse Urien. He started hollering at her to get Urien's inhaler, thinking he'd had an asthma attack, but Lisa just stood there, frozen to the spot.

'She kept saying that it hadn't worked, and she was shouting out your name, going in and out of rooms, before she started screaming at me, "Where's Iona, where is she? Why has it not worked? How could she get away?"'

Eurov by now was doing CPR on Urien and couldn't think of anything but trying to save his son. He kept screaming at her to call an ambulance but she kept shaking her head, saying that an ambulance would not save them, it would not save anyone in the end, and that she had to go.

'Where was there for her to go?' he says now, reliving the moment. 'With a dead son on the landing? There wasn't anywhere to go. But she always knew where she was going, Iona . . . And I didn't even know then, about . . . Bri. Oh god, our poor, darling Bri . . . '

Eurov's words seem stuck in his throat now, as though they are expanding there, choking him. Iona sits down next to him and takes his hand. His skin is rough like sandpaper.

She urges him to go on.

Eurov tells her that he had watched in horror as Lisa headed towards the bathroom where the overflowing bath was waiting; an invitation. He knew, then, that if she closed that door on him, that would be it, it would all be over. But suddenly she stopped in her tracks. Because Lisa saw Skylar. Her very own mirror image at the bottom of the stairwell.

While he cradled Urien in his arms, he watched as Skylar approached Lisa and tried to calm her down. 'We can sort this,' Skylar told Lisa, throwing Eurov a look of desperation, unsure

233

herself now what to say to a mother – her mother – who had seemingly killed her own child. 'I am your daughter and I will support you,' she said, lifting Lisa's hand up towards her face, so that she could trace her features. 'Look at us,' she said. 'Look how similar we are. I did a stupid thing too, once. Back in the States. Threatened people. Said I would kill them. But I never would have. I think I just wanted to be seen, you know?'

And that's when Lisa finally erupted, letting out a bellow that was worse, more brutal somehow, than the sounds Eurov had heard her make during childbirth. Her head shook violently as she screamed at Skylar that she did not want her help, that it was too late now to change anything. Skylar had been better off without her. Her children were Bri, Urien, and Iona, and nothing could be done to change it. Then she began muttering to herself, saying she knew she'd been selfish to have brought all these children into their lives, that they never asked to be born into this awful world, where they were always in danger of being drowned.

The river was coming for them, she said. Eventually. It would come for them all. And she would not be drowned.

She would not have it.

But Skylar would not have it either. She had not come so far for it to end like this.

Eurov could not remember when exactly he realised there was nothing more to be done for Urien, only that he became aware of the absence in his arms as he walked towards them both, a feeling that has stayed with him ever since. Lisa was trying to get into the bathroom again now, to shut the door on them, and they both, together, pushed against it. Skylar was so much more forceful than he was, as if her determination not to lose her mother all over again had endowed her with some kind of superhuman strength.

But Lisa wasn't going to let them win. Her love for her children was powerful; she seemed at one with the river that was bursting its banks a few hundred yards away from them, taking everything with it.

When Eurov thinks back on it now, he realises the most painful thing in the world for Lisa would have been to survive what she'd done. To be brought back from the brink, to be made well again, to face the emptiness – it was the worst thing imaginable. And at some point he had realised it, too, and had decided not to fight anymore. He had stepped back from the door and decided to head into Bri's bedroom, still hoping, at this point, to find her asleep. But Skylar was not so accepting. She had managed to slip inside the bathroom, and Lisa had screamed at her to get out. And when Lisa had run to the top of the stairs, Skylar had clung to the mother she had been ripped away from, all those years ago, and refused to let go.

And the thing that Eurov regrets most of all, he tells Iona, is that while he had already made the decision to let Lisa go, he should have realised that he still needed to fight for Skylar. The girl he had left for dead eighteen years ago in a hospital corridor. It was his job, at that moment, to be her father. To pull her back from the precipice. To tell her he would look after her. That everything would be OK.

But he didn't. He watched in horror as she kept grappling with her mother on that landing. And even when the first, precarious step was missed, and it was obvious the tumble down the stairs would begin – even then, he did nothing. He just watched as Skylar went down with Lisa, anchoring herself to her. And though he could not be sure, he was convinced he had seen something in Lisa's eyes, just as she lost consciousness at the bottom of the stairs: a moment of lucidity, a belief – however misguided – that she had succeeded in her mission after all, in making sure that not a single one of her chicks had been left behind in this terrible nest of a world.

And then he had heard a sickening snap as Skylar had rolled over on top of her. And knew that what he feared on a corridor eighteen years ago had now come true.

'I'm so sorry,' he cries, holding on to Iona's hand for dear life. 'I'm so sorry I didn't see how ill your mother was. She accused me of taking her pills, but it wasn't me . . . She hid them from herself . . . and when she found them again, I think . . . she saw them differently . . . Convinced herself they had some . . . higher purpose . . . '

He could not remember much of the hours afterwards. He had ambled around in the dark, carrying the bodies of his wife and his daughter up the stairs, and placing them in the bed and in the bath, while the storm raged on outside. He had lain the encyclopaedia on Skylar's chest. Then, he had headed back onto the landing, knelt down by Urien and wept, thinking how peaceful he looked as the water continued to gush around his body, anointing him somehow. Lisa's bath had kept running, spilling out across the landing and dripping its way down the stairs, and the rhythms of the water had made him think of his village being drowned, and of his father's grave underneath all that water, and he had the sense that there was nothing for it but for them all to be truly submerged. It would be history repeating itself, a story of drowning across multiple generations. And it comforted him in that moment – the very thing he'd been so opposed to all these years – that Pont Sulyn would soon be evacuated and decommissioned and that their whole history would be undone.

He had gone to get his axe from the shed, he had piled those sandbags up by the doors, and he had smashed those pipes, every single one of them. Each blow had felt as if he were cutting his own veins, letting the blood drain slowly from him.

But then, just as he was deciding how to erase himself from his own history, he had heard Iona's key in the door.

'And then, none of it made sense,' he says. 'Because I could not leave you. I have loved you, Iona, from the moment I took you. And I couldn't make you face even more loss, even if I deserved that death myself, you . . . You did not.'

He does not yet know, Iona thinks, that her mother was not dead when he put her in that bathtub. That effectively, he killed her by doing so. She thinks of an expectant Skylar turning up at their house that evening, thinking that she was walking into the future. Of Urien at the top of the stairs, confused and losing consciousness, the benzodiazepines raging through his veins. Of Bri going to sleep dreaming of ballet and school friends. The water that never meant them any harm, that cleansed them, sustained them, sinking deep down into everything just as their mother had feared.

And yet none of this should have meant anything to her. She should have read about it online, from her home four thousand miles away. It should have occupied her mind for no more than a few minutes.

Clickbait. To be clicked, just as suddenly, away.

43. CAIN

'Good god,' *Mam-gu* says, reading the paper as she munches. 'Poor Iona. To find out your own mother is capable of . . . '

She swallows down the rest of her sentence with her toasted tea cake.

'She was ill, wasn't she . . . ' I say, quietly. 'I guess like . . . Elaine was.'

I don't know why I call her Elaine, instead of my mother. It seems easier somehow to detach myself from her. My grandmother lets out a heavy, cumbersome sigh. It is fifteen years exactly from the day my mother drove her car into the river. *Mam-gu* and I are doing what we always do on that day: we go out for tea to a café in town that overlooks the water. The café's right at the top of a department store, one of the very few buildings to have remained intact in Pont Sulyn over twenty years while many of the other buildings around it have been bulldozed, smashed up, rebranded or repurposed into other things. I always feel that we owe this building something, because, despite the many franchises that have come and gone, it defiantly kept being a department store café, its window booth remaining intact, making it possible for us to peer down at the river from this colossal height.

The decor here used to be red and at some point it changed to green, and then it became yellow, then went back to red again. And it's more or less the same setup, the same tables and chairs, the same old remembrances of teas and meals past that still come to the fore when we take our window seat – haddock and chips, steak and ale pie, bubble and squeak – and our booth is curiously always empty, as if it's ours, as if no time at all has passed since our last visit.

Mam-gu is actually acknowledging that this is the day my parents and brother died, which is something I've never heard her do before. We usually pretend we're just two ordinary people, sitting in a café window seat, looking out. But not this time. This time, she seems to want to talk about what sets us apart from other people, saying things like 'Do you think it's normal for us to keep doing this?' and 'Do you think the people in this town still refer to us as the people the awful thing happened to?' She talks and talks and talks – while her cake goes untouched – about the fact that we're only sitting here now because my mother drove a car into the river on this exact day fifteen years ago, which makes it a day impossible to ignore, one that will never be ordinary again. I can't seem to stop the words coming out of her mouth. At one point I lift the cake and reach forward, as if I'm going to insert it into her mouth, to block the next sentence. It seems that talking about the Griffri murders has opened a whole can of worms.

'Something happened to him, you know,' she says, looking away from me suddenly. 'To your dad. After your brother was born.'

It's the first time I've heard her say 'your dad', perhaps ever. She always calls him Nick. I have always assumed that having to say those two words was too painful for her, that remembering him by the name she gave him was easier, because saying 'your dad' was a reminder of his other role in life. By calling him Nick he's somehow always that silly little boy of hers. *Nick, stop it now. Nick, will you get down here now!*

'Toby,' she mutters. 'Bless him. It wasn't his fault. You know, sometimes, there's nothing more dangerous than a birth. Because it's true what they say: one comes, another one goes. From the moment he was born, God bless his little soul, I knew something terrible would happen. Poor little Toby. He didn't ask to be born, did he?'

This is also new. Calling Toby, 'Toby'. Not 'your little brother', not 'the baby'. For years and years I've just assumed she could never remember his name. I mean, he'd not been here long, so it's under-standable. *Mam-gu* seems different now, vulnerable all of a sudden, with these truths surfacing from a sunken car that she's kept submerged for all this time. And I'm not sure I'm completely com-fortable with it. Or where it's taking us. I imagine that the people in the café are turning their heads towards us, that even the mention of the name 'Toby' has set off some alarm. But in reality it's the faraway pinging of a kitchen microwave I'm hearing, a dessert being reheated to within an inch of its life.

'Your dad was not the same after the baby arrived,' she says. 'I'm not sure anyone else could see it. He kept saying there was some-thing wrong with your mum because it covered up the fact that there was something wrong with him.'

'I don't remember there being anything wrong with him,' I say, and my voice comes out all small, once again a child. It's prepos-terous to think I could have intuited anything at that age and yet the memories of him are still so vivid; the clamour of his keys as he came in from work, crashing metal in a porcelain bowl. Big hands reaching out for me. And then putting me down in order to assuage Toby's whimpers; poor Toby, who always wanted to be picked up, his small arm hooked around my dad's torso. And yet when *Mam-gu* says there was something wrong with him it gives rise to other memories: I remember spotting my dad once outside the house, having just come home from work, just standing there in the drive, as if he was glued to the spot. He had this odd sort of look on his face, and he kept shaking his head, like a dog fresh out of the water. And then, rather than coming in, he turned around, got back in the car, and drove off. And I didn't say anything to my mum about it, because I remember she was just pacing back and forth in the kitchen with Toby, watching the clock and waiting for Dad to come home and I worried that if I said I'd just seen him and that he'd gone away again that she'd drop Toby and he'd smash into a million pieces.

So even as I'm sitting here saying 'Nothing was wrong', I guess I must have always known that something was.

There was nothing wrong with Elaine. It was Nick. It was always Nick.

'He was getting on top of it,' *Mam-gu* continues, too afraid perhaps, to lift her head to meet my gaze now. 'He was. But then, you know, you think you've got a handle on things and then suddenly you haven't. No one wanted to go to that wedding, and yet they went. It's beyond me why so many people in this world do things they don't want to do. Fancy invitations arriving in the post and people having to fake-smile their way through a social event that is almost unbearable to them. Just because they are worried what people will think if they say no. What's wrong with saying no? What's wrong with wanting to stay at home? I mean, I'm old fashioned about these things Cain, I know. But sometimes staying at home, it's nice and safe, and there are worse ways to spend your life.'

'Is this about the Griffri family?' I ask. So much in town now is about the Griffri family – people telling me how terrible it is, how unlike the Griffris they are – everyone who knew them now frightened of acknowledging themselves as friends, colleagues, acquaintances. The Griffri story has become the barometer for disaster.

'It is a little bit,' *Mam-gu* says. 'I mean, what Lisa Griffri did, you know, to her kids – she must have been very, very ill. Because no one just wakes up and decides they're going to kill a whole family. That's a whole lot of unravelling that's been happening there, perhaps over decades. But it wasn't the same with your mum, you know? I don't want you to think it was. Because I saw her, I saw what it was she had. I recognised it. Mothers know. I could spot it a mile off because I'd been that same way when your father was born. You check everything twice. Is he strapped in? Does he look too pale? The thing about anxiety like that, it makes you focused, alert. Super alert. Stupidly alert! It means death is always lurking but you're going out of your way to avoid it. Doesn't mean you'd drive right into it wilfully.'

'But they said —' I start.

'What did they say, eh, Cain? In all honesty? What could they tell us? No one told us much of anything. They presented us with what they thought would be the easy facts. Easy! As if any of it was easy. She had alcohol in her system. OK, that was a fact. But did anyone tell you she was drunk Cain? No. Over the limit? No one said anything like that, did they? Your mother had a bit to drink the night before and that's all it was. I think she insisted on driving because . . . because she was scared of what would happen if your father did.'

Mam-gu pauses. This is the most open I've ever seen her, words flying out of her at random. She can't help herself somehow.

'I think that maybe your dad was having some sort of episode, you know? I think, maybe, he reached over and tugged that steering wheel. A really stupid thing done in a rash moment, not thinking clearly, not knowing fully what the consequences would be. I mean, we won't ever know, because there wasn't any CCTV, but one of the police examiners suggested as much to me. That there was an altercation in the car. That the way the steering wheel was tugged, it had to be by force, and from the direction of the passenger.'

'No,' I say, unable to take it all in. 'No.'

'It isn't easy for me to say this, Cain. He was my son. I knew there was something wrong. I said to Elaine – don't take the baby with you, leave him with me. But she wouldn't. She thought I didn't trust her with her own child. But it wasn't that. I didn't trust *him*. *My child*.'

I don't know why I'm so angry about what she's just said, but no one likes their version of things to be challenged, not if they've clung on to it for as many years as I have. The images in my mind, of my mother's dishevelled hair, the disaster waiting to happen – they have been a strange comfort over the years. The line *'There's something wrong with Elaine*' has always made me feel that it was nothing to do with me, that it was a matter of time, that no one could stop it from happening. It hurts me to think of *Mam-gu* worrying herself sick that weekend, because I do remember how she picked up the phone time and time again and then decided not to ring anyone. Had she been telling herself that it was her own anxious mind dreaming up these things? Is that what stopped her from saying, 'Cain get in the car now, we've got to go, now. Now, Cain!'

We could have gone to meet them. We could have arrived at the bridge before they did, we could have created a barricade between them and the balustrade. We could have stopped it.

But then there wouldn't have been anything to stop. *Mam-gu*, they would have said, was the problem. Her anxious mind playing tricks on her. She was not fit to look after their child. She was mad. And so in order to not appear mad, she forced those feelings to go away. She pushed them down into herself, as deep as they would go.

'I need you to know. Before I go, you know? Because you can't . . . cling on to me forever, you know Cain. At some point, you will lose me. And you need to crack on with things. Find someone. Begin your own life.'

'My life has begun,' I say, confused as to what she means.

'Has it?' she says. 'You go to work at that mortuary, you spend your evenings with the misfits in that group, you don't date anyone, you don't have friends.'

'I have friends,' I say.

'Name one friend who isn't in some way related to death.'

I can't say Manny. I can't say Iona. Carol's gone. I see her point, but am reluctant to tell her she's right. Everyone I have gathered around me has been marked by death, in some way. But this makes sense to me. 'Why surround myself with the living, who haven't suffered any kind of loss? Who are still living in blissful ignorance of their own deaths and the deaths of those around them? What good will that do me?'

'A lot of good, believe you me, Cain. It's time to start living your life. To feel something.'

I tell her I feel a lot of things. That I may even have felt something resembling love over these past few weeks, with Iona. And that I feel determined that *Mam-gu* can go on forever, if she chooses to do so. If that isn't some kind of belief in life, then what is?

'Oh Cain,' she says, brushing the sugar crystals off the table and into her palm. 'Oh dear, dear Cain. We still have a long way to go with you.'

44. IONA

Iona is on her way to meet Cassie at Bianchi's Gelateria by the river. Cain offered to come but she said no, she needed to do this alone.

Something inside her has shifted since they found Eurov. A loosening of her grief, somehow; its tendrils spreading out inside her rather than being a solid, knotted ball at her core. He had seemed so utterly, genuinely broken, lying on the dusty floor of that bridge, that she wanted to scoop him up in her arms and tell him it would all be all right, no matter what he'd done. 'We will find a way through this,' she told him, as Miri arrived to take him into custody, warning her to tell no one that she had kept Eurov for all those hours before informing the police.

'You brought him straight to me, OK?' Miri had said calmly, with kindness in her eyes. 'That's our story.'

Miri is no longer a stranger to them. Her face at their door is so utterly, completely, familiar that it's hard to believe she hasn't always been part of their life story, arriving daily to deliver the worst things in the gentlest of ways, as if she's parcelled them up with chiffon paper. The Griffri family phone records show how her mother sought help in those last few days, how she'd tried, and failed, to get through to her local surgery. Further tests have shown that Lisa had stopped taking her pills several weeks before, and that she was more than likely experiencing a psychotic episode. Iona cannot stop thinking of Lisa and Skylar, entwined, hurtling towards their death, a daughter cushioning her mother, a mother cushioning her daughter, rhythmic patterns of flesh and hurt and love and desperation and defeat. Was that not what had driven Lisa to do what she did in the first place? That need to be close to her family, close in death in the same way they had been in life?

And perhaps what Eurov had seen had only been a figment of his imagination, but perhaps he was also right, perhaps Lisa had been satisfied, at the end, that it had all turned out as she'd wanted. That in those final moments, she had finally let go of Iona, as Iona must now let go of her.

Odd to think that Lisa, this woman she's mourning, is just a random stranger. One she should never have met. It bothers her when Anna points this out, as if it means she's absolved from something. Absolved from caring. *We are where we are*, she would say, Cain's mantras have now become hers.

I am where I am, she says to herself, as she walks across the path next to the river, taking the scenic route into town.

Perhaps it's as simple, and as complex as that. *We are who we are.* Just a person in a place in a moment in time, with all our history flowing away from us, like a river.

*

It's a quiet occasion, in the end, and not the explosive one she has been imagining. Cassie is sitting there, head bowed, reading, when she enters. It's what Iona herself does when she's waiting for someone or something – she'll pass the time by becoming transfixed on something else, so that she forgets herself, forgets even what she's there to do. It isn't until she's right at the table that Cassie lifts her head. And it isn't that Cassie's emotionless, exactly, but more that she's exhausted, perhaps from the grief, and she blurts out that there's so much to process that she doesn't know where to start.

'Do you ever get like that,' she asks, even before they've sat down, 'where you're just so nervous about something that it transcends into a different state, almost, and it's as if you can't feel a thing?'

'It's how I get at the beginning of an exam,' Iona says, wishing she hadn't said it, blushing at her own youthful frame of reference.

'Sheer terror at first and something else takes over. Adrenalin, my mum says.'

My mum. The word has floated into the conversation right there, so early, without Iona having considered the impact it would have on them both. Lisa is right there at the table somehow, with them, as if they manoeuvre respectfully around her as Cassie takes hold of her hand and tells her to sit. Something in her touch is electric, it almost scalds Iona, though Cassie's hands are cold, colder than even her own.

'Hypotension,' Cassie says, as if she's read her mind. 'Low blood pressure runs in our family.'

Our family, Iona thinks. Will it ever feel that way to her?

'I'm sorry, I'm sorry you lost her,' Iona manages. 'Skylar.'

'I lost Skylar a long time ago,' she says, her eyes brimming with tears.

Cassie tells her how she always knew there was something wrong but had blamed it on her own selfishness. She told herself she was a bad mother, that she worked so much because she didn't want to be home with the baby. But her mother thought it was something more than that.

'My mother – your grandmother – she thought I should have had some counselling, for the shock of having her, of having *you*, the way that I did. Not just suddenly, without warning, but at a time in my life where I was determined to be child-free. It was all I talked about when people asked me if I wanted kids. I was so defiant about it. You see, don't take this the wrong way, but I *knew* I didn't want a baby, I knew that this wasn't the world I wanted to bring a child into, and no matter what people said to me, I knew I wouldn't change my mind. And then suddenly, there I was, holding the baby. And I tried my best to make sense of it all. I tried so hard to be a mother to her, but I kept getting it wrong. And I thought, it must have been me, because I had never wanted it, and she'd sensed it, you know? But I think Skylar, on some level, always knew she was in the wrong place. Maybe I did, too, but we didn't have any explanation for it, so we just . . . muddled along, the best we could, you know? It wasn't perfect, but then, so many relationships around us weren't either, so . . . '

Iona wonders why she has never questioned her own life. Why she didn't have Skylar's intuition. She accepted the truth presented to her. Was it the fact that Urien and Bri were always there, and that she loved them fiercely, more so than she loved her parents; was that it? That when you were brought up in a gang, a tribe – a *llwyth* as her father would have it – you just went along with it, without question?

'The thing is, though,' Cassie says, reaching in her bag for a tissue, 'is that she was wrong about me. About the way I felt about her. I think she convinced herself all her life that I was distant, not wanting to engage, when really, I really, really loved her. God, did I love her. Just because I never wanted her, doesn't mean I didn't fall head over heels with her. The love was awful, almost – it was all consuming. I'd cry at night when we fought because I loved her so much and couldn't bear it. But I think I was always afraid of losing her. Because once your children exist, you know that losing them has the capacity to shatter you. To break you. To make life unbearable. And when you live in a place like I do, where there are all these awful things . . . school shootings . . . you just assume, one day, it's going to be your kid. But what I hadn't seen was that she was so frustrated, she felt so unloved . . . She almost *became* one of those kids, you know . . . ? The ones who could . . . '

Cassie pauses, and grips the table, as if she's gathering strength for the next instalment of Skylar's life story. Slowly, cautiously, she tells her about the day Skylar went into school with a knife in her bag and began waving it around in the corridor at school, threatening to kill everyone, and then how, when she was chased out of the school, she went and stood in front of a yellow bus to end it all.

'What I never told her about that day – because she'd blocked it out you see, some kind of amnesia, because of the brain

injury – was that we had one of our big fights that morning . . .
We used to have them all the time, which became worse and worse
as she became older . . . But that morning we were just screaming
at each other – oh god it was really awful – and she accused me
of never really seeing her, for who she was. And I said, and I will
always regret it – I said to her "I wish you'd never been born . . ."
God, it hurts to think of that now, but she looked at me then as if
she was going to make me regret saying it, you know? That's why
she did it, to get my attention . . . But she was right . . . I didn't .
. . perhaps, see her, *show* her . . . how much I loved her, because I
was scared of that love, a little bit . . . and I think . . . well, I think
she did what she did to prove a point to me. She never meant to
harm any of those kids in the school, but she did want to make
herself visible to me, in the worst way possible, and after that . . .
when she stood in front of that bus . . . Well, I think she did it not
so much because she wanted to die, but because she wanted me to
feel the guilt of what I'd said to her . . . And now she's gone, all I
can think of is that image of her waving a knife in the air because
she so badly wants her mum to notice her . . . the mum who never
wanted her to be born . . . '

Cassie breaks down now, reaching for more tissues from her bag,
her shoulders heaving.

'But, you know . . . However badly I messed up her life . . . I
messed up yours more, didn't I? I just let you . . . go . . . I'm so so
sorry.'

Iona tells her that there hasn't been a moment in all this when
she wishes she had not been raised by her family, in Pont Sulyn.
Whatever has happened, she says, cannot take away what she has
been given. Urien and Bri and Lisa will be imprinted on her heart
forever. They have moulded her and shaped her, as has this town of
Pont Sulyn and its people, their language, their dialect, their weird
and wonderful ways. Even the water, she says, is part of her. But it
doesn't mean that it's all she can be. Or all that she has space for.

'I'm so glad to hear you say that . . . because . . . I know it maybe sounds odd to say this, but that night in the hospital, your father . . . Well he was really, really kind to me. I was in such a mess, you know . . . I mean, imagine it: one minute you're on a date in a restaurant, having a glass of wine, the next minute . . . God, I don't even want to fucking think what I looked like when that first contraction came at me, it was like a meteor from outer space, and the whole thing was just so shocking. I was reeling, you know, pushing you down that corridor. Reeling. And there was something kind about him. A drowned look, almost, you know, like he was really trying to keep his head above water, you know?'

Iona nods and smiles, in spite of herself. Yes, she knows.

'And I said all sorts of awful things to him about how I felt about the baby, and about what it would do to my life, I mean . . . I was still high, I guess, still on the drugs, still confused, but he just listened and took my hand, and said everything would work out the way it was meant to. And though I can't forgive him for what he did after that . . . there's part of me that thinks I led him there, to that conclusion, that to take that baby from me; that it was the best thing for everyone.'

There is silence between them after this; as if they are both trying to retreat back into that hospital corridor to see how it would have played out differently. And when Cassie regales the rest of the story – how a left turn she made in the corridor, now screaming with the realisation that her baby was dead, led to her finding a junior doctor who instantly performed CPR on the dead baby – they both then wonder whether Eurov would have, in fact, taken the same left turn had he been the one looking for help, and whether Skylar's life would have been saved at all, if the babies had not swapped places that night.

'So Skylar . . . she was . . . actually dead, then? That wasn't a lie?'

'Oh yes. I'll never forget it. They called it a brief resolved unexplained event – but yeah, I mean, I guess she was as good as dead until that doctor saved her.'

A brief resolved unexplained event, Iona thinks. As if it were nothing. But it had been brief enough to bring a whole world crashing off its axis and careering in a completely different direction.

'I'm so, so sorry for letting you go,' Cassie says, her voice now faltering. 'But I've got you now. I've got you. I will be a better mother this time, I promise you . . . '

And Iona – not-Iona – knows that this is where they start from, her and Cassie. Not from the moment a man lost his mind in a hospital in Scranton; they start from here, now, from this table, from this realisation that, as they get up to hug each other, there is always a way to wipe the slate clean, to reach across this great chasm between them, and travel back to a time where nothing was decided or firmed up, right back to the moment when an unsuspecting baby sprung to life in darkness, against all odds.

S – SCRANTON: a Welsh epicentre in the heart of Pennsylvania. Between the late 1800s and early 1900s, it was reported that around 80,000 Welsh immigrants flocked to the United States – and many of those were drawn to the coalfields of Pennsylvania, settling in the city of Scranton. It is what drew me there in the first place, to complete a relatively uninteresting research project about the Welsh diaspora in the US.

I followed in their footsteps because I was curious to see what it looked and felt like; what hold such a different place could have on you, a place that was so unlike your own, that seemed to offer all these opportunities. Would I feel free? Would I understand it? And instead of the academic enlighten-ment I had hoped to have, I found love; long after I had stopped dreaming of it, at a time that even the prospect of having a family was something I no longer allowed myself to think of, or even lament the loss of.

Journeys always lead to unexpected encounters. We go in search of one thing and come away with another. Instead of the ghosts of the Welsh migrants, I found instead a bright, beautiful, American girl at the top of a stairwell, gently sketching the faces of her friends, and knew instantly that she would determine the direction of my life from there on. She was not plagued by her history, or bogged down by it. She was free to move from the big country to the small country, to choose another reality altogether.

And somehow it seemed that the whole thing was predestined from the moment those first migrants dreamed of those bigger, more lucrative coalmines, fuelled by a desire to be taken seriously elsewhere.

It comforts me now, my love, that in some ways you lived the faraway dream of those first Welsh migrants.

Minus the burden of carrying the loss of a place in your heart, like a lump of coal.

45. CAIN

Iona, Nerys and I are the only mourners at Carol's funeral. It's a quiet, understated affair, as she wanted, at the crematorium just outside town.

'In and out, there, isn't it,' I remember her saying to me and Manny when we sat down with her a few weeks back. 'Half an hour tops. No hanging around. You can choose the hymns. Just make sure they're not ones that drag, you know.'

Hymns are not my forte. But Manny knows them inside out. He knows which ones will be tricky for an audience, especially a tone deaf one, and which ones will be sung with gusto. He knows which ones work best for a bilingual audience, and he knows which ones give rise to the best four-part harmony. When the preacher whispers to him in concerned tone that the organist has been caught in traffic, he doesn't flinch. He just takes off his shoes, heads over to the organ himself, fires it up, and launches into a hymn he'd played to Carol off his phone, two days before her death. She had just about enough energy back then to curve her dried lips up into a smile to indicate her approval. It's a tune that's mesmerising and beautiful, an easing out of life rather than the dramatic exit some of the other music choices imply. Both Iona and I read short passages to commemorate her life, poems of her choice, in both languages.

Iona squeezes my hand as the curtain closes around the coffin and it isn't until then that I realise I'm crying, my tears dashing across the order of service. But they are tears of happiness, too, in a way, because for the first time for a long time, I'm at the funeral of someone I knew intimately, and being here feels right.

After the funeral, Iona tells me about meeting her mother. It went well, apparently, so much so that she's considering returning with her to the States for a while.

'Just to see where I'm really from you know?' she says. 'To try to understand Cassie a bit more, too. And maybe, Skylar.'

Later on, we talk and talk and talk until all the light has left the room and it's almost time for my shift. We muse on who we have become because of what has happened to us, and wonder how we can try to change the narrative. Who is this ghost of a morgue worker, she asks me, earnestly, if it isn't someone shaped by feeling himself to be somehow half-dead? And who is she, I ask, this lost girl who belongs to no one now, who still feels anchored to a history that isn't even hers?

And then she looks at me. And we both seem to know what comes next, as her lips meet mine in the darkness.

I don't have to think about what my body is doing, about what she wants or expects because we have been moulding ourselves around each other for months now, and this is just the confirmation of it all, a connection which doesn't feel frantic or desperate, but feels natural. And by the end of it we are both crying, crying into each other with an odd sort of relief, in a way that grieving bodies only can, realising that there is something hopeful and enjoyable and pleasurable to be found among the rubble of our lives. 'Romance is not dead, eh?' she says, as our cries morph into helpless giggles.

And though there is nothing I want to do more than to stay there with her, there are deaths to attend to, still. And so I gently untangle myself from her sleeping body to get ready for my shift, relishing the thud of her heartbeat next to mine, the regularity of her breath, the pulsing of her body; the particles of life that radiate towards me.

I carry the warmth of her memory with me into the coldness of the morgue.

*

I call in with *Mam-gu* on the way home from my shift, and find her sitting grumpily at the table, looking at a letter from the hospital. She's been having tests for a tumour at the base of her spine.

'It doesn't matter how many times you read it, it won't suddenly change,' I say, glancing over it. Benign, it says. It's what most people, half her age, would like to hear. It's a lottery, as far as I can tell. Some bodies let disease run rife, some won't be letting it get a foothold, even if it tries. *Mam-gu*'s constitution has always been more solid than most, though she's never without a complaint.

Now that she knows she isn't going anywhere for a while, her main concern is what I'm going to be doing with the rest of my life. She says I can't continue to work with the dead as though my life depends on it.

'That isn't a way forward, for anyone, Cain,' she says.

I try to argue that there's nothing but a way forward for death, that it's the one thing that's going to be with us, forever and ever, the only guarantee. A job for life. Because death keeps on going. Only this week there's been a twenty-year-old girl killed on a bike, a forty-year-old mum dead from colon cancer, a sixty-year-old granddad killed by a ladder falling off a speeding van on the opposite side of the road. While the rest of us have just managed somehow to sidestep it all. And someone needs to tend to them. Someone who won't be broken or traumatised or changed by it, but who is comfortable enough to live alongside it, to give the dead the care they deserve.

And that's when *Mam-gu* shakes her head and leaves the room.

*

I head back down to the river where my parents met their end, where I've promised to meet Iona. We decided we'd just sit it out, this one last time, look the water in the eye and tell ourselves it isn't who we are, it's just what happened to us. That although we know

257

it has the potential, at any time, to burst its banks, wash away families, fill up homes, drown entire cultures, it can just run alongside us for now, not through us.

And as Iona's reflection trickles into the flow of water next to me, it strikes me that while our faces seem almost tangible in it, as though they could never be removed, the water doesn't feel them at all – it just moves on.

T - TRYWERYN: what can be said about Tryweryn that has not already been said? Everyone knows the story, or so it seems, until you head out of Wales, and people have no idea what you are talking about, or what those hundreds of red and white graffiti signs all across walls and rocks in Wales are all about. *Tr-uh-where-een*. The drowned village. The village that sacrificed itself on the altar of oppression, so that an English city could have water. More water than they needed, it transpired, in the end, an abundance of it, while a whole community were left fractured, displaced, and made to forge their way in life, angered and rootless. But in a sense, some good came of it too, because a whole nation rose up to rally against the sheer indignity of it, and decided they would not take it anymore.

Those graffiti slogans smeared on our walls and rocks carry the words: Cofiwch Dryweryn / Remember Tryweryn. Yet there are those who have forgotten. My mother, for example, who died having forgotten any of it ever happened.

Sometimes I think it's not the events themselves, but the constant remembering, that drives us mad.

And yet it is not over. Another Tryweryn could well happen in the future. Wales still has no real control over its own natural resources. There is nothing to stop them from flooding us, over and over.

From removing us from the map altogether.

46. IONA

Iona is in the air. Leaving Cardiff airport for Schiphol in Amsterdam, where she and Cassie will spend the next two hours waiting for their connecting flight. As much as Schiphol has always been a nowhere place for her, sitting there mindlessly scrolling on her phone while waiting with her family for their flight back home, it is now significant, because she learns she is one quarter Dutch – that her Dutch great-grandmother who named her (not-her) *Schuyler* – is still alive. The origin of her first name, she learns, is scholar – a curious baby born into the world, searching for knowledge. It seems ironic that she was then raised knowing nothing of her origins, that so much essential knowledge was kept from her for eighteen years.

Not a Welsh bone in her body, is a phrase that keeps whirring through her mind. And yet, she is, she can feel it, bound, indelibly, to this country she is rising above right now. She feels almost a magnetic pull towards those hill-forts and lakes and fields and crumbling old castles; as though that bulging river is inside her somehow, streaming through her veins. As the countryside below becomes smaller and smaller in her line of vision, she herself seems to become larger, suspended above it, now having doubled in size, carrying the secret of having two whole lives within her.

All around her people are speaking English and Dutch, and her own language stays dormant, in hiding, until a child in the aisle in front hurls a soft toy, an eyeless rabbit, over his seat, and into her lap.

'*Ymddiheura iddi,*' she hears the Mum saying. Apologise to her.

Up pops a small face, which hosts a pair of bright, inquisitive eyes so much like her sister's that it takes her breath away.

'*Dwi'n flin,*' the boy says. Sorry.

261

'*Hedfan bant 'na'th e, ie?*' she says, trying to control the tremor in the voice. He flew away, did he?

The boy laughs, as she makes a flying motion with the toy rabbit and delivers him back into the boy's eager, tiny hands. And that's it – a moment of connection over. She hears his mother commend him for the polite way he spoke to the nice lady. '*Da iawn cariad.*' Well done my love. Iona instinctively reaches her hand into her rucksack to feel for Briall's toy piglet, stored there in the darkness; a talisman she will keep with her always, along with Urien's running wristbands that are placed firmly, tightly around each pale wrist. Being up in the air with their possessions has bestowed her with a kind of peace; she feels closer to them, despite not having any delusions about heaven or a higher being, as though being freed from land, from the dark, plodding earth on which those terrible things happened, will allow her some space and time to get to grips with the fact that she will not be returning to her (not-)brother or (not-)sister, nor they to her. Yet they are revenants, of sorts, as her father would have it, who will be around her always – not haunting her exactly, but living alongside her, deep within her, forever.

As they ascend higher again she can see Cardiff city in the distance, and the faint outline of the secure hospital that is her father's new home, while he awaits his assessment. She thinks of him sitting there, in his room, alone. In so many ways, she thinks, Eurov has been in a closed off space of his own making, for years and years. Finally being found out for taking her, all those years ago, seems a relief to him.

'Don't worry about me,' he'd said, when she's visited him to say goodbye. 'I'm going to be fine, whatever comes of this, however many years of this I'll have.'

He'd gone on to tell her that it was the best place for him, now that there was no going back to the life they'd had before, and that this is what he wanted for her, too. He'd urged her to take up her place at university next year, and to spend whatever time she needed getting to know Cassie. Not that she'd agreed at the time, either. There was still the age-old father-daughter push-pull between them, where she'd refused to meet his gaze, and told him that she was going to do what she wanted, not what he had laid out for her; hadn't he done enough of that for eighteen years? He'd gone perfectly quiet then, and simply nodded his head.

'Just be you, and be free,' he'd said, just as the alarm chimed to tell them that their time was up. 'But please, please . . . try to forgive your mother. She was not well.'

It had forced her then, to have to think of her mother – not-mother – to face all the conflicting feelings she had bottled up about this woman who had supposedly been her mother. Her anger, her pity, and then her rage at the whole world for being such a terrible place that it led a woman to believe it was better to remove herself and her family from life, than have to face whatever horrors would be coming for them in the future.

Anna had been waiting for her in the hospital car park, her eyes like a lost little girl's, and she remembered how her (not-) aunt had hugged her, capably, then, without awkwardness, letting her sob loudly against her body, and had told her that she would always be her aunt, for as long as Iona wanted her to be. That you did not unpick eighteen years of love like a tapestry gone wrong. That she was right to get out of Pont Sulyn, and all its problems; that by the time she got back, it would probably have ceased being Pont Sulyn anyway.

Her life as she knows it, Iona thinks, has been decommissioned. It has been removed from service. She is free to start again, somewhere else.

And yet. There is Cain. Cain who is so rooted in place his body is melded with the bricks and mortar of Lincoln Avenue, Smallbrook Street, and the Pont Sulyn morgue. Anchored to the spot. Cain who feels he cannot just up and leave because he must care for those who are past caring. Cain, who, when she was trying to convince him last night that there were all sorts of jobs he could do in the States – working with cadavers used to test out car crash injuries or to help further medical research – had laughed, and said 'Iona. It isn't about the dead people! It's about doing what I can, being part of this place. I'm not just going to traipse around the world looking for corpses.'

And they'd talked long into the night, exploring all their options, until Cain had eventually said that Manny was looking for an assistant funeral director to join the company, and that his dalliances with the living over the past couple of weeks had convinced him that being with actual living, breathing people, wasn't all that bad. And she'd kissed him feverishly then, and he'd rolled into her, and Iona had clung to him thinking how different this was to any other relationship she'd had, how her loss always felt lighter when their bodies were conjoined, as though their two hollowed-out halves could somehow bear the weight of it together, and attempt to become whole again.

Pont Sulyn and Wales have dispersed in a puff of cloud. As if her country and her past were a magic trick, a conjured-up life. Across from her, in the adjoining aisle seat, sits Cassie, quietly reading. She doesn't know whether Cassie booked these seats purposefully, so that they wouldn't have to sit right next to each other for the flight, but it seems an appropriate amount of distance somehow. Odd to think that there should once have been no space between them at all, cushioned as she was right inside Cassie's body, an instinctive, natural thing, but that now they must measure it out, work out how much is too little, too much. For now, it's as if Cassie wants her to know that she's there, for whenever Iona is ready.

Iona turns back to her own reading, carefully unfolding the document from her bag. Once it became clear that Eurov would eventually be pleading guilty to taking her, there was no further need for the encyclopaedia to be held by the police. On the plus side, the fact it's been in their possession these past few weeks means that it's been cleaned up and restored professionally. The errant P and Q pages have been placed back neatly in order, and the pages have been laminated smoothly, so that they detach nicely from one another, and make for a smoother reading experience. Eurov's handwriting is even almost legible, now that the smudges have been removed. As she skims over the final sections, she sees how the entries are becoming increasingly fragmented and frantic towards the end. *U for Uxorious*, she reads: *having or showing a great or excessive fondness for one's wife.* She bristles slightly in reading this. Had this really been the truth of Eurov's feelings towards Lisa in those final months? He admitted to ignoring how ill she was, of neglecting her. Yet he had never stopped loving her, he had said. *I have come to the conclusion that the love I felt for Lisa was responsible for the most unwise thing I have ever done.* He had evidently wanted Skylar to know that he had not given her away, but he had given Lisa someone to love, in lieu of what he thought was an absence, a loss.

She turns over the page to the V – V *for Vitriol*. This was to do with the vitriolic attack on the language. That it shocked Eurov that it could be present anywhere, not only outside Wales, but within it too. That people had been colonised so successfully that they claimed to hate the language of their own country. He seemed to be telling Skylar in this entry that she was lucky to be free of having to justify her own tongue, to have it under attack from those who used statistics to minimise its importance, those who had never been present in a family home where the language was a natural, even mundane part, of daily life.

Eurov has struggled with the W section, she can see. He has first written 'Wales' and then crossed it out, noting to himself that it is *too obvious*. Water, too, he feels no longer needs elaboration, and the ink has petered out to nothing. X is for xenogenesis – *the production of offspring completely unlike either parent*, as though he has tried to explain Iona away as a scientific fact, rather than a crime. In the Y section he has delved briefly into a description of the Y chromosome before crossing it out aggressively. The final letter, Z refers to Gen Z, his older children – *sliding carefree down the curved flume of the last letter of the alphabet like they may actually be the last generation on this earth* – he writes, *the digital natives, born with iPhones for hands and USB sticks for fingers, who do not need sentences and paragraphs when a computer gen-erated emoticon can express it for them.* Iona sees now, how the written word can show her the slippages, the excess of someone's personality, whereas a word on screen gives you no indication at all of the person's state of mind. If it were not for Eurov's desire to sink himself so deeply into these pages, she thinks, they may never have found him alive.

Iona knows that there's nothing for it now but to head back to the P section, the one she's been avoiding, ever since the document examiners printed out a clean, decoded version for her. As the seat-belt light pings off, she reads:

P – Parent: *being a parent is perhaps the greatest responsibility of all. And to have made a decision to bring a child into a faltering, crumbling world, from which there will then be no escape, is con-sidered by some to be an entirely selfish decision. To have to look into the eyes of an unsuspecting baby, who does not yet know what life is, what a complicated and fraught thing the future can be, is to feel the worst kind of wringing of one's organs, and the heav-iness in one's flesh, the same flesh that has now doubled, trebled, and unleashed whole new beings from its core. Yet there is also a flipside to this in some cultures – a child represents the hope that certain languages, traditions or customs are now able to prevail, and needn't be lost, now that they live inside a whole new being – one generation huddled within another.*

To know that you will leave the world without your children is the natural order of things, yet to conceive of it is torture. To not know their end, when you have known their beginning, feels unnatural. And yet there is no guarantee of how this is going to go. The timing and length of one's life, once it is bound to another, can be erratic, unpredictable and potentially ruinous. Once you have entered into this bond, where one cannot imagine life without the other, each day is just a ticking time bomb which has the potential to destroy everything.

And yet there will be happiness, so heartfelt and unbridled that it will eclipse the fear. And a child will unquestioningly accept the reality presented to it by its parent, which defies any biological or geographical fact previously considered integral to its identity. A child can root itself anywhere, at any time, in a multitude of languages and cultures, and can embrace the life it is given with gusto. Out of their lack of choice they develop their own choices, and forge ahead with their own decisions – including whether they want to reproduce or not. Are they a Matryoshka doll that engenders others or a single entity wanting to leave room inside for other possibilities?

In so many ways I failed as a parent. Yet I loved my children, deeply, through it all, and succeeded in feeling what I was meant to feel as a parent. I walked alongside them through life, in presence and absence, and never once wished they had not been born.

I even silently, secretly, parented the one I thought I had lost.

My love, I thought of you every single day, even those days when I tried my best not to.

Iona places the encyclopaedia down on her lap. She tries to visualise Skylar reading the entry, and imagines the confusion and hurt she would have felt in knowing she had been loved, yet abandoned. A girl who had been denied so much, clinging on to this piece of paper to prove her worth. And yet still, even though Iona knows all the facts now, there isn't a part of her that can detach herself from that upbringing, in that house, with those people she loved. And it comforts her to think that despite the fiction of her life, under the wallpaper in the house of water lie the markings of her changing height across the years, along with Urien's, and Bri's, the ink forever embedded there, as truthful and real as veins under a canopy of skin.

And as her hand falls, now, at her side, weak and spent in taking it all in again, she suddenly feels another hand closing around hers.

Her mother's hand, reaching out, closing the gap. And hovering as they are now, not on any patch of land but in this strange, in-between place up above the clouds; it feels as though they are finally free to map out their own journey.

ACKNOWLEDGMENTS

Thanks to the Orion Publishing Group for their permission to quote 'Drowning' and 'Night Sky' by R.S. Thomas, both taken from the *R.S. Thomas Collected Poems 1945–1990* (J.M. Dent, 1993). I am also indebted to a number of publications that have been instrumental in researching and inspiring my own fictional encyclopaedia in this novel, namely *Termau Iaith a Llên* by Morgan D. Jones (Gwasg Gomer, 1972), *Geiriadur Prifysgol Cymru* (A Dictionary of the Welsh Language, *Volumes I to IV*, Gwasg Prifysgol Cymru, 1967–2002), *The Long Field* by Pamela Petro (Little Toller Books, 2021) and of course, *The Welsh Academy Encyclopaedia of Wales* edited by John Davies, Nigel Jenkins, Menna Baines and Peredur Lynch (University of Wales Press, 2008). For me, any book about an encyclopaedist would not be complete without giving a special mention to my former colleague, the late Nigel Jenkins – poet, writer, encyclopaedist – and I often wonder whether this story would exist had I not been so inspired by his passion for telling Welsh stories and exploring the narrative of Welsh history. *Diolch*, Nigel.

A heartfelt thanks to the numerous early readers of this book who shared with me honest opinions, insights and corrections: Menna Elfyn, Jane Fraser, Kate Woodward, and Daniel Westover. Also to Graham Bartlett, police advisor extraordinaire, for his invaluable insight into police procedures, and to Dilwyn Williams from the National Library of Wales for sharing with me his expertise on restoring water damaged manuscripts. Thanks also to Richard Rees for providing me with a copy of his excellent documentary 'Yr Afon Dywyll' which has informed much of my thinking about the fictional Sulyn river.

A huge debt of gratitude, as always, also to my agent, Euan Thorneycroft, to whom I pitched an early version of this novel as far back as 2008. Your patience and support over the years means the world. Thanks to all at Hodder & Stoughton for taking me on and welcoming me into the Hodder family, especially my editor Tallulah Lyons, whose shrewd choices and wonderful observations have allowed this book to flourish.

Special thanks also to my ever supportive screenwriter soulmate Lowri Hughes for the banter and supportive daily nonsense via voice notes and texts. I couldn't have survived the maelstrom of writing and rewriting without you.

I am also grateful to Beca and Luned, my daughters, for the distraction from writing, and for the daily dose of silliness, love and laughter. And finally, for the generous insight into the funeral director's world, and for keeping me sane through the writing process, thanks to my husband, Iwan Evans, who has taught me all I know about kindness and compassion. It's a special job which takes an extraordinary person to do it. Funeral directors really are my favourites.

This isn't the world you know.
This isn't the story they expect.

Read on for an extract of *The Library Suicides*,
Fflur Dafydd's captivating locked-room thriller,
where there is more at stake than meets the eye.

Ana and Nan

9PM

The twins always saw themselves in the seagulls, even as children. Their feathered doppelgängers would come and sit on the bathroom ledge every evening and stare in at them as they had their bath, watching them with their curious pink-rimmed eyes. There would be a flash of recognition between both parties. Something vermin-like, something poisonous, would pass between them. Rats with wings, their mother would shout, before shooing them away. But the birds always came back; unlike their mother, who – six months ago – wasn't able to navigate her own drop from the ledge with quite the same ease.

There was a strange comfort in it now for Ana and Nan; to have the seagulls there during their bathing ritual, those webbed feet padding confidently across the cramped space where their mother had once stood. The twins watched these rolling resurrections with fascination, gazing at their feathered aggressors jostling each other, pushing each other off, with each ousted bird returning seconds later as though the fall meant nothing.

Ana and Nan could see the gulls trying to decipher – with every twist of their ugly, slanting heads – why two identical women would sit opposite each other in the bath every evening, conjuring stiff white peaks from their fingers until the suds obscured each one's view of the other. The shape afloat on the water was a replica of that building on the hill where the twins worked. They saw themselves as architects of foam, carving out from the amorphous mass the contours of a library in miniature – weaving windows from the fine white webs, moulding

I

scented stacks and stairwells, their fists firming up each angle, their fingernails scraping away space for reading rooms and archives, all the while ensuring the egg-white roof was sturdy enough not to collapse on top of it all, and wash away their efforts.

What the gulls could not see was that this was more than mere bath play. Tonight, Ana and Nan were preparing themselves for the day that was nearly upon them, a day when they would take charge of the library, and expose its delusions of grandeur, of safety, for the soap-mirage it always was.

'When do you think we'll next have a bath?' Nan asked, as she straightened her right palm in order to forge a lower level into the structure, a squeaking subterranean corridor, the concrete version of which they would soon enter.

Ana knew what Nan was really saying was: *There will be no baths in prison. None of this intimacy, none of this togetherness. No more of each other.*

'Could be years, I suppose,' said Ana, wiping sweat from her cheek. 'A small sacrifice,' she added, taking her fingers for a leisurely stroll around the back of the building, imagining herself entering there as they had planned, Nan around the front. She used her left thumb to smooth out another step, then her right pinkie to make an outline of the doorframe.

'I know you're thinking about Mum,' Ana said, moving a little too suddenly so that her left breast bulldozed away half the North Reading Room. 'Wondering what she'd make of all this, aren't you?'

Nan sunk lower into the foam, kicking the library basement away with her toes, her hair morphing into a dark overgrowth on the library's roof. The structure was crumbling now; the suds having become limp and shapeless, even the gulls no longer interested. Nan hated the way Ana insisted she could read her mind, as if Nan's brain were a vacant room through which Ana was

2

free to roam as she liked, opening and shutting doors, ransacking through cupboards, running her fingers over everything. Nan could never read Ana's mind; the doors were always shut, the windows dark.

'Yes, I suppose I am,' Nan lied, relieved that if nothing else, she owned her own mind.

'I think she'd approve, you know. Of all this. It's what she would have wanted. I don't think we need to be scared.'

Nan was not scared. If anything she was excited. Whatever happened, however things eventually played out, it would be the end of something. The start of another.

'If we just stick to the plan,' Ana continued, 'we'll be fine. Nothing's going to go wrong.'

Everything would go wrong, Nan thought. And this is how she knew her sister couldn't really read her mind. Because her sister still believed that Nan would carry things out in exactly the way they'd planned, when Nan had no intention of doing so – she was going to do things her way, even if it meant a longer sentence; and forgoing her right to a bath forever more. She had long imagined herself with that gun in her hand, taking control of it all; desperate to know how it would feel when she finally got to pull the trigger.

'Whatever we do, we do together,' Ana continued. 'After all we're the same person, you and I, aren't we?'

Ana's foot swam towards her. Nan lifted her own foot and pressed against it. She knew Ana saw this as a moment of unity, but for Nan it was the opposite: a real, physical sign of the boundary between them. Where one thing broke away and became another.

'Ana and Nan. One person. One soul. Palindromes.'

Nan hid her smile in the froth. Ana was obsessed with the fact that their names could be read forward, and backward, that they could formulate no other possible sounds. Ana was convinced that their mother had chosen them so that no one could interfere with

3

their names; that their identities remained strong, unshakeable. Nan didn't see it like that. She saw their names as dull and uninspiring in their plainness; neutral as anything. As a young child she'd always dreamed of having a longer, greater title, something complex, multisyllabic. Something that spoke of revolt. Something like Arianne – a silvery wheel of a name; or Gwenivere – a girl glowing in the dark. Something that enticed yet terrified you.

'Palindrome,' Nan echoed quietly, as she opened her mouth to ingest the rest of the soap ruins.

*

As she tapped on the bath plug to drain the water, Ana saw that the doppelgänger gulls had flown away, leaving in their place a strange, black-headed seagull. She'd seen him several times before, parading the promenade near the flat, squawking at day-trippers, boasting his tar-tipped head. He'd never dared to come and stare at them like this before, either. Ana thought he must know what they were up to, wanted to be a part of it.

'Just ignore him,' Nan said. 'He's desperate for your attention; don't give it to him.'

Ana couldn't resist, somehow. She found herself sneaking a look at him every now and then as Nan finished rinsing the soap out of her hair. It felt like he was mocking them; the way he'd scared off the gentler gulls, just to assert his individualism, his singularity. It was as if he was saying that the sisters' doubleness wasn't right in some way – for there to be no birthmark, no scar, no blemish that set them apart, it was as if he was making out they were the freaks, rather than him. She stood up suddenly, hoping her nakedness would scare him off, but he wouldn't budge.

'Shoo!' she shouted, like her mother had once done. 'Shoo!'

'You've still got a bit of conditioner in there,' Nan said. 'Sit back down.'

4

'Shoo!' she said again, now determined to get rid of him, her breasts squished up against the window.

Still the black-headed gull refused to budge. He cocked his head; again Ana felt that he was waiting for something, waiting to be consulted about their plans, perhaps.

'OK, well you can sort your own hair out, then,' Nan said, standing up suddenly, hoisting one leg out of the water.

'Help me get rid of him,' Ana pleaded with her, grabbing on to her sister's slick, wet arm.

Nan reached over to open the window wide, knocking the seagull off his perch. It should have been the end of it. But the gull saw the open window as an invitation and glided smoothly past them and into the bathroom. They both went into a blind panic then, the bird flapping and squawking in the air above them as they grappled with him, entangled in one another's nakedness, their fingers sticky with feather and soap, both shrieking, the gull breaking away, fleeing this way and that before suddenly coming to a halt at the bathroom mirror.

It was perhaps the first time the black-headed seagull had seen his own reflection. Perhaps he thought this was the way of things; that in entering the twins' world, this is what happened – everything, everyone doubled. Became a perfect, clear, luminous reflection of each other. He perched there on the side of the sink a while, staring, trying to work things out.

'Grab him,' Nan said quietly, as though the bird might hear their intent. 'Do it now.'

Ana was frozen to the spot. She couldn't take her eyes off him, as he began to peck away at the reflection, disturbed by how easy it was to replicate himself. Nan eventually pushed her out of the way and grabbed him herself, but instead of hurling him back out of the window, she pulled him towards her and forced him down into the diminishing bath water. Ana backed away, watching as he thrashed relentlessly against Nan's hand, knowing somehow that if he held fast the water would soon be gone. But Nan had other plans, swiftly wringing his neck as the last of their soap structure died in the plughole.

'I didn't know you knew how to do that,' Ana said. Her sister was, for this one moment, no longer a twin; suddenly merely herself, just like the black-headed seagull.

'Neither did I,' Nan replied, with a curious calm.

There was a strange smell in the room now, the stench of pavement and death mingled with the perfumed steam coming off their bodies. Nan handed the bird to Ana.

'You can get rid of it,' she said, wrapping herself in a towel and marching out of the room, leaving Ana alone with the executed bird hanging limply from her hand.

Ana almost couldn't bear to touch it, and so she hurled it back out through the open window as fast as she could. She shut the window firmly and leaned her head against it. She tried not to think of the dead bird's ungraceful descent through the air, the final, dirty slap. How it had come in alive, and gone back out dead, all because of them.

A few minutes later, after checking the doors and the lights, Ana returned to their bedroom to find Nan already fast asleep, her back turned away from her. She was disappointed that the evening had ended so abruptly, but she supposed that the incident had exhausted them both, and they would need to conserve their energy to carry out all they had planned, for they had not slept well these last few months. She clambered in next to Nan, shuffling around to see if she could rouse her; but no, she was a dead weight across the mattress. Ana lay down next to her and tried to clear her mind and assume the inertia of a normal person, a person for whom tomorrow was just another working day. But those people were all fools, she thought; because their lives would never be the same. And there would be one fool in particular walking among them along that red carpet. The fool who had brought all this upon them in the first place; the fool who was finally going to get what he deserved.

Before long, she found herself entering the deadening dark that was both her friend and co-conspirator, the only place she could really be alone. Where only one vision awaited her, a vision that recurred all night, just beyond the thin veil of her eyelids; that of the library of soap and feathers evolving, sud by sud, feather by feather, brick by brick, into the National Library up on that hill; a building shining brightly into the darkness, bold and fearless in the face of night, without the faintest idea of what the morning would bring.

Eben

7AM

Eben had decided that today would be the day he would make a start on those daily affirmations his therapist was so keen on. He had attempted, and tried countless times before, of course, but because she had insisted that these affirmations needed to be carried out first thing, he had not been able to face it. The mere thought of having to heave his early morning, blotchy, bloated self over to the mirror in his pants and T-shirt was too much for him. No one in their right mind, he imagined, would consider it an image worth affirming.

Today, however, he knew he had to put those anxieties to one side. It was absolutely paramount that he walked into the National Library with his head held high, convinced of the fact that he belonged there and that he was not doing anything wrong. And in the absence of anyone else around him to affirm his decision – apart from his disinterested cat – it was simply up to him to tell himself that there was nothing sinister in his request to access these materials in the National Library. And that it was a means of atoning for something he knew he hadn't done. A kind of belt-and-braces response to the accusation.

He had been awake for hours, just staring at the Artex swirls on the ceiling, trying to avoid the moment when he would come face to face with his own awfulness. What the therapist simply didn't consider in all this was how much it actually took to get him functioning in the morning in the first place. He had a crick in his neck that needed rectifying before he could do anything else, and so he hauled himself to the bottom of the bed to grab his trusty rolled-up towel, placing it behind his neck and hoisting it up until he felt the familiar clunk of his head sliding back into place. Then he reached for his nasal spray to relieve some of the congestion that had built up overnight, but somehow managed to squirt most of it into his eye, leaving him squealing in pain as he tried to redirect it into his nostrils. The final undertaking in his self-assembly was to choose between his contact lenses and his glasses, a decision made easy by his watering eyes, but he paused before putting them on, as the thought struck him that the therapist hadn't actually specified that he had to take 'a good look at himself' with twenty-twenty vision.

He approached the mirror with caution. In front of him was a blurred image. For all his therapist's smugness, she obviously hadn't foreseen this particular loophole in her self-affirmation nonsense. He now realised he could cope with talking and looking at himself if all he was dealing with was a haze of colours and contours, which could very well have been anyone. Even someone worth affirming. He kicked himself he had not thought of it before, this half-acknowledgement of himself, half-blindly accepting he was enough. 'Perhaps I'm simply a person who *does* do things by halves,' he said to himself, quietly congratulating himself on coming up with this rather original affirmation.

'I feel,' he said out loud now to the blob in the mirror, trying to get used to the sound of his own nasal voice in the dry air of the flat. 'I feel confident in every situation.'

He was suddenly aware of the cat staring at him from the corner of the bathroom, unconvinced.

Eben lowered his shoulders, trying to assume a more authoritative poise.

'I like who I am,' he said, with more conviction this time, although he considered it to be the least true of the many affirmations on his therapist's list.

And finally, at the therapist's request – because he needed to utter a minimum of four, she said – he forced his parched, reticent mouth to deliver the words:

'I am not responsible for the death of Elena Oodig.'

He felt the heat of shame prickling up his neck, imagining a cacophony of other voices echoing across the town, all uttering the affirmations they'd been prescribed by the town's one and only therapist. What power she held, from that battered-looking leather chair of hers, knowing everything about the people in this town, hoarding every little secret they had. Who else did she have telling their reflection that they had not killed anyone? He imagined he was not alone in this; yet at the same time he had felt hopelessly alone in the whole debacle for months. It brought to mind another affirmation he had been asked to try, but quickly disregarded: *Nobody else has my unique skill set.* That, at least, was true. Nobody else had been accused of snuffing out an author on the basis of several scathing attacks in the press; no one else's words had been hailed as a 'hate crime', said to have driven a woman out of a window, out of her mind, and then over a ledge.

Today, however, he hoped to put all that behind him. Or at least to put his unique skill set to good use. It was his interest in her, the therapist had eventually convinced him, that had led to what others erroneously considered to be his *annihilation* of her. He had come around to the idea that he had been simply doing his job; was it not a critic's job to dissect a writer's work, draw those weaknesses to the surface, bring them to the attention of the less observant reader so that they could demand more of their writers in future? Was he not also trying to get Elena's attention by doing so; highlighting that he expected more from her; that, in fact, he knew she was capable of something deeper, better? Had his intent not been to push her to the brink of her own genius, rather than off the ledge of her bathroom window?

He shuddered again at the image, recalling the details of the fall he had read online. How some of her brain had been exposed on the pavement. The frontal cortex – that brilliant place where all her plots had been concocted – rolling right out of her skull, before being descended upon by seagulls.

Stop it, Eben, he told himself, trying to breathe through it and erase those images from his own, still-intact brain. All that mattered right now was that he was, at last, going to be able to read Elena Oodig's diaries. The very first person to get access to them.

He'd sent several requests of course; all of which had initially been denied. Eben eventually realised he needed a project in order to justify his research, and had written a lengthy letter to her daughters to ask for their permission to write Elena's biography; a task he insisted would be near impossible without access to private materials. After a long silence, he'd received confirmation via the library that they were happy to grant permission – and that he alone would be given the exclusive right to undergo the research, with a view to publishing her biography, if her girls approved of his angle. He saw this as an absolution of sorts: it perhaps indicated that her daughters were sensible enough not to hold him responsible for her death, the way others did, and that they, perhaps, saw better than most that there was no one better positioned to write about her than her most involved (not obsessed, as others said) critic.

He took a shower, deciding against a shave for fear of mishaps – under the circumstances it was hardly appropriate to arrive at the library dripping with blood – and then set about putting on his suit. The formal outfit was a departure for him, as he never usually gave any thought to his library attire, but he felt like the occasion demanded it. You had to dress properly if you wanted to be taken seriously as a biographer. A crisp, navy-blue blazer and a mustard-coloured tie to show that you had a modicum of personality, but not too much. No one wanted a biographer to have too much personality, for such a thing could eclipse their subject. But you wanted something for onlookers to latch on to. Your subject was dead after all; you were the only visible link. That's why he chose the mustard colour. And it wasn't the colour of the strong, brash mustard like you'd get in the bigger countries, the kind that would get up your nostrils and make you cry – but a gentler, taste-bud-teasing thing like they still made here in his own country – mixed in with honey.

It was exactly the sort of endorsement he hoped the book would get. *A honey-mustard offering of a biography, sweet and sharp.* He would ask a friend of his, Frankton, to write it. Frankton had made himself an expert on all things literary in this country, despite having no literary credentials of his own. He had fashioned himself into a critic, using the internet to create just the right persona, while he sat in his pants at his laptop eating jam tarts, typing away with little care or consideration for others. He was always open to offers; writers could actually pay him to write a good review and to rubbish their rivals – a great system that a certain group of male writers had benefited from for decades, boosting sales of the most mediocre books. But everyone knew you had to keep him onside. Having someone like Frankton offside simply was not an option. He was a word-filled grenade waiting to go off in your face and his castigations would fly your way like shrapnel, to lodge in your literary reputation forever.

Eben had met Frankton at one of Elena's book launches around a decade ago, where Frankton – his teeth blackened with red wine stains – had grilled him on his thoughts on Elena's work. Having seemingly passed some sort of test he hadn't been aware of, Eben was then invited by Frankton to be part of an underground collective called 'The Smotherhood', a group of reviewers who could snuff out the writers who annoyed them, making sure they were too insecure to write anything ever again. It didn't work with all writers of course. It made the odd one more determined, drove their success even; but there had been some small triumphs. And one great big colossal victory, depending on which way you looked at it.

'I am not responsible for the death of Elena Oodig,' he told himself again in the mirror.